KHAN

MIKE BARON

WOLFPACK PUBLISHING
— EST 2013 —

**WOLFPACK
PUBLISHING**
— EST 2013 —

Paperback Edition
Copyright © 2022 Mike Baron

Published in the United States by Wolfpack Publishing, Las Vegas

Wolfpack Publishing

5130 S. Fort Apache Road, 215-380
Las Vegas, NV 89148

wolfpackpublishing.com

Paperback ISBN 978-1-63977-910-9
eBook ISBN 978-1-63977-909-3
LCCN 2022931234

KHAN

CHAPTER 1

EISELY

Roth Eisely was a builder. He bought up farmland west of Madison and turned it into developments with names like Faraday Heights, Belgravia, or Notting Hill. Five thousand square foot houses, winding cul-de-sacs, an HOA, and a clubhouse with pool, tennis courts, and gymnasiums. Notting Hill had a par three golf course.

Eisely had been married three times. His most recent wife, who had appeared on the cover of *Vanity Fair*, was suing him for alimony. But that wasn't the reason Josh Pratt kicked out in front of Eisely's house, dubbed the "Darth Vader" house due to its futuristic design. From the outside, it looked like Vader's helmet. Massive mansard roof hunched seven feet above the lawn.

Two weeks ago, Roth got in a fistfight with Madison City Councilman Mickey O'Shaugnessy after a city council meeting. The fight took place at Ino Vino, in the downtown

Marriott. O'Shaugnessy had been vocal in his support for defunding the police. Roth got in his face and called him a commie rat, and the drunk O'Shaugnessy, whose faith in his innate toughness as a drunken Irishman, swung on the builder, who had played nose tackle for Notre Dame and had boxed Golden Gloves. Result: O'Shaugnessy had a dislocated jaw. Although the Irishman swung first, virtually everyone in the bar, which included most of the City Council, swore that Eisely had provoked it.

O'Shaugnessy sued. O'Shaugnessy's lawyer Steve Fleiss hired Josh to deliver the subpoena. It was a warm July day just before noon as Josh walked the flagstone path to Eisely's front door, recessed beneath the glowering roof. He pushed the doorbell and heard a faint buzz followed by barking. Minutes later, the door swung open, Eisely in dungarees and a sleeveless shirt holding a rottweiler by the collar.

"Thor! Stay!" Eisely stepped outside shutting the door behind him. "What can I do for you?"

Josh handed him the subpoena. "Sir, you've been served."

Eisely stared at the paper in his hand as if it were a cockroach. "What the fuck is this?

"It's an order to appear in court to answer charges of assault."

"Is this from that asshat O'Shaugnessy? He swung on me first!"

"That's not what the witnesses say."

"Well, isn't this just perfect. I never should have entered that den of thieves. Who the fuck are you?"

"I'm Josh Pratt. I work for Steve Fleiss, counselor at law."

Eisely looked him up and down. The biker boots, the tats, the shaved skull. "Are you supposed to intimidate me?"

"No sir. My job is done." Josh turned to go.

Eisely grabbed him by the shoulder and dragged him around. Josh saw the punch coming, ducked under and drove his right fist into Eisely's taut gut. Eisely whirled, slamming his elbow into the back of Josh's head. They squared off. Eisely's neighbor, who had been tinkering with a sit-down mower, pulled out his cell phone. Josh put his hands up in a placating manner.

"Sir, you're only making it worse for yourself. Your neighbor is filming this on his camera."

Startled, Eisely looked next door, and put his hands up. "Whoa! Jess! We're only fooling around!"

Reluctantly, the neighbor lowered his camera. Eisely turned to Josh. "Come inside."

It was twenty degrees cooler in the house. It looked like something out of a James Bond movie, with the cool blue lighting, multiple stairs, gleaming blue railings, clear Plexiglass angling out from balconies. In the center was the hexagonal pit, with gleaming blue sofas surrounding a free-standing fireplace with a steep copper hat. A gray blue wall rose from the ground floor twenty feet. On it were mounted game trophies including longhorn sheep, a lion, and a moose. There was a framed picture of Eisely kneeling proudly next to the lion wearing a bush hat, holding a rifle, in the bush.

Eisely walked to a sideboard.

"You want something to drink? A beer?"

"I'll take a soda. Ginger Ale, if you got it."

Eisely looked in a copper-colored fridge. "You got it."

He gestured for Josh to sit on the gleaming blue sofa. Eisely returned with two Canada Drys. He sat at an angle.

"I'd like to apologize for my behavior just now. I could say I'm having a bad day, but that's no excuse."

Josh saluted with his can. "No prob. I admire a man who admits his mistakes."

Eisely had a bulldozer chin and close-cropped white hair. Race Bannon. He wore a sleeveless yellow BSA T-shirt, revealing massive biceps. "That your chop?"

Josh nodded.

"What is it?"

"Ninety-four Road King."

"What all you do to it?"

Josh drew a deep breath. "Engine: 88 with oil cooler. Changed the cams to S&S gear drives with 510 lift. Took out the fuel injection and replaced it with an S&S Super E, Yost Power Tube, S&S manifold and Pingle High Flow petcock. S&S Tear Drop air cleaner cover with a K&N filter. Screaming Eagle Hi Performance ignition unit with a 6200 rpm rev limiter. Accell Super Coil, Fire Wire plug wires and spiral wound metal core wires. Accell Platinum tip plugs. Five speed tranny with Barnett kevlar clutch, self-adjusting hydraulic chain tensioner. Screaming Eagle dualies. Progressive springs in front with higher viscosity, Progressives in back. Changed the rear swing arm bushings to "STA BOW" nylon high density. SBS semi-metallic disc brake pads and the brake lines are stainless steel braids. Went to tubeless wheels."

"Whoa," Eisely said. "That's a lot."

"I'm glad we got that out of the way."

"Did you do it yourself?"

"Pretty much. You ride?"

"I got an Indian Chief and a Rocket 3. Went to Sturgis fifteen years in a row. Haven't had much time lately. I guess I should look at that subpoena. What a bonehead."

"Mr. O'Shaugnessy's pressing charges."

Eisely grunted. "What a piss ant. We need to bring back dueling."

"Where did you bag that lion?"

"Tanzania. Maasai tribal lands. They're fighting to carve out sovereign territory, like American Indians have. Cost me three quarters of a million dollars, but it was worth it."

"Ever hunt tigers?"

"No. They are an endangered species found mostly in Asia. A few have been spotted in Alaska."

"Huh?"

"They swam across the Bering Strait. Perhaps they'll flourish. You hunt?"

"No."

"My hunting days are over. I don't want my house burned down."

"Do you have a card?"

Eisely got up, went into a den and returned. He handed Josh his card. Eisely Construction. Josh gave the builder one of his, carried the empty can up the stairs and set it on the sideboard. "Thanks for the drink."

CHAPTER

2

FREE BIRD

Ray's Prius was parked in the driveway. Josh rode up a slight incline into his two-car garage. His 300 occupied one slot, four bikes the other. He kicked out and went in through the kitchen door. Ray stood at the counter wearing short-shorts and stirring something delicious in a pot. Her cat Sid Vicious twined between her legs.

Josh pointed. "What's Sid doing here?"

Ray turned the gas off, covered the tureen and put her arms around Josh's neck, grinding her hips against his. "How about you and I go in the bedroom and I make you forget all about the cat because you are a man, and your primitive lizard brain is now overwhelmed with lascivious thoughts?"

Josh cupped her ass in his hands. "Works for me."

Sid jumped on the bed while they were making love and bit Josh on the leg. Not hard enough to break skin, but just enough to let him know where Sid stood. Josh showered, contemplating the Big Move. Ray had been transferring her stuff in stages and was almost moved in. She planned to rent her condo on Lake Monona to friends she knew from her Rise Up Dance Company. It was a big change for Josh and he wondered how he felt about it. On the one hand, he was crazy in love with her. How much was physical attraction he didn't know. He'd never been deep. He'd always lived for the moment, until he landed in Waupun. He'd become a Christian in prison. When he was released, and pardoned by the governor, who was a good friend of his lawyer, he had turned his life around. He bought his one-story pale yellow ranch house with proceeds from a motorcycle accident. He was lucky that there had been no lasting physical injuries, and he thanked God every night before he went to bed.

When he'd moved to Ptarmigan Road on the far southwest side, his was the only house on the tree-lined street. Within two years, Phil Bass had decreed an upscale community called White Oaks and begun surrounding Josh with five thousand square foot McMansions. Josh's house looked like some antediluvian pygmy compared to his neighbors. The White Oaks Home Owners Association had been trying to buy him out for years. The offer was up to seven hundred and fifty thousand dollars. But Josh was there first and he'd be damned if he'd let a bunch of insurance executives and university professors drive him out. His current employer, Steve Fleiss, told him it was always better to have the cheapest house in an expensive neighborhood, than the most expensive house in a cheap neighborhood.

The subject of marriage had yet to rear its ugly head, but Josh knew it would. He'd met Ray's university professor parents. They tried to hide their dismay when they found out he was a devout Christian. The prospect of parenthood lurked in the back of his mind like a forbidden attic room. One thing was sure. He knew what not to do. His father Duane had abandoned him when he was fifteen. Now Duane was in Danville serving life for murdering a family of five. They had the poor fortune to take the room next to Duane's in a cheap motel. Their children had been rowdy. They kept Duane up at night. Rather than complain, he waited until after midnight, drove his car around the back, and ran a hose from his exhaust pipe into their bathroom window, filling the room with carbon monoxide.

Don't think about it.

Josh put on clean jeans and a clean Foreign Films T-shirt. In the kitchen, Ray put out two salad bowls while Josh's dog Fig did mock battle with Sid. At least the pets got along. Josh got a beer from the fridge.

Josh sat. "Whatcha making?"

"Venison stew. I hope you don't mind. I found your venison steaks."

"Smells delicious."

Ray put down two bowls, filled a wine glass with a Cabernet Sauvignon, and sat opposite. She picked up her fork.

"Do you mind if I say a prayer?"

Startled, Ray put the folk back down. "It's your house."

Josh bowed his head. "Lord, for this food we are about to receive, we thank You. And thank You for bringing Ray into my life, or I'd be eating a Swanson TV dinner."

Fig sat at Josh's feet and begged. Josh fed him a chunk of venison on a fork.

"You shouldn't do that. You're rewarding bad behavior."

"We will survive."

"It's Thursday night. You've already been laid. What should we do?"

"Let me see who's playing."

Josh put his empty dishes in the sink and went into his office, a spare bedroom with a buffet table on which rested his computer, hard drive, and a pile of debris including advertising brochures, political brochures, motorcycle brochures, magazines, books, pens, spark plugs, and a Florida Man hat. There used to be several local publications which listed all the acts, but one by one they'd fallen, leaving only *Isthmus*. The Wickershams were playing the High Noon Saloon starting at eight.

Josh pointed at Sid Vicious. "Is Sid gonna piss all over everything?"

"No. His litter box is in the other bathroom. Don't leave your shirts out."

Josh closed the door to his bedroom and they went out through the garage. They took the Road King, Ray's hands wrapped tight around Josh's flat belly, as they rode through the warm evening, up Ptarmigan to Midtown, up High Point to Mineral Point, east on Mineral Point to Speedway where they cut north east toward the isthmus. It was still light as Josh backed to the curb between a Wide Glide and a Beemer. A sign on the door said MASKS ARE REQUIRED. They went inside, helping themselves to the free pale blue masks on a counter. About half the crowd wore masks. They snagged a booth and ordered beer. There was no smoking in the bar, but the scent of high-grade marijuana lingered. Photos of performers lined one wall: Delbert McClinton, the dBs, Trolley, local bands.

The Wickershams fooled around with their equipment for twenty minutes.

"If they don't figure it out soon, I'm gonna slap 'em," Ray said.

"You still studying with Nelson?"

Ray threw her arms out in wedges and semaphores. "Hoo! Hai! Ho!" she shouted.

"Impressive."

"Nelson says I'm a natural. He wants me to be in the lion dance next week."

"And hide your lovely face behind forty pounds of paper mache?"

She frowned. "I can't do it anyway. I'll be in the middle of *Kung Fu Musical.*"

"How's it going?"

"Had our final rehearsal last night. First show next week."

Josh rubbed his hands together. "I can't wait."

The spots went on the band, hunky lead guitarist, hot blond drummer, bear-like bassist, and a sylph-like keyboard player. The guitarist nodded. The band played a fanfare segueing into a hard boogie. The guitarist played legs splayed, bent over, hair in his face. Each song flowed into the next. By the fourth song, everybody was on their feet and shouting. Ray pulled a silver dollar out of her purse and rolled it between her fingers. Josh raised his eyebrows.

"I'll bet you I can toss that into the tip jar."

Ray eyed the tip jar, fifteen feet away on the lip of the stage. "Oh, come on."

"Seriously. If I can't, I'll take you to Second Story."

"Big deal. You'll take me there anyway. What if you win?"

"You have to shout 'FREE BIRD!' at the band."

Ray flipped him the coin. Josh effortlessly tossed it through the air and sunk it with a clink. Ray cupped her hands.

"FREE BIRD!"

CHAPTER
3

THE JOB

Fig barked from inside. They went in through the kitchen door where Fig waited excitedly, wagging her tail, tongue lolling. Sid Vicious lay in supine splendor on Josh's living room sofa. Ray went into the big bathroom and returned.

"Sid's using the litter box."

Josh stared at the floor looking for cat piss. He'd left the door to his bedroom shut.

"Are you still worried about the damn cat?"

"I don't trust him."

Ray fitted herself to him and ran a finger. Instant boner. She took his hand. "You're so easy."

Josh woke at nine, made coffee, thought about nuking some Jimmy Dean pork sausage sandwiches. His cell phone buzzed, lying on the kitchen counter where he'd left it. He didn't recognize the number.

"Pratt."

"Mr. Pratt, my name is Mandy Palmer. I work for the Wild Animal Initiative. Have you heard of Queen Tiger?"

"You mean the Amazon who runs that tiger sanctuary?"

"Yes. Gena Kropenski. 'Queen Tiger' was her fighting name, I believe. Her partner, Fabian Fitch, has been indicted for attempted murder. Miss Kropenski runs the day-to-day operations, and a Wisconsin state court has ordered her to turn it over to us. She was served papers five days ago."

"What can I do for you, ma'am?

"We are preparing to go to the Tiger Sanctuary in Clark County and take custody of their animals. We're afraid that the animals aren't doing well. Not getting enough food, medical care, or even water. These people who ran this thing, they're not animal lovers. They do it strictly for the money."

"Yeah."

"We want you to go with us as security when we go in."

"Ma'am, I'm just one guy. Do you know what you're going up against?"

"Kropenski, a former carnival roustabout named Archie Chuck, a woman named Mona, and maybe a couple of others."

"What about Fitch?"

"Fitch has disappeared. There are warrants out for him for transporting wild animals across state lines. In Wisconsin, they're legal, but Wisconsin is an exception."

"You need the police."

"We have the police. We want you to come in with us

while we go enclosure to enclosure."

"I don't get why you need me."

"We need you because these people are capable of anything. They may be armed."

"Where are the police?"

"The gentleman with whom I spoke explained that they are experiencing severe under staffing. He can send one squad car with two officers. That's all."

"You think they're going to fight to the death over their zoo?"

"It's quite possible."

"Where'd you get my name?"

"You were recommended to me by Edwin Hotchkiss."

The Seventh Earl of Hotchkiss had begun manufacture of his revolutionary motorcycle, powered by a five-cylinder engine that rotated around the drive shaft.

"Huh," Josh said.

"Could we possibly get together to discuss it? We are willing to pay whatever you ask, within reason."

"Sure."

Josh looked at the wall calendar, a babe stretched out on a chopper. "I can meet Monday."

Ray entered the kitchen. "What was that about?"

"The Wild Animal Initiative wants me to help them rescue a bunch of mangy zoo animals. You ever hear of the Tiger Sanctuary?"

"Sure. It's a Wisconsin institution like The House On the Rock."

"That's the place."

Ray's mouth went round. "Oh! I'd love to come with you!"

Josh barked. "Dubious."

"When are you going?"

"Don't know. I'm going for a run with Fig."

"Hold on. I'll join you."

Ray put on sport shorts, a sports bra, and a Badger T-shirt. Josh wore old sweats, no top. It was already eighty as they set out toward Madison, Fig loping behind them. They ran on the broad shoulder. No sidewalks. The neighborhood was too classy for sidewalks. Phil Bass passed on his way into town and honked his horn. He bore no grudge for having to shoot self-proclaimed guru and cult leader Brian Pils, who'd tried to break into his house. In fact, Bass' stock had risen considerably among the carriage trade. They made loud noises about defunding the police and nobody should have a gun, but they secretly admired a man who had the guts to stand up and defend his own.

They turned around at the 7/11 and headed back. Ray showered and left. On Saturdays, she ran dance workshops. She left the cat behind.

Josh showered and put on clean jeans and a Norton T-shirt. He nuked a Jimmy Dean muffin with egg, cheese and sausage and ate it in the kitchen while Sid Vicious twined between his legs purring and Fig watched, tongue lolling.

"Oh sure. Now you like me."

At twelve-thirty, Josh kicked out on Langdon Street across from the Student Union. He and retired MPD detective Heinz Calloway had lunch there every Saturday. Josh walked around back by the lake. It was in the mid-eighties with a dozen Hoofers scattered in the blue water, white sails slightly heeled. Across the broad lake, motor boats pulled skiers and board riders. Paddle boaters eased off the end of the long white pier. Most of the tables were taken, leaving a handful without umbrellas under the baking sun. Heinz had got there early and secured a table beneath the massive oak on the patio next to Paul Bunyan's chair.

Last fall, Josh had helped Calloway recover his daughter Ashley from the God's Breath cult in Colorado. Heinz had turned in his papers. Josh dropped his backpack on the ground and sat in one of the distinctive Union chairs, with its sunflower pattern.

"It's my turn. What do you want?"

Calloway rose. "Your money's no good here. What, a brat and a beer?"

"Sure."

Calloway stood in line at the outdoor grill with a dozen undergrads and a smattering of faculty. At six one, he was still trim, with a shaved skull. He had a wandering eye that had served him well during interrogations. He wore a Hawaiian shirt with flying saucers and creased Dockers. He returned with a tray holding two brats and two beers in plastic cups. All around them, undergrads, summer students, and faculty stared at their phones or debated the merits of plant-based meat. Many of them wore face masks.

Calloway looked around. "You see the same faces from twenty years ago."

"How's Ashley doing?"

"She made the Dean's List. She's majoring in law. I think Scipio scared the shit out of her and now she wants to be a cop."

"No shit. Well, that's better than a philosophy professor."

"I just hope she'll find a job when she graduates. The issue isn't whether she's qualified. The issue is whether there will be any police forces."

"What are you gonna do, Heinz?"

"Doreen and I just bought twelve acres outside Barneveld. We're going to raise horses."

"Horses?"

"Doreen's crazy about 'em. She got me up on 'em a couple times. Everybody loves horses."

"Hey you know Queen Tiger?"

"I'm aware of their difficulties."

"The Wild Animal Initiative wants me to go with them while they rescue the animals. Said they can't spare the cops. Low priority."

"It's Clark County. It's not like Milwaukee or Beloit. I don't know why they can't spare the police."

"Apparently they're stretched thin. They think there's a meth lab that's supplying most of the Upper Midwest."

Calloway looked at the lake. "It's like the whole country's gone mad."

"Are you selling your house?"

"Eventually. The property has an old farm house which we're gonna fix up. How you doing with that dance instructor?"

"She's a keeper. Except for her cat. It pisses on my shirts."

"We ought to get together one of these days. Doreen's dying to meet her."

"We'll have you guys over."

Calloway looked at his watch. "Got to get going. Doreen's dragging me to American TV."

"Maybe you'll get a free bicycle."

Calloway barked. "Fat chance."

CHAPTER

4

ONE HUNDRED AND FORTY-FIVE POUNDS

The Wild Animal Initiative had an office on the southwest Beltline, next to the Zor Temple, which featured a bronze camel kneeling in honor of the Zor Shrine Circus. At ten Monday morning, Josh kicked out in the parking lot and entered the two-story beige brick building. A slim, middle-aged woman with sandy hair in a wave, reading glasses hanging from her neck, rose from a bench to greet him.

"Thank you for coming, Mr. Pratt. I'm Mandy Palmer."

Josh wore a knit Lacoste shirt, a concession to business, and crisp new blue jeans. She extended her hand. She had a grip like a stevedore. He followed her down a corridor to an office with a window looking out on the Beltline. On the wall behind her was a framed Ph.D. in Animal Sciences from the University of Wisconsin, a picture of her posing with a yawning lion, like one of Hemingway's women, and a picture of her posing with a compound bow, in sunglasses and a Not Lame cap. Six archery trophies rested on top of a bookcase.

"Would you like coffee?"

"Sure."

Josh followed Palmer to a break room with several dispensers, a coffee machine, and a tray of doughnuts. They returned to Palmer's office. She sat at an institutional gray desk while Josh sat on a cloth sofa that had seen better days. Framed photographs of wild animals lolling, shaking off water, or playing hung on the wall along with certificates of appreciation. A flat screen TV hung opposite.

"Edwin Hotchkiss speaks very highly of you."

"How do you know Ed?"

"He is a great supporter of our cause, and many other worthwhile charities."

"I have no experience with tigers." Josh had killed a mountain lion with his bare hands once, but that didn't count.

"The court ordered Fitch to vacate his premises in April and turn the sanctuary over to the Wild Animal Initiative. Fitch has failed to act, and now we have an order of confiscation which we intend to serve on Friday. I know this is short notice, but we're hoping you can join us."

"Where's Fitch?"

"No one knows. He was there last Friday. We know because he picked up the land line."

"What's this attempted murder?"

"Fitch has been feuding with Anastasia Vukelov, the

owner of Big Cat Rescue in Tampa, Florida. It started on-line, and it escalated to the point where Ms. Vukelov began accusing Fitch of being an opportunist who irresponsibly breeds hybrids, has no real interest in conservation, and is only in it for the money. It's been going on for years. Ms. Vukelov alleged that Fitch hired a hit man he found online to kill her. She found out about it, went to the police, they picked up the hit man who confessed. Do you think you'll be able to join us?"

"I'm available, but again, I have no experience with wild animals."

"We want you there in case the remaining employees, including Queen Tiger, try to intimidate us. I've obtained the criminal records of several of their employees. Are you familiar with the Wild Animal Initiative?"

"I may have heard of it."

"We are dedicated to providing a natural environment for wild animals from North America and the world. We have acquired many of our animals from zoos and carnivals, and many of them have been mistreated. We have two com-pounds in Colorado, our public center in Wallis, and our new two-thousand-acre facility in Fremont County. This is our twenty-second year. The court ordered the sanctuary to permit us to rehome the animals, but that hasn't happened. Fitch stonewalled. He gave numerous interviews. Two weeks ago, the indictment came down. We really have no idea who's still there."

"Have you tried using a drone?"

"Yes, we have skilled drone technicians. We sent one up last week and it got shot down."

"I would take a look at those criminal records. Those people should not possess firearms."

"We have looked into that. The Clark County Sheriff's Department says they can send one cruiser, two officers. We have no idea how many people are inside the compound, which consists of five acres. That's woefully inadequate for the number of animals they claim to have on hand. Previous flyovers revealed that many of the animals are housed in small cages with concrete or gravel floors. We're concerned that they're not receiving proper medical care, and many of them may be swallowing gravel with their food, which the keepers toss through the bars."

"Where would you like to meet?"

"We will rendezvous at the Neillsville City Hall at nine o'clock Monday morning. The state troopers will meet us there and accompany us to the reserve. We are bringing in three long trucks to begin moving animals."

Josh nodded. "If we get in there, it would be helpful if you record whatever happens."

"No worries."

Josh went home and looked up the WAI. Their eight-hundred-acre refuge in Wallis, Colorado was home to 500 lions, tigers, bears, wolves and other rescued large carnivores. No dogs allowed. Day passes cost fifty bucks for an adult, twenty for seniors, and thirty for children. A mile's worth of aerial walkway traversed much of the property, twenty feet above the ground. Animals didn't recognize the "sky," so overhead visitors caused no alarm. This was an innovation previous sanctuaries never recognized, and opened the sanctuary to unlimited visitors.

The virtual tour showed the office, the aerial walkway, videos of animals lolling, playing, eating, a group photo of volunteers. There were a lot of volunteers. Josh had never been to a zoo. He respected wild animals, but they weren't a main feature. He admired people who volunteered to preserve as much of the natural world as possible. It seemed to him that too much of the natural world was disappearing. When he'd moved to Ptarmigan Road, it had been the country. Now the housing developments had engulfed him and stretched west and south as far as the eye could see.

Fitch made a fortune breeding big cats and charging people to play with the cubs. They sold a few to drug dealers and rock stars. Siegfried and Roy bought a liger.

Fig sounded off. Minutes later, the front door opened and Ray entered carrying four plastic grocery bags. Josh kissed her, and took the bags into the kitchen. Lettuce. Onions. Spinach. Asparagus. All organic. All Whole Foods. Josh had never shopped at Whole Foods. The closest he got was Brennans.

"Hey Ray! You ever go to the zoo?"

"Not since I was a little kid. Why? Do you want to go to the zoo?"

"I'm thinkin' I should see what a tiger looks like before I go out there."

"You know what they look like."

"I know, but now I'm curious. I've never been to a zoo."

Ray gaped in disbelief. "Never?"

"Duane wasn't into family outings. He took me to a couple strip bars. Let's go to the zoo."

"When?"

"Tomorrow?"

"No can do, big guy. I have rehearsals all day. But I can do Friday."

"We'll make it a date! We'll eat whatever they sell at the zoo and like it."

"It might be a good idea for you to watch *Queen Tiger*, to get to know the people."

"She has a show?"

"Oh yeah. It's wild. I kind of like her. But he's a dick."

"I don't get Netflix."

"I get it on my laptop. I'll set it up for you. There are five episodes. You can watch one a night and you'll be all caught up by the time you have to go."

Josh shrugged. "Why not."

"Get yourself a beer and settle down, big guy. I'll be right back."

"Right now?"

"What else have you got to do?"

"What about my primitive lizard brain?"

"Oh that."

A half hour later Josh plunked himself down on the sofa with a can of Capital lager, a bowl of peanuts, and Ray's laptop on the table. *Queen Tiger* began with a powerful, intense woman in black sports bra and shorts holding a tiger around the neck.

"This is Genghis Khan. Genghis is the largest tiger in captivity in the world. Genghis came from Siberia. Give mama a kiss, Genghis."

The tiger slurped the woman's face.

Theme music and a tiger pacing back and forth in its enclosure. "This is the Tiger Sanctuary," said an announcer who sounded like Sam Elliot. "A controversial tiger breeding facility in central Wisconsin run by Fabian Fitch and his girlfriend Gena Kropenski, aka 'Queen Tiger.' Before Gena devoted herself full time to the sanctuary, she was a top-ten ranked mixed martial artist and in line for a featherweight title fight."

One hundred and forty-five pounds.

CHAPTER
5

ZOO

Henry Vilas Zoo lay on the north side of Lake Wingra near the University Arboretum, a swatch of green bordering the South Beltline. It was one of only ten free zoos in the United States. Josh backed his bike to the curb in the zoo parking lot next to a dirty springer with leather saddlebags and a skull painted on the tank. He and Ray walked hand in hand to the arched entryway with a cut-out of an orangutan on the left and a tiger on the right. The smell hit them in the face. The tang of wild animals and exoticism. It was a warm Friday morning and the zoo was filling up with families with young children, kids on skateboards, uniformed zoo employees. A map mounted on a board inside the entrance showed the various animals, the gift shop, the restaurant, the restrooms.

The tiger enclosure looked woefully inadequate in size, but at least it had a natural habitat with big rocks on which a tiger sunned itself, a pool, and trees. Compared to what Palmer had showed him of the Tiger Sanctuary, it was a five-star suite. They paused in front of the tiger enclosure with a half dozen other visitors including a family with two young children who gaped in awe. The enclosure was surrounded by a chain link fence and roof. A plaque on the wall said

HABITAT

They live in the far east region of Russia in the boreal forest (taiga), and in northern evergreen forests where there are bogs, marshes, and shallow wetlands.

DIET

Amur tigers have a carnivorous, meat-eating diet, consisting mostly of large animals such as elk, deer, and pigs. One tiger will eat 20 – 60 pounds (9 – 27 kg) of meat in one meal.

FAMILY LIFE

After 3 – 3.5 months, a female will give birth to 2 – 6 cubs (the average is 2 – 3 cubs). The female cares for the cubs by herself. After three months, the cubs begin to accompany their mother on hunts. At 18 months old, the cubs are capable of hunting for themselves, though they don't leave their mother until they're 2 – 3 years old.

The back of the enclosure was a green wall with a door. In the door was a square foot hatch. The hatch opened and raw meat flew through the air. The sunning tiger leaped down and was immediately joined by another. They wolfed down the meat.

"Mommy," the boy asked. "What are they eating?"

The mother turned to a passing zoo employee. "Excuse me, ma'am. What do you feed the tigers?"

The woman stopped and smiled. "We used to get about two hundred pounds of meat from Oscar Mayer. Since they closed, we send a truck twice a week to Armour meats in Milwaukee. They donate three hundred pounds at a time which is enough to feed our big carnivores, including tigers, lions, bears, and wolves."

"What kind of meat?" the boy demanded.

"Pork, mostly."

"What's pork?"

"Pigs."

The boy seemed stymied. The employee moved on.

A man in blue jeans, biker boots, black leather vest and ball cap, with a lean, vulpine face, arms and neck with tiger tats on each arm sauntered up to the enclosure and stared at the tiger. "Chainsaw, amirite?" he said out of the side of his mouth.

Josh's skin prickled and he went icy calm. A furrow appeared on Ray's brow and she instinctively edged away, to stand on the other side.

"Who are you?" Josh said.

The man turned, pointing to a red patch on his vest. Dogbreath.

Josh grinned. "You're the third Dogbreath I've had the honor of meeting."

"I may be your last."

Josh stepped into Dogbreath's space. "You have a problem?"

Ray put her hand on Josh's arm. "Come on, Josh."

"You better listen to your woman before you bite off more than you can chew."

Josh allowed himself to be dragged away.

"That's right. Walk away, pussy."

Josh's back was an iron triangle. He'd never backed down from a challenge in his life but he understood this was not the time or place.

"Take a picture of that guy," he said. "Be discreet."

They walked around the corner to a bench. Ray took out her phone and wandered like a tourist back the way they came. She returned.

"I stood behind some trees. I don't think he saw me."

"Send me the pics."

She sat on the bench and poked. "Done. That man seemed to know you."

"I don't know him, but I'm going to find out."

"How?"

Josh stared at his phone. "These pics should be good enough for face recognition software. I'll send it to Ninja."

He called the last number Ninja had given him. "That

number is no longer in service at this time."

They returned to the parking lot. On a hunch, Josh photographed the skull chop and its Wisconsin license plate.

"Can you take me to the studio?" Ray said.

As they cut across State Street at Johnson, many small businesses remained boarded and shuttered following the riots. The newspapers referred to it as the "recent unrest." They rolled northeast past ranks of new townhouses painted pale yellow and white with planters on their decks, past the ancient three-story wood homes that had been divided into student apartments, and cut across the isthmus. As they rode east on Ingersoll, Josh felt his phone vibrating in his pocket. He knew who it was. He backed to the curb in front of the Rise Up Dance Studio and turned off the engine.

Ray hopped off. "Are you coming in?"

"Nah. I gotta take a phone call."

Ray kissed him, went up the steps and unlocked the front door. Josh walked down the tree-lined East Wilson. The call was from an unknown number. He called back.

"What do you want, what do you need?" Ninja answered.

"Those pics I sent. Can you find out who it is using face recognition shit? I'm also sending you pictures of a motorcycle with license. Can you give me the name and address of the owner?"

"Give me twenty-four hours. I'm on a job."

Ninja Preston was a hacker. He could get into any data base in the world, a skill which brought him notoriety and a great deal of trouble.

"Where are you, Ninja?"

"At an undisclosed location."

"Yeah, if you can find out who that guy is and get me the skinny in a few days, that would be great."

"I don't work for free, your hospitality notwithstanding."

"No prob. Sending you the bike pics in a sec."

"I'll get on it within twenty-four hours."

"Thanks, Ninja."

"How are you?"

"You heard of Queen Tiger?"

"Oh yeah. Crazy bitch raises tigers. I saw her fight in the World Series of Fighting. I don't know why she quit. She was the number one challenger."

"Later."

"Next time you call me, use one of those burners."

"What burners?"

"In your gun safe."

"There's no burners in my gun safe."

"Yeah, there are. They're in that ammo can. I left them there."

"You opened my safe?"

"I didn't take anything."

"Yeah, okay."

Josh got on his bike and headed home.

CHAPTER 6

LIFE OF PI

Fig and Sid Vicious lay on the sofa together, Sid Vicious licking Fig's ear. Josh stopped in the entryway from the kitchen.

"I turn my back for a minute and find you consorting with the enemy."

Fig leaped off the sofa and grabbed her Frisbee. Josh went out back in the fenced-in yard and tossed the Frisbee to her for fifteen minutes. When he went back inside, Sid was curled up in a cardboard box Josh had used to carry groceries from Woodman's. He checked his mail. Nothing from Ninja. He brought the Tiger Sanctuary up on Google Earth. A big rectangle with a small rectangle jutting to the east. It lay on Bremmer Road in Clark County, the entrance facing west. Josh zoomed in on the facility. He saw the tin roofs of the enclosures, but the animals themselves could not be seen because they were confined to cages. The only animals he saw were a pair of black bears lolling in an open topped pen by a muddy pond. Two vehicles were parked in front of the administration building, a converted ranch-style. One appeared to be some kind of four by four, the other a recent Corvette.

Wiki:

> "The Tiger Sanctuary is a five-acre petting zoo/breeding facility for tigers and other big cats, created by Fabian Fitch in 2014. The park began as a shelter for endangered and exotic species of animals, and is home to over 24 species of animals and 50 big cats, such as lions, pumas, ligers, tigons and tigers. In 2016, Anastasia Vukelov, owner of Great Cat Rescue outside Pensacola, Florida, accused Fitch of malpractice and cruelty to animals and demanded that the Sanctuary submit to an audit and investigation to be jointly conducted by the Wisconsin State Police and Circus World Museum, located in Baraboo, Wisconsin.
>
> "Fitch sued Vukelov for slander, libel, and defamation. Vukelov responded by releasing video footage, shot by drone, of Fitch using an electric cattle prod to force a tiger back, inside its cage. The video outraged animal lovers, who demanded an investigation. The State of Wisconsin threatened to withdraw its certification for the park. Wisconsin is only one of five states that permit private individu-

als to own any exotic animal they wish. The others are Alabama, Nevada, North Carolina and South Carolina. Fitch was found in violation of Wisconsin animal welfare laws and ordered to appear.

"When Fitch failed to appear, a warrant was issued for his arrest. His whereabouts are currently unknown. His girlfriend Gena Kropenski is currently in charge of day-to-day operations. The Sanctuary no longer allows visits. Gena "Queen Tiger" Kropenski is a former woman's featherweight MMA top ten contender for the World Series of Fighting. She was in line for a title shot when she abruptly quit the ring and went to live with Fitch at the facility in Wisconsin..."

His phone rang, number unknown.

"Pratt."

"The man at the zoo is Jeff Gunter, Chief Enforcer for the Hessians in Arena."

"Oh man," Josh said. "They're real bottom feeders. I ran into them a couple times at Sturgis. Mean and stupid."

"Gunter is forty-seven, has been Chief Enforcer for nine years, and lives in Arena. Makes his living cleaning houses."

"You're shittin' me."

"Hey. Guy's gotta pay the rent. They also distribute meth for the Gargoyles, in Midlothian. In 2011, four Hessians smashed their car into a gun shop in Cross Plains in the middle of the night and made off with about thirty weapons. The whole thing was caught on video, and they were all apprehended. They're out now. Gunter was one of them. His club name is Dogbreath. I found his mug shot. He had most of his teeth knocked out in a fight and wears dentures. I'm sending you his rap sheet. Might take a while because it's encrypted and has to go around the globe."

"I thought that shit traveled at the speed of light."

"Nah. It travels instantly, but once it gets to the next router, it has to re-encrypt itself which is kinda like a column of red ants working their way through a straw maze. It should be there in about three hours. What's goin' on?"

"The Tiger Sanctuary has been taken over by the state. They're turning the animals over to the Wild Animal Initiative. That's a boneroo non-profit in Colorado that treats their animals right. No cages, no pea gravel. They live on a huge property in their own enclaves."

"Yeah? So?"

"So Queen Tiger's still there with some of her buddies and she ain't about to just hand over her tigers. You saw her in that show. She's crazier than a coyote on crack. The WAI wants me to go out there with them in case the queen and her pals try to intimidate them."

"What about the cops?"

"They can only spare one car. Omma accompany the WAI as they go cage to cage. They're transporting the animals to their reserve in Colorado. It'll probably take a week 'cause they only got so many trucks and drivers."

"Mike Tyson had a tiger. It ripped somebody's arm off."

"Can you find a link between Gunter and the queen?"

"I'll look into it."

"Send me an invoice."

Ninja laughed. "Send me a thou in a hollowed-out book. Use priority mail."

"What book should I use?"

"Use Michener. There's always plenty of room."

Josh retrieved ten hundreds from his gun safe in the basement. As a convicted felon, he wasn't supposed to have guns. He was a free man because his lawyer got him a gubernatorial pardon. The maniac Moon had killed his lawyer, three cops and Josh's girlfriend Cass, among others. Moon had died at the hands of his own son.

Ray was his longest-lasting girlfriend. Before prison, he only had hook-ups. After prison, all his girlfriends had died. He hoped Ray would break the chain. And then what?

Sid Vicious entered the office and wound around his legs purring.

"Don't pull that shit with me. I haven't forgotten how you keep pissing on my shirts."

Fig stuck her head in and barked. Josh changed into shorts, T, and running shoes and headed southwest on Ptarmigan, Fig running a step behind. They passed the stone arch entry to White Oaks, Phil Bass' project. Mature oak and elm shaded the smooth boulevard. Behind the trees lay some of Madison's most exclusive neighborhoods. They passed the closed wrought iron gate, suitable for Buckingham Palace, entrance to Moritz Acres. A little bit of France right here in Wisconsin. The mailboxes were set in a brick frame.

A pickup passed them heading toward Madison, the driver waving through his open window. Josh waved back. Two bicyclists rode past wearing primary color spandex and teardrop-shaped helmets, butts in the air. Their patches read Sprint Seltzer Bike Club.

As they climbed out of a slight depression, a deep blue BMW passed going in the opposite direction. As the car drew level, an aluminum can sailed from the passenger window and bounced into the ditch. Josh picked it up. Blam Energy Drink.

"Come on, Fig. That's far enough."

They retraced their steps heading northeast. When they rose out of the depression, they saw the blue BMW parked by the side of the road and a man unlocking a mailbox. Josh stopped and held out the can.

"Sir, you dropped this."

Up close, the driver was a gym rat with biceps bulging through his knit shirt, buzz cut, tribal tats creeping down from his short sleeves like kudzu. He sneered at the can.

"So the fuck what?"

Josh was a statue, holding out the can, looking the man in the face. Fig growled. The man did an infinitesimal double take and took the can. "Thanks man."

"No prob."

Josh showered, fed Fig, cracked a can of Fancy Feast tuna while Sid Vicious walked around yowling. Stifling a

gag, he forked the food into a plastic bowl and lay it on the
kitchen floor. He turned on the AC, went around the house
shutting all the windows, and settled in the living room in
front of the flat screen. *Life of Pi* was on Hulu.

He had never seen such a beautiful movie.

CHAPTER 7

COULDN'T HURT

Fabian Fitch grew up in Brookline, Massachusetts, the son of BU Professor of History Cosgrove Fitch and Harvard Psychology Professor Eunice Gabbard. His mother kept her maiden name and insisted she be addressed as Doctor Gabbard, except among close friends. Fabian 's older sister Nanette excelled at tennis and eventually turned pro, and played Wimbledon, the US Open, and the French Open. She suffered a career ending injury jumping the fence to do battle with an opponent. Had she not torn her meniscus, the United States Tennis Association would have banned her for life.

Nanette was famous for cursing at spectators, reporters, and rivals. At the ripe old age of twenty-nine, she married rising stockbroker Nathan Rabinowitz and became a Long Island socialite, championing various charities and serving Long Island iced teas in elaborate parties that often included

Robert DeNiro, Spike Lee, and Glenn Close.

Fabian attended BU majoring in political science with vague thoughts of joining the legal profession, but spent most of his time partying with his fraternity, Yamma Tau, aka "the llamas." Although he received a generous allowance, Fabian supplemented that by dealing cocaine to his Yamma brothers and other fraternities. His clients included the son of a Supreme Court judge, an actress who went on to win an Emmy, and an aspiring banker who was later convicted of a massive Ponzi scheme and sentenced to federal prison.

In his junior year, his father was accused of impregnating the daughter of a powerful alumnus. Faced with the prospect of humiliation and jail, Cosgrove shot himself in his home office in Brookline. Eunice resigned under pressure. Cosgrove's gambling habit had eaten out the family fortune like a cancer, leaving his children a small inheritance. Eunice found solace in the bottle and lived on in their eighteen room Brookline manse until taxes and the mortgage forced her to sell, downsizing to a miserable apartment on Buckminster Road which she could barely afford on her pension.

Nanette and Fabian were not sympathetic. Like many children of the rich, their childhoods had been consigned to live-in helpers and baby sitters. Fabian could count on one hand the times his father had ever sat down with him for a manly heart to heart. Cosgrove failed to explain the facts of life, which Fabian learned first from his tony private school chums, and later the fraternity.

A trust fund for the children survived the lawyers, leaving Fabian seven hundred and fifty thousand dollars. One of his frat buddies had invented a new stereo speaker called the Quack. John sought investors to manufacture the speaker. A lifelong rock fan, Fabian took a chance and invested fifty thousand dollars in the Quack.

Fabian blew through his inheritance. He bought a classic Cobra. He threw lavish parties. Booze and cocaine every night. High priced hookers. He was expelled when he was caught cheating on an exam. He had to downsize. Fabian was forced to give up his lavish digs in Back Bay and rent a basement apartment in Brighton. He dealt cocaine. One night at a party at a friend's house, a man with a goatee and a pea jacket showed up. He formed a human question mark, hands in pockets, looking around like a lighthouse, lower lip protruding. The beam swept past Fitch and returned.

"Hey, man. I'm Dallas. Brick told me I could score some blow."

"Brick? Who's Brick?"

"You know. Donald Foster, man! He said you were in the same fraternity."

Fitch stared into the distance. "Brick. What's he doing now?"

"You won't believe this, man, but he's doing tile work."

"No way."

"Yeah. He went to work for his old man, Thornton Tiles. Turn your bathroom into an Arabian delight!"

"Sorry, man. I ain't dealing."

Dallas looked around, pulled a wad of hundreds from his package. "Come on, man. I'm cool."

"I could maybe do a gram to help you out."

"A gram? Oh mannn. I need a lot more than that."

"How much more?"

"I need a K."

Fitch looked Dallas up and down. Very authentic. Tie-dyed Nirvana T-shirt. Motorcycle boots. Blue jeans and a Harley wallet.

"Well, I ain't the man. I can do you one gram for a hundred."

Dallas pulled more hundreds from his pocket. "That's eighteen thousand dollars. Do you think you could find me a kilo of cocaine?"

Fitch 's brain was a hamster wheel. Tony. Tony Capadona, his main supplier, could move that kind of weight. Last time Fitch had copped, Tony had been sitting on a pile of blow.

"Half now, half when I deliver."

Fitch returned to his basement apartment, pulled out the nine thou, pulled out the blow and the vodka, and partied by himself.

Fitch woke in the morning with a massive hangover. His apartment looked like it had been hit by a tornado. He poured himself a shot of Jack and did a line. All right. Things were looking up. Like his bank account, his supply was running low. Time to see Capadona. Capadona was tied in with the Casuto Crime Family which controlled the North End, Back Bay, South Boston, everything down to Brockton. The Casutos' tentacles extended to Columbia. Fitch didn't want to know any more. It was ten in the morning when he phoned Capadona.

It was two in the afternoon when Capadona returned his call.

"Whaddaya say, whaddaya know."

"Tony, I need a Buick."

"Fabian, I told you there was nothin' happening until August at the soonest. The DEA's up my dude's ass and he's laying low. We're all feeling the heat. I went to Mass last Sunday and talked to the priest. You know what he said?"

"No. What did he say?"

"He told me I should say twelve Hail Marys, give a million dollars to the church and turn myself in."

"You're shittin' me."

"Swear to God."

"What did you do?"

"I cut out the middle man and went straight to the Big Guy. I went home, got down on my knees, and prayed for a way out of this fakakta fuck-all that is devastating our business from here to Providence."

"What did He say?"

"He said he couldn't do anything for me. This was my mess, and I hadda clean it up myself without breaking any of His commandments."

"The Big Guy told you that?"

"Swear to God. So don't come whinin' that you don't have an eight ball for some fraternity brat drivin' his father's Porsche."

"Oh mannn, what am I gonna do?"

"Don't go to Karenga. You do that, you're out. I'll personally take out an option on your head. We're at war with Karenga. Don't call me. I'll call you when things cool down."

"Come on, Tony. We're tight! I got a really big one on the line here! I know you got keys stashed. Just this one time, man. I'm begging you. It would mean a lot to me. I'll make it up to you. Anything you want, I'll do it. You know me. I'm a man of my word. I'm good for it."

Fitch heard Capadona breathing. "Just this once. Fifteen thou to you."

"I can give you seven fifty now and the rest when I collect."

Heavy breathing.

"I don't know why the fuck I let you talk me into this. But this shit was going to Brandeis and then my contact, she gets hit by a car! Can you believe that? Out running like a fuckin' moron at nine o'clock at night when nobody can see her! I wouldn't do this, but for some reason the stars are aligned. Meet me at ten o'clock tomorrow night at Reventlo's."

"Beautiful, man. I owe you one. I really appreciate this."

"Yeah yeah."

Capadona hung up. Holy shit. Fitch had to get his shit together. He was in no condition to go anywhere that night. He could get himself straight in twenty-four hours. River Phoenix could get straight in twenty-four hours.

He eyed the amber bottle on his linoleum kitchen table. Fuck it. One more. Couldn't hurt.

CHAPTER 8

THE SANCTUARY

Josh got up at five, did a couple miles with Fig, and was on the road by six. It would take three hours. Josh drove the 300. This was not a pleasure trip. He took the Interstate to Black River Falls and cut over to Neillsville on Highway 73. City Hall was a blond brick Romanesque revival, main entrance framed by asymmetrical towers. A Statie was parked out front, with three semis pulling long trailers parked on a side street, one per block.

Mandy Palmer stood on the steps before the arched entrance with a half dozen members of the Wild Animal Initiative, along with two staties in Smoky hats drinking coffee from cardboard cups. Josh went around the block and parked in the city hall parking lot. He walked around front.

"Good morning," Palmer said. "Would you like some coffee?"

"Sure."

She pointed him to a card table set up next to the front door with a half dozen capped cardboard Starbucks cups, artificial creamer and sugar. A cardboard box of doughnuts was down to three. Josh took a coffee and a cruller.

"Josh, I'd like you to meet the rest of our crew, and the state police who will be accompanying us. This is Brian Floyd, our drone pilot."

Josh set his goods on the broad cement rail and shook hands. Floyd was a slight, balding man wearing a knit shirt and glasses.

"Have you taken a look today?" Josh asked.

"Not yet. We're going to do a flyover before we drive up to the gate."

Palmer stood next to a diminutive woman, her long brown hair in a ponytail, wearing a white T-shirt and cargo pants with bulging pockets. "Jennifer is our veterinarian. These are our wranglers,

Burt Pennison, Ray Cleary, Phil Davis, and Wilson Southgate."

Josh introduced himself to Sheriff Leach and O'Riordan, big men who looked like they could handle themselves. Leach was the county sheriff. He wore aviator glasses, tan uniform and a Smokey hat, straight out of central casting.

"Miss Palmer explained your role here today. You understand that you're assuming risk by going into the compound, and we advised against it, but we were overruled. Fitch threatened to wire the cages with explosives. As soon as the court ordered his arrest, he disappeared. That was a week ago. There's only the two of us, and we're there primarily to enforce the eviction notice, but we can't be everywhere at once. There may be as many as eight people in the compound, three of which we know for sure. They all have criminal records. They may be armed. I can lend you a bulletproof vest."

"No thanks. I'll take my chances."

"You change your mind, let me know."

"Hey everyone," Palmer said from the steps. "We're moving out in five minutes. The state troopers will go first, followed by me. Josh, Jennifer, and Burt will ride with me. Ray, Phil and Wilson will ride in the trucks."

Leach stood next to her. "I want you all to stay back until Brian and I have ascertained if anyone is on the property. We'll let you know when it's safe to proceed. Please wait outside the gate until we give you the word."

They watched the troopers get in their car and take off. Josh finished his doughnut. He followed Palmer to her Dodge Ram four door, the bed filled with furniture blankets, veterinary equipment, and hardware. Josh took shotgun with Jennifer and Burt in the rear seats.

"What are we gonna do if we get in?" Josh said.

"The first thing we're going to do is check on the animals. They are likely malnourished and possibly dehydrated. We're prepared to administer fluids intravenously. We will start transporting animals as fast as we can load them."

Palmer started the engine and headed north on Main Street.

"What, exactly, is the warrant?" Josh said.

"It's a court-ordered confiscation because Fitch failed to adhere to a previous court order preventing him from buying and selling more animals. He was making hundreds of thousands of dollars from breeding, selling, and public interaction with his animals. Now obviously, you can't pet a full-grown tiger unless it's sedated. Hence the constant breeding. People come in, pet the tiger cubs, have their pictures taken. Fitch was renting the cubs out for private parties. A local citizen succeeded in getting an injunction against that behavior, so Fitch started hosting birthday parties at the compound."

They drove north on Seventy-Three past farms and cornfields. The corn was four feet tall and would be ready for harvest in a month. Spidery irrigation machines whirled water from long tubes. A sign at Twenty-Six Road pointed left. A big, circus-style billboard featuring a snarling tiger said:

THIS WAY TO TIGER SANCTUARY
FEATURING GENGHIS KHAN
THE KING OF BEASTS

"The USDA revoked Fitch's license in January, but he appealed and was allowed to continue. Then the Wisconsin Attorney General filed suit to shut it all down. They had proof, including drone footage, of animals living in awful conditions. The AG tried to liquidate the Sanctuary's assets and prevent Fitch from ever owning animals again. The court has yet to rule on that motion, but we learned that one of his tigers died and got another motion, which is pending. PETA has also filed suit. We suspect he has killed a number of tigers and buried them on the property."

Twenty minutes later, they turned south on Bremmer Road and saw the compound on the east side surrounded by eight-foot hurricane fencing, the gate open. The sheriff parked in front of the administration building, a one-story wood farmhouse that had been extended to double its size. There was a barn next to it. Josh saw an older blue Corvette and a backhoe through the open doors. Palmer parked in the gravel lot. Josh walked over. The 'Vette was a '96. He'd always liked that model. Two white discs lay on the saw-dust-covered floor. Thirty inches in diameter, they showed the head of a ferocious tiger snarling beneath GENGHIS KHAN in circus-style lettering. The lower rocker said, THE TIGER SANCTUARY. A rectangle indicated where a vehicle had been parked.

The staties were talking to five sanctuary employees, four men and a woman with one arm. One of the sanctuary employees glanced over and then looked hard. It was Jeff Gunter. Three staties stayed with the men while Leach came their way.

"These gentlemen claim neither Kropenski nor Fitch is on the property. They say Kropenski left yesterday, and Fitch months ago. We're going to let you go ahead and inspect the animals, but if you see something unusual, please notify us immediately."

Floyd hoisted himself into the truck bed and opened the carbon fiber case carrying a four-rotor drone. "Officers, with your permission, I'm going to do a flyover. Would you like to watch?"

"That's a good idea." Leach boosted himself up into the bed. "Let's hold off on that inspection until we take a look around. This shouldn't take long."

"Officer, Leach," Josh said, "that guy with a face like a hatchet is Jeff Gunter, Chief Enforcer for the Hessians in Arena."

"Who are the Hessians?"

"One percenters out of Arena."

"We're running them all through the system and if there are outstanding warrants, we'll take them in."

"Hey!" O'Riordan said.

Gunter sprinted toward the end of the office building and disappear around the corner. O'Riordan took off after him.

"Aw shit," Leach said.

AT THE ZOO

"Okay, nobody's going anywhere until we figure out what's what," Leach said. "Get that drone up. Let's see where he's going."

Floyd sat on the tailgate with the drone yoke in his lap. "Here he is." He turned the yoke so that Leach could see the man racing through the compound, past cage after cage, until he came to a locked gate at the rear. He leaped, gripping the hurricane fencing with both hands and scrambled up and over, dropping on the far side, racing across an irrigation ditch and disappearing into the woods.

"Shit," Leach said. "We just don't have the manpower."

Josh looked over his shoulder. "Can you use face recognition software to track him down?"

Leach grinned wryly. "I'm just a country sheriff. We can put in a request to the Wisconsin Division of Criminal Investigation, but it will be low priority."

"What about Fitch's phone number?"

"Don't know it. Can't find it unless we know what carrier he was using."

"What about Gena's?"

"Working on it."

"Sir, we need to find whether Kropenski or Fitch are on the property."

Leach turned to his deputy. "James, get everyone together. Be careful. These people are a little crazy."

"Sheriff," Palmer said, "Jennifer and I need to check on the animals."

"Okay. If you come across anyone, notify me immediately." Leach handed her his card. He went back to his car and sat in the front seat looking at the computer.

Outside the main gate, the semis pulled up on the side of the road. Fifteen minutes later two state cruisers entered the compound and four men got out. The head statie, face like a granite cliff, approached.

"Howdy. I'm Sergeant Patterson. Heard you could use a little help."

Leach stepped forward and shook his hand. "Sheriff Leach. We sure could, Sergeant. Thank you for coming. We have a fugitive, Jeff Gunter, wanted for assault and dealing meth." He handed Leach a print-out from his car. "We were tracking him via drone but he disappeared into the woods just west of here. He's wearing blue jeans, black boots, and a yellow Tiger Sanctuary shirt. Those woods stretch for a quarter mile and stop at Bingham Road. Any possibility of getting a car out there?"

Patterson turned. "Craig, get over to Bingham. See if you can spot Gunter."

Craig got in his vehicle, pulled a Y turn and booked.

Palmer nodded toward the cages. "Let's go. Jennifer, you and Josh come with me. Burt, you and Ray, Phil, and Wilson take a look at that line over there."

Jennifer hunched into a heavy backpack and followed Palmer toward a long line of cages stretching back to their right. The first cage held two black bears lying on concrete, their eyes barely open. Their water bowl was empty.

"Josh, see if you can get a hose in here. I saw one lying next to the administration building."

Sickened by the bears, Josh sprinted to the admin building, found a fifty-foot hose attached to a faucet and knew it wouldn't reach. He sprinted around back, found another fifty-foot hose, unscrewed it, hooked it up to the first, turned the water on and rushed back to the bear cage. Jennifer crouched next to one of the bears administering an IV.

"I'm afraid this one isn't going to make it. Here. Give me that hose."

Josh handed her the spurting hose. She gripped to reduce water to a trickle, and gently filled the water bowl before the other bear. Lying on its side, its tongue flopped into the bowl and curled water into its muzzle. Josh looked away.

Palmer's phone rang. She listened intently for a few minutes. "All right, thank you Burt." She returned the phone to her pocket. "Burt has found a dead liger in a cage with a gravel floor. It appears to have been dead for some time. Flies have been at its eyes."

The phone rang. Pennison reported two tigers alive in a gravel-floored cage. "We're gonna have to tranquilize them before we load them."

Palmer phoned her drivers. The first of the big rigs backed expertly through the gate into the compound. Volunteers opened the rear door and pulled out a steel ramp. The trucks were refrigerated. A volunteer would ride in the back with the animals to monitor their health.

Mona beelined toward Palmer.

"Genghis Khan is missing."

"I'm not surprised. He's their star attraction. Fitch isn't going to give up Genghis without a fight. Where is Miss Kropenski now?"

Mona shrugged. "She left yesterday morning. I didn't talk to her. I was sleeping."

"Do you live on the property?"

She pointed to a silver airstream waist deep in weeds.

"How do you hide a tiger?" Josh said. "You can't keep it in your house."

"That cat needs thirty pounds of raw meat a day. The local Walmart was supplying the refuge with past-their-date chicken, beef, and pork, but they stopped when the court issued its injunction. We have techies who might be able to get a hand on food deliveries or purchases, but it's a long shot."

Ray Cleary called. "We've got two black bears in a cage full of five-foot weeds. You can only see the bears when they stand. We're gonna have to tranquilize them."

"Let me make sure we're ready to transport them," Palmer said.

"Mona," Josh said. "Was there another vehicle in the barn? Where did those magnetic signs go?"

"Yeah, Fabian bought a Mercedes Sprinter to move the animals around. It was his pride and joy."

"Where is it now?"

Mona shrugged. "I don't know. He may have snuck back in and taken it."

"Wouldn't someone have noticed?"

Mona edged closer and dropped her voice. "These guys get shit-faced every night. They do a lot of blow. I mostly stay to myself in my trailer."

"Could Miss Kropenski have taken it?"

"It's possible."

"When was the last time you saw Fitch?"

"Last Friday. He said he was driving into town to get some meat and he never returned."

"What was he driving?"

"An old Subaru wagon."

"Okay." Josh fished a card out of his hip pocket. "If you think of something, please call me."

Leaving Jennifer with the bear, Palmer and Josh returned to the front yard where Palmer spoke with Ernie, one of the truck drivers, a short man who looked like a Russian nesting doll. They spoke intensely, with lots of hand motions. The driver scratched his head. Palmer stiffened up, crossing her arms and tapping her foot. Josh could see the trucker was a goner.

"All right," she said through gritted teeth. "We're moving the three black bears as soon as possible. Josh, I'll need you to help push a cage."

"Fine."

The trucker unloaded a wheeled cage down a ramp at the back. Very faint red, white, and blue paint remained on the bars. It squeaked like a bad shopping cart all the way to the bear enclosure, where Jennifer's bear was too weak to stand, an IV drip going into its forepaw. While Jennifer held the IV, Josh and Ernie carried the bear into the transport. The bear weighed about one hundred and sixty pounds and clearly suffered from malnutrition.

"Whatcha gonna do with these bears?" Josh said.

"We're transporting them to our preserve in Colorado. You should come. You should see the animals. They don't remember the bad times. They live in the moment. Oh, we had some real problems. Animals that had been abused so badly they would do anything to get away from a human. And if there was no way out, they'd rip the human to shreds."

"Where's Fitch make his money?"

"Petting zoo. He sells hybrids. Ligers, mostly. Also breeds Tabby tigers and Goldens."

"Huh?"

"Special colors. There are no albino tigers. All the white tigers you see are the result of cross breeding."

"Can you get any color you want?"

Palmer laughed. She took a deep breath. "Wow."

"What?"

"It's been quite a day and it isn't even noon."

Sergeant Patterson cruised their way. "Folks, I'm gonna have to ask you to temporarily vacate the premises. We just found a meth lab."

CHAPTER 10

INTO THE RING

As long as she could remember, Gena Kropenski had been fascinated with tigers. It started on her grandparents' farm in Iowa, where she spent many happy days with her brother Wayne while her father Reggie, a long-haul trucker, was on the road. Grandpa Deke had once worked as a carnival barker and had framed circus posters in the living room. Barnum & Bailey. Ringling Brothers. Circus Royale. An old abandoned grain elevator stood next door where Gena, Wayne, and some neighborhood kids would play hide and seek, cowboys and Indians, or, when Wayne chose, Moors and Crusaders.

Her parents took her to the Omaha Zoo, where she saw her first tiger in the Asian Highlands exhibit.

"The Amur or Siberian Tiger is native to Far Eastern Russia, Northeast China, and North Korea. It once ranged throughout the Korean Peninsula, Northeast China, and

Eastern Mongolia. The population currently inhabits mainly the Sikhote Alin Mountains in southwest Primorye Province in the Russian Far East. In 2005, there were 331–393 adult and subadult Siberian tigers in this region, with a breeding adult population of about 250 individuals. The population had been stable for more than a decade because of intensive conservation efforts, but partial surveys conducted after 2005 indicate that the Russian tiger population was declining. An initial census held in 2015 indicated that the Siberian tiger population had increased to 480–540 in the Russian Far East, including 100 cubs.

"Male tigers can weigh as much as six hundred and seventy-five pounds, and females three hundred and sixty-eight."

Gena glued her nose to the glass wall, staring at the great cat lounging by a pool, occasionally flicking its tail. She had never imagined such a thing. When her folks wanted to move on to the next exhibit, she said, "Oh please, Daddy, let me just stay here and watch the tiger."

They watched the tiger for forty-five minutes before her father looked at his watch.

On the ride home they stopped at a Dairy Queen. Seated in the backseat (Wayne had begged off on the grounds that he had to attend football practice,) licking her ice cream cone, she said, "Can I get a tattoo?"

"Absolutely not," her mother answered without turning.

"But Daddy has them."

"When you're an adult you can make your own decisions. But as long as you live under our roof, there will be no tattoo."

On her eighteenth birthday, Gena got her first tiger tat.

Gena's older brother Wayne wrestled in high school and was runner up to the state champion. From there, he moved to boxing. Stanley's Gym was on the second floor of a red brick industrial warehouse down by the Jepperson tracks. Jepperson, Illinois, population twenty-two thousand. Gena was a big girl. No fat. She started tagging along and soon she was taking boxing lessons from Joe Crenshaw, a wizened black homunculus who claimed to have trained Tyson.

She worked the heavy bag. She worked the speed bag. She boogalooed the ropes and sparred with her brother. Gena was five eight and a hundred and thirty-five pounds. She started begging for a fight.

"No one want to fight a white girl," Crenshaw said. "'Less you got some other white girl I don't know about. You the only white girl in this town crazy enough to fight."

"I don't care. Get me an Inuit."

"Whatuit?"

"I'm not looking for a championship bout. I'm not even looking for money! I just want to get in the ring."

"Well, if you feel that strong about it, you mind getting' in the ring with my boy O'Neil?"

They were in Crenshaw's office, with a dirty picture window looking out on the floor. O'Neil was a lean, red-headed and freckled welterweight with a wicked right cross. He'd boxed Golden Gloves and tried out for the Olympic Team.

"Let's do it."

They entered the gym, where O'Neil was working with Davante Adams, a middleweight who looked like a Rob Liefeld drawing, and was two and oh professionally. Adams held the pads, leading O'Neil around the ring, throwing fast hooks, making O'Neil bob and weave. O'Neil worked the pads like an upholsterer. Bam bam bam bam. Crenshaw and Gena walked over. Adams let the pads fall.

"What?"

"Gena wants to spar with O'Neil."

O'Neil, gleaming with sweat, sneered. "You have got to be shitting me."

"What'sa matter, O'Neil?" Gena said. "Afraid I'll show you up?"

"My momma taught me to never hit a woman."

Adams grinned. "Well hell, Frankie. We got transgendered weight lifters, soccer players, and wrestlers. You don't wanna go insulting this fine young woman by denying her a chance to prove her abilities."

"Are you shitting me?"

"Come on, O'Neil," Gena teased. "I promise to take it easy on you."

"We're just sparring, right? You're not gonna film this, right? I can't have no video out there of me sparring a girl."

"I'm all woman, baby."

O'Neil took a good look. "I guess you are. Why a good looking woman like you wants to get her face messed up, I don't know."

"Ain't no one looking to get their face messed up," Crenshaw said. "Just a light round of sparring to see if this here white girl has got what it takes."

"You want to be a boxer?" O'Neil said incredulously.

"I want to be a complete, well-rounded fighter."

"She's Wayne's sister," Crenshaw said.

O'Neil nodded. "I get it. What the hell. Two minutes."

O'Neil pulled off his bag gloves. Adams helped him wrap his hands and put on the twelve ouncers. Crenshaw did the same for Gena. Five other men stopped what they were doing to gather around the ring.

Crenshaw leaned in. "Remember what I taught you. Bob and weave. Footwork. Don't be a stationary target." He slipped Gena's red mouthpiece in. O'Neil and Gena got in the ring.

"Ready?" Crenshaw said. The fighters nodded. Crenshaw rang the bell.

They came out circling, O'Neil obviously reluctant to hit a woman until Gena juked forward and smacked him on the nose with her jab, ducked under his cross and punched him in the gut. O'Neil tried to run her over, but Gena danced out of the way, always moving at an angle, peppering him with machine gun jabs and uppercuts. Crenshaw mercifully rang the bell early.

"That's all," he said. "Gena take off your gear and come into the office."

O'Neil leaned on the ropes. "I can't go against my momma. You hit pretty good for a girl."

Adams muttered, "Man, she smoked you."

Crenshaw shut the door and tossed Gena a towel. "So what do you want to do? You want to box? Ain't much money in women's boxing."

"No. I want to compete in MMA."

"Well, this here's a boxing gym and I ain't no MMA trainer, but I could recommend someone. Austin Bear runs Bear MMA over in Omaha. Want me to make a phone call?"

"Yes, please."

"This mean you ain't gonna grace us with your presence?"

Gena smiled. "I know you love me, and just having me here is gonna bring in a lot more members, amirite?"

"I don't know about that. You start winning and you're right. But it's a big step up from the amateurs to the pros. I think you should probably compete on the amateur level first, see how you do. You start racking up a record, we can ramp up the PR, look to get you a pro fight. You got six organizations to choose from. All American MMA and Rumble run amateur MMA tournaments throughout the Midwest. In fact, Rumble has one coming up in Winnetka in September. That's five months away. You start training now, maybe."

"I need a manager."

Crenshaw held up his hands. "I don't know nothin' about that. Let me make a few calls."

"You think O'Neil was pulling his punches."

"No ma'am. I think you got what it takes."

"Thanks, Crenshaw."

"Maybe when you're a big shot, you'll come back to my

gym and say hello."

"I'll never forget this, Crenshaw."

"I just got one question. Why in the hell does a good-looking girl like you want to be a fighter?"

"My heroes have always been fighters. Muhammad Ali. Joanna Jędrzejczyk. Ronda Rousey. Paige Van Zant."

"And they're raking in the big bucks. All you have to do is win, and not get your nose plastered all over your face."

Wayne was at work when Gena returned to the faded duplex they shared. When she came out of the shower, Wayne was parked in front of the TV watching *Pawn Stars* and laying out lines on a hand mirror.

"You want a line?"

"Don't mind if I do."

She snorked up, threw her hands in the air and sighed in satisfaction.

"What?"

"We got any Jack?"

"There's a bottle in the cupboard. What you been up to?"

"Wayne, I'm going into MMA. How'd you like to manage me?"

"Yeah right. Look at me. I can't manage myself. You want to turn pro, you'd better lay off this shit."

Gena headed for the kitchen, returned with a bottle of bourbon and two mismatched glasses. "I can handle it. I'm treating myself. I just smoked a pretty good welterweight."

"Who?"

"Tim O'Neil at Crenshaw's Gym."

"No shit?"

"No shit. Ask Crenshaw."

"Well, you go, girl, but I ain't got time to manage you. I'm building up my stake so I can buy the Elkhorn. Oakley wants to retire."

"Now that's funny. All this time I thought you wanted to turn pro."

Wayne pointed to his cut eyebrows and flattened nose. "A man's got to know his limitations."

"There you go, quoting Clint Eastwood again."

"I know what you're thinking."

CHAPTER
11

VEGGIE BURGERS

The staties called in the crime lab specialists. While they waited, the Wild Animal Initiative loaded four bears, two ligers and two emaciated tigers into their long trucks and headed for Colorado. Palmer and her veterinarians booked rooms in Neillsville.

Josh caught up with her at the second truck, where they were loading two lions. "If you don't need me anymore, I'm heading back to Madison."

"I want you to find Genghis Khan," Palmer said.

"Excuse me?"

"The missing tiger. We are committed to bringing him to the preserve."

"I wouldn't know how to track a tiger."

"You find people, don't you?"

"Sometimes."

"Do you think Genghis Khan is traveling alone? He's

with Gena. Fitch doesn't give a damn about the tiger's welfare."

Josh turned a palm up. "What else I got to do?"

"Thank you."

"Do you still need me here?"

"I want you to find Genghis Khan as soon as possible."

"I'll need a list of everyone who worked here."

"I will get that to you as soon as possible."

Ray answered on the first ring. "Hello!"

"Baby, I gotta track down a fuckin' tiger. Can you take care of Fig?"

"Excuse me?"

"Excuse my French. They had this tiger. Genghis Khan. He's missing. He's not the kind of pet you can smuggle into a hotel. The people who took him are batshit crazy. It's a bad mix. Can you take care of Fig?"

"Of course I can. I'm here now. Where are you?"

"Neillsville. I'm helping the Wild Animal Initiative round up tigers. Some of them are in bad shape. You wonder how Fitch got away with this for so long. Don't people notice malnutrition when they see it?"

"He's not going to charge paying customers to pet sick animals."

"Well, it's over for him. He won't be coming back here. Now I have to find Genghis Khan."

"They hired you to track down a missing tiger?"

"What else I got to do?"

"It could be anywhere! What if it's loose?"

"If it were loose we'd hear about it by now. I'm really

tracking Gena Kropenski. Queen Tiger."

"Who?"

"You heard me."

"Is she dangerous?"

"Don't know. She shouldn't be hard to find. Where do you hide a seven-hundred-pound tiger?"

"You'd need space. And meat."

"We're looking into the meat. Did you know there are Siberian tigers in Alaska? They swam across the Bering Strait."

"Oh come on."

"Roth Eisely told me."

"Who?"

"I served papers on him last week. Big shot developer. Notting Hill."

"I have a friend who lives out there. Don't worry about Fig. She's in good hands. I'd rather have you, but I'll take what I can get. When you coming back?"

"Tonight."

"I'll show you a good time."

"I'm leaving now."

"Don't get a ticket."

Josh pulled out one of the burner phones, called Ninja, got "this number is no longer working." Five minutes later Ninja called.

"Speak."

"They want me to find this tiger, Genghis Khan. Ever hear of him?"

"I've heard of the Mongol warrior, of course. But not

the tiger."

"A monster. Seven hundred pounds."

"What do you need from me?"

"I'm sending you pictures. Gena Kropenski, Fabian Fitch, and the tiger. Kropenski may be driving a Mercedes Sprint van. Maybe you could tap into Facebook's face recognition system, see if you can get a hit."

"You think if I put Genghis Khan in the system, it will find him? Like it could pick him out of a crowd of hundreds of tigers?"

"You should do Comedy Club."

"Five hundred a day, and that's only because you're a friend."

"I'll send you as soon as I get home, in about three hours."

"I'm looking at you right now."

"What do you mean?"

"Google Earth real time. You're at the Tiger Sanctuary."

"Fuck me."

"I'll send you a link. Upload the data to the link."

Josh saw Leach heading toward the gate. "Sir, can I hitch a ride with you back to Neillsville?"

"Come on."

They got in Leach's Dodge and headed east, passing the two parked semis that had yet to load up.

"When Miss Palmer asked if you could come along, I accessed your criminal record. Is it true you found Christ in prison?"

"Yes sir, thanks to Pastor Mike Dorgan. I wish I could

find him so I could thank him."

"I met Dorgan once. We were touring the state facility. He always struck me as a good man, the right man in the right place at the right time."

"He was for me."

"Good to know."

"Did you find a meth lab?"

"Yes. In the pole barn, along with some ostriches."

"Ostriches?"

"I hope they weren't giving those ostriches meth. I do not want to deal with any cranked-up ostrich."

Josh laughed.

"We're gonna charge Fitch and Kropenski with cruelty to animals. I wish we'd got on that sooner. We're live and let live around here. If a man wants to raise ostriches, he can do so. I should have known something was up. I picked Gunter up a month ago for drunk and disorderly and assaulting a police officer. Someone paid his bail."

"I'd like to know who paid his bail," Josh said.

"Me too."

They rolled into town. There was a Hereford painted on the water tower. Leach dropped Josh off at city hall. Josh walked to his Chrysler and headed south. Josh slipped a Four Seasons disc in the player and sang along, reaching for the high notes. He turned on to the Interstate at Black River Falls and rolled at seventy-five, five miles over the limit, along with everybody else. He knew enough cops to know they'd give you five miles over the limit. Otherwise they'd be stopping ninety per cent of all traffic.

He took the Interstate to the Beltline, headed west, and pulled into his driveway at five-thirty, next to Ray's Prius. Fig barked in excitement. Josh left the car in the drive. The front door opened before he got there, Ray wearing a Fire Town T-shirt. She grabbed him by the front of his shirt and pulled him into a liplock. Fig capering around, they went into the bedroom and shut Fig out.

When Josh came out of the bedroom freshly showered and wearing clean laundry, he found Sid Vicious curled up in the cardboard box on the kitchen floor.

"He sure does love that box," Josh said.

"I'm grilling veggie burgers."

"You don't have to cook."

"But I want to."

Josh resigned himself. He and Fig went out on the deck. He phoned Roth Eisely.

"Eisely."

"Mr. Eisely, it's Josh Pratt."

"What can I do for you?"

"You heard about the raid on the Tiger Sanctuary?"

"It's all over the news."

"It seems their star attraction, a seven-hundred-pound tiger, is missing. Would you have any insights on how I might go about locating it?"

"Tiger needs twenty-five pounds of meat a day. They can eat up to a hundred pounds, but then they just lay around."

"So I should look for the meat."

"It's just a thought. Ask the zoo how they feed their big cats. If it's spotted out in the open, that's when you call me."

"That would be a permanent solution, wouldn't it?"

"Not necessarily. I can shoot a tranquilizer dart as well as a bullet. I've done it."

"Seriously."

"Yes. Tanzania, 2014. A lion was terrorizing a village. Hadn't killed anyone yet. A wildlife fund flew me over. That lion can be seen in the National Zoological Gardens of South Africa in Pretoria. Its name is Gerald."

"How do you track a tiger?"

"They mark their territory. The smell is very distinctive. They scratch trees. You look for their droppings."

"What does it look like?"

"Would you like me to send you a picture?"

"Yes please."

"What about the urine?"

"Smells like boiled basmati rice. You can find it at Whole Foods."

"I'll get some and cook it up."

"There's one other thing you should know about tigers. Unlike other wild animals, they're vindictive. They recognize humans who have mistreated them and will try to kill them."

"Thank you, sir. I'll let you know if we need your services."

THANKS FOR UNDERSTANDING

Reventlo's on Charter Street in Cambridge was a college bar with a stage. Fitch had seen Otis Rush and Jonathan Richman there. On a hot Saturday night in July the joint was jumping, every parking space taken, bicycles chained to the rack out front. Raw metal spilled out the open doors where college students, blues aficionados, small time dealers and bewildered tourists hung out on the sidewalk shouting to each other to be heard over the sound. Cesium, a Deep Purple tribute band, was playing.

Capadona was one of the owners. Fitch entered the dark, smoky bar. It was like walking into a boiler factory. Bar on the left, tables and booths straight back to the stage, a foot off the floor, where a quartet of inked long hairs bent over their instruments wanging out industrial strength rock. Fitch worked his way toward the back, sliding between seat backs, smelling marijuana and beer, past the stage to a door that led to the manager's office, up a level, with a one-way glass looking out toward the front of the club. There was a landing at the top of the stairs, a locked door and a peep hole. Fitch knocked. A minute later the door swung open and he entered the big room with a red shag carpet, mismatched chairs, a scarred table on which sat a mirror off which a lubricious redhead snorked a line. A man who looked like a Mario Brother let him in. Capadona sat with heeled cowboy boots on the desk, drink in hand. He was boyishly handsome with curly black hair, but there was something about the twist of his lips when he smiled, and he smiled often, that bespoke an interior rot. As soon as the door shut, the corrosive din receded to a rumble. The room smelled of high-grade reefer and cocaine.

"Hey Fabe!" Capadona sang. "How they hangin'?"

"Long and low."

"Come on over here. I want you to meet my friend Tania. Tania, say hello to the man."

The redhead looked up. She had fashion cheekbones, green eyes, and lashes that looked like palm fronds. Her arms were fully inked and most of her calves. She stuck out her hand. Fitch shook it.

"How the hell are ya?" she said.

"Fine."

"Tania here sings in a band. The Buzzkills. I'm thinking of managing them."

"What kind of music?"

"Industrial thrash. But don't let that fool ya. She's really a very good singer. Tania, sing something."

"I was so much older than, I'm younger than that now," Tania crooned.

"Wow," Fitch said.

"I know, right?"

"That's not exactly industrial thrash."

Tania slid the mirror toward Fitch who bent over and hoovered a line through a plastic straw.

"We do a Byrds tribute. It's more thrashy when you hear their lead guitar. Benny sounds like a buzzsaw."

"Great. Say Tony. Got a mo?"

Capadona ran a finger under his nose. "Sure, Fabe. Come with me."

Capadona rose from his desk and led Fitch through an oak door into a windowless room with a sofa, a forty-eight-inch screen, and a coffee table on which rested a gold Panda coin and a series of plastic food containers, the kind you get three for a buck at Dollar Tree. He picked one up and tossed it to Fitch. Inside, a gleaming chunk of white was wrapped in plastic.

"Half now, half tomorrow, right?"

Fitch pulled the envelope from his inside jacket pocket. "You bet."

Capadona took the envelope, removed the wad, sat on the sofa and counted it, laying out each hundred neatly on the coffee table.

"Half tomorrow, right?"

"Yeah, man! I'm meeting him tonight! You want, I can

come straight back and give you the rest tonight."

"Well, I'm not going anywhere."

"Well, all right then!"

"Your buyer's cool, right?"

"Man, he is the coolest."

Fitch picked up the coin. "What's this?"

"Chinese Panda. One ounce pure gold. You buy those when the Fed floods the market with worthless paper."

"Nice." Fitch set the coin down.

"Okay. See you later."

"Thanks Tony."

Fitch passed through the office and said goodbye. No one looked up. Dallas had texted him earlier to meet him at Rutabaga at eleven. Rutabaga was a blue-collar bar in Charleston with one wall covered with autographed pictures. Bobby Orr. Yaz. Brady. Ted Williams. Bird. Bill Russell. Randy Moss. Troy Brown's jersey was framed above the bar. Fitch parked his ancient Toyota Supra on a side street in front of a triple decker that had seen better days. Rutabaga was kitty corner. Fitch beelined through the intersection. Two jokers in a sprung Impala honked at him and swerved around, cursing and throwing the finger.

Fitch fired right back. The driver stood on the brakes, put the car in reverse and ratcheted rearward. Fitch jumped on the sidewalk and stood behind a light pole. The Chevy stopped in the middle of the street. Fitch could see the occupants arguing and hear them cursing. After a second, the Impala moved forward down the avenue until it disappeared.

Fitch stood there heart pounding wondering what just happened. It wasn't like he was some great fighter. He knew how to take a punch. But that was just plain stupid, him shooting the bird like that, carrying a key of blow.

"You stupid shit!" he cursed himself. He took a moment to compose himself on the sidewalk as two dudes with shaved skulls that looked like light bulbs, and green shamrocks on their arms pushed by and entered, releasing a snippet of "Beat It" and the smell of beer. Fitch clutched the plastic container under his right armpit and went in. It was dark, with the jukebox blasting and people shouting at one another. A third of the crowd was women. Fitch went to the end of the bar near the door and ordered a Sam Adams, eyes sweeping the bar. He spotted Dallas down at the end talking to a pale woman with a black buzz cut. Dallas looked like he'd stepped out of the Summer of Love. Fringed jacket, wide-brimmed hat, pink aviators.

Fitch drank his beer and watched. The woman smiled. Dallas leaned in. She laughed. They were having a good time. Fitch checked his watch. It was eleven-thirty. He walked down the bar and stood behind them until Dallas noticed.

"Oh hey. Hey, man! Hey, Fabian! This is Midge. Say hello, Midge."

"Hello."

"Hey man, I hate to be a drag," Fitch said, "but I gotta fly."

"Oh. Oh okay. Excuse me, Midge. This won't take a minute."

He got off the bar and nodded toward the rear. They passed two pool tables. Bikers and bus drivers. They went down the corridor past the rest rooms, a supply closet, through a store room in the rear, out a metal door into a narrow alley between School Street and Elm. Oily puddles on the pitted concrete reflected the night sky. Rats skittered among green dumpsters lined up against the wall.

Dallas headed for School Street.

"Hey. Hey. Where you going? I got it right here?"

"Yeah, man, I'm a little spooky about the money thing, okay? It's in my car. It's just around the corner."

Fitch got vibes. He knew the smart thing to do would be to turn tail and run. Tony wouldn't be happy about getting his key back, but Fitch could live with that.

"That's far enough, man."

Dallas turned with a pained expression, hands by his sides. "What?"

The beat-up Impala, lights off, turned into the alley and accelerated. Dallas froze. Fitch leaped behind one of the reeking dumpsters. The Chevy flashed its brights. Thunk. Dallas flew over the hood and off the trunk. The Chevy screeched to a halt and backed up over him. It rumbled forward, mangling Dallas' arm. It stopped. Two guys got out. The driver was a dark little guy with moussed hair and a vest. He went to the broken body which lay like a discarded doll.

"C'mere, numbnutz."

Fitch shrank back. The second guy, the guy in the shot-gun seat, came around the dumpster and grabbed Fitch by the ear, dragging him into the middle of the alley to where the body lay. It was near midnight. They could hear traffic from up the block but there was no one else.

The driver ripped Dallas' shirt open revealing a micro-phone taped to his rib cage with a wire running down into his pants.

"This dude's a narc, fuckwad."

The second guy, who had a faded anchor inked on his arm, a broken nose, and a shaved skull, said, "Give it up."

"What are you talking about?"

The second guy punched him in the gut so hard he bent over and puked. The plastic container dropped from his jacket. The second guy picked it up, pried off the lid, look at the plastic-wrapped flake in the moonlight, and put it back.

"All right. Thanks for understanding."

HIGH NOON

Tiger Sanctuary personnel included animal tender Les White, who had a rap sheet for kiting checks and selling meth, Mona Davis, a one-armed animal activist, Matt Durham, a former rocker who had a regional hit with his band The Messerschmidts, and Jeff Gunter, whereabouts unknown. Palmer had also forwarded everything she could find on co-owners Kropenski and Fitch, whereabouts unknown.

Fitch had screwed around in college, dealt cocaine, got in bed with the mob, and probably would have been dead except for a fluke. As an undergrad at BU, he had invested part of his inheritance in a friend's start-up company. The friend invented a new type of speaker, the Quack. In 1998, Quack went public. Six months later, KLM purchased Quack for sixteen million dollars, giving Fitch a three thousand per cent return on his investment. One point five mil. Fitch used the money to buy land in Grant County and began collecting tigers.

Kropenski quit the MMA circuit to join Fitch. She had a lifetime fascination with the big cats and a desire to do *something*. For Gaia. For Earth.

Josh looked up each party on the internet, learning what he could. He was no Ninja. He could barely work his computer. In trying to locate Khan, several thoughts occurred. First, and obviously, the cat was either with Kropenski or Fitch, or both, if they had hooked up. Face recognition software only worked if you showed your face. If Fitch and Kropenski were in rural America and had an ounce of sense, they wouldn't show up. Josh needed a description of their vehicles and license plates. He needed to know whether either party owned land in the Midwest, and under what name. He needed to know a whole lot of things that only Ninja could find.

Twenty-four hours had passed since he'd called Ninja. He called again. The number he dialed was no longer in service. Five minutes later, Ninja returned his call.

"I got no hits. What else?"

"I'm sending you a list of people connected with the Tiger Sanctuary. They abandoned all the animals but Genghis Khan, a seven-hundred-pound Siberian tiger. Kropenski's got the tiger stashed somewhere in the Midwest, 'cause you don't want to drive cross country with a tiger. I'm particularly interested in rural properties to which Kropenski might have access. See if you can locate anything that may have been purchased or rented through a dummy corporation or a third party.

"Also, Fitch is driving an old Subaru, and Kropenski may have taken the Sanctuary van, which is a Mercedes Sprinter. See if you can find anything about them."

"Will do. I'm combing through their social media posts. Twelve days ago, Fitch deleted his Facebook, Twitter, and LinkedIn accounts. There's a lot to go through. Kropenski's accounts are still up but she hasn't posted anything since July 14."

"Kropenski's family lives in Omaha, Nebraska. Reginald Kropenski was a long-distance trucker. He's retired. Her mother Edie works for Artisan Home Care. Her brother Wayne owns the Elkhorn Tavern in Waterloo, Iowa. He was a star running back in high school and at the U of Nebraska, tried out for the Green Bay Packers, didn't make it, and runs his bar. Has a coke problem."

"How do you know that?"

"Staties picked him up for erratic driving, found an ounce in his glove compartment. His lawyer got him released on a technicality. They think he gets his blow from a biker gang called the Hessians, headquartered in Arena. He's not on social media. He and Gena are tight."

"Are you someplace we could meet?"

"What for?"

"I'd like to pay you in cash."

"I'll come by your place tomorrow afternoon."

"Thanks, Ninja."

Ninja couldn't be far. He'd left East St. Louis after pissing off a mobster named Johnny Torreo. Torreo was awaiting sentencing for racketeering and murder, after tracking Ninja to Josh's house last fall. The Torreo gang was not a factor.

Ray entered Josh's office. "Let's go."

"Where?"

"High Noon Saloon. Side Effects is playing."

"Who?"

"They're an amazing power pop band."

"I'm beat, babe. I've been on the go since six a.m."

"Poor baby."

"I have to get some sleep. I have to run down to Waterloo and look for that tiger."

"What's in Waterloo?"

"Gena Kropenski's brother. Who knows. I might get lucky."

"Come on! It's not gonna take you all day to get there. You can sleep in."

"I don't sleep in. Fig wakes me at six for her breakfast. Then she wants to run."

"If I run with you, will you go see the band?"

Josh saw there was no way he was going to win this one. "All right."

"Come on. I'll drive."

They got in Ray's Prius with the Obama stickers. They parked on East Washington, took two more free masks, and scored a table in the back. At eight-thirty, the place was at eighty per cent, mostly locals, East Side hippies who walked from their tiny houses on the isthmus. A couple of chops pulled up at the curb. Ray handed her backpack to Josh. That was one of the things he liked about her. She never carried a purse. She carried a backpack.

"Whaddaya want?"

"Giant Jones."

Josh watched Ray walk to the bar. So did most of the men. In tight blue jeans and a tucked in Not Lame T shirt, she was hot. Josh watched in amusement as a slick dude in a fade away and Tommy Bahama Hawaiian tried to chat her up. Ray smiled, talked to the man, nodded toward Josh. Josh waved. The man turned to the woman on the other side. Ray came back with beer.

Marijuana drifted through the room. The band took the stage, a loose-limbed guitarist with Buddy Holly glasses, a svelte lead singer in hip huggers and a halter top, a bass player with a flop of brown hair in his face, and a thick drummer with a blond haircut. The guitarist nodded his head and the band launched into Cheap Trick's "Hello There," earning instant delight, segued into Angel City's "After the Rain" followed by Rick Derringer's "You Can Have Me."

A lissome blond named China came over and pulled out a chair and pulled down her mask. Josh recognized her from Ray's dance company. "Hi Ray! Hi Josh! Ray, can I ask you a question?"

"Go ahead."

"For this number I'm doing, 'Bangin' On A Pangolin,'

don't you think I should downplay my sexuality and do it as a kind of nerd? I'd like to wear glasses, no makeup, and dance in Buster Brown shoes."

"What do you mean, Buster Brown shoes?"

"You know. Clunky."

"Can you dance in clunky shoes?"

"Sure. I put taps on the bottom."

"Show me tomorrow. You're coming tomorrow, aren't you?"

"Of course. This show is more important to me than my job! I can always get a job."

Josh looked up at one of the flat screens that circled the dining area, usually tuned to some sporting event. The sports fans cleared out around eight thirty, just in time for the music lovers. The World Cup was on. Nobody Josh knew liked soccer. Suddenly the view of athletes lying on the ground clutching their calves was replaced by a stern-looking woman standing in front of a row of tract houses. The sound was off but the trailer at the bottom of the screen read:

ESCAPED TIGER TERRORIZES HORTONVILLE.

Josh nudged Ray.

"What?"

He pointed at the screen. Stock photo of a snarling tiger.

"Oh my god."

"I have to go."

"What? That's bullshit! What can you do? Are you going to run out there and wrestle the tiger back into its cage?

Forget it, pal. You're staying here."

He knew she was right, but he was crazy to find out what was going on. What if it were Genghis Khan? He pulled out his device and tuned in WMAD. Katy Varner at the desk, staring intensely. This was serious business.

Josh stood. "I'll be right back."

JOSHTOWN

Josh sat on a bench in the garden out back and went to the *State Journal*. The big cat had been spotted on the outskirts of Hortonville. Residents were advised to stay indoors, and keep their pets inside. Authorities didn't know where it came from. Dozens of would-be big game hunters, who usually just shot deer, volunteered, showing up in pick-up trucks with rifles and scopes. The Sauk County Sheriff's Department thanked them and sent them home. Baraboo was in Sauk County. Baraboo was home of Circus World Museum, the civic-minded descendant of Ringling Brothers, Barnum and Bailey Circus.

Ray tracked him down. "Come on!"

"What about my tiger?"

"Forget the tiger. I can't believe I'm having this conversation! Who do you think you are? Tarzan? Come on!"

Josh let her yank him back into the saloon where the

band was playing "Route Sixty-Six," one of Josh's favorite jams. She dragged him out on the dance floor. No one was watching him anyway. He shaked and boogied for one song and headed for the table. He drained his beer. Ray was flushed and happy.

"I love to dance!"

"Me too!" China said.

"Good. Why don't you two chicks go dance with each other?"

"Chicks?" China said.

"Forget it, China. It's Joshtown!"

Josh put his hands behind his head and stretched, watching the two women gyrate on the dance floor. Whistles and catcalls. They didn't just bop and dip. There was art in the way they moved, the subtle pause between motions, the elegant arms in sync with the music. Josh returned to the patio where ancient east side hippies sat smoking marijuana and debating the relative merits of Herbert Marcuse and Howard Zinn. Josh walked to the rear and called Sheriff Leach.

"This is Leach."

"Sheriff, Josh Pratt. You remember me from yesterday..."

"I remember. What can I do for you?"

"Did they catch that tiger?"

"No. However, we know where it came from. It escaped from Circus World Museum in Baraboo. Animal rights activists set it loose. They used a bolt cutter to open the gate.

They're lucky it didn't maul them to death. We have video and it's only a matter of time before we track them down."

"The Wild Animal Initiative has asked me to find Genghis Khan."

"I expect you to notify law enforcement if you do."

"I will."

Josh's phone rang. "Pratt."

"I'm in your house," Ninja said.

"How did you get in? The security system is supposed to alert me."

"I installed the security system. I need to hunker down for a few days."

"What's the problem?"

"I'll tell you when you get here."

"I wish you'd checked with me first, Ninja. Ray ain't gonna be happy."

"Ray loves me."

"She loves you in small doses."

"You want my help?"

"It's fine, Ninja. See you shortly."

"I'm whacked. I'm crashing. You won't see me."

Josh returned to the saloon. Ray and China were dancing up a storm, the center of attention. When the song ended, Ray returned laughing to the table.

"Okay, I'm beat. Let's go."

"Ninja called. He's staying at my place."

"Really?"

"Sorry, babe. I need him and I owe him."

"How long is he staying?"

"Don't know. He's trustworthy. You won't even see him. He's sleeping in the basement."

Ray frowned, hands on hips. Josh knew what that meant.

"Listen. It's not that I don't like Ninja. It's just that, in this stage in our relationship, I would prefer that you and I have the house to ourselves."

Uh-oh. Red flags appeared.

"I really need to work with him on this."

"You know what? Why don't you just go on by yourself for now."

Josh bit his tongue. "All right. I'm sorry."

Ray flicked her hand. "Whatever."

Josh called an Uber. A ratty old Denali was parked in the driveway and the basement lights were on. Fig greeted him at the door with a fusillade of barks. Techno thumped from the basement. Josh opened the door and went downstairs where Ninja had arranged two folding tables in an L formation and covered them with routers, screens and keyboards. Ninja was a lean black man wearing gray sweat pants and a white muscle shirt

"Hey!"

Ninja jumped and turned. "Didn't hear you come in."

"That's because you're blasting shit at one hundred and twenty decibels."

Ninja turned it down. "Hope I ain't intrudin'."

"Whadja find out about Fitch?"

"Shady past, made some money off Quack speakers, sold

cars, moved around. He bought that place upstate in 2014. He got the idea for the tiger sanctuary on a trip to Florida in 1994, where he visited Big Cat Rescue near Pensacola, one of the first big cat sanctuaries that offered petting zoos. Funky earth mother Anastasia Vukelov owns Big Cat. At first they got along fine, but then Anastasia got word of the situation at Fitch's place and started bad-mouthing him. Saying he was irresponsible and mistreating the animals. Rank shit. They started feuding over the internet. One day PETA shows up at Fitch 's place. Anastasia sicced them on him. So Fitch hires some muscle to scare them away."

"Would that be Jeff Gunter?"

"Don't know yet. For fifteen dollars, you got to spend fifteen minutes with a tiger cub. Photographs extra. Fitch bought his first tiger in '14 from the R.D. Rosen Circus, on its last legs in Florida, drove it to Wisconsin himself. He musta studied up 'cause it survived the trip. Then he went on a spree, buying bedraggled lions and tigers from private collectors all over the country. He hired a drunken vet from La Crosse. Bill Peterson. Started breeding and selling to private collectors. Illegal in most places, but not here. A liger is the offspring of a male lion and a female tiger. They're white. Sold a couple to Siegfried and Roy."

"How does that help me find Genghis Khan?"

"Fuck if I know. I just thought you'd want to know. How things goin' with that sweet ass girlfriend?"

"When she found out you were here she told me to take a hike."

"Oh no. Oh man, I'm sorry. You want me out of here?"

"Just tell me what kind of trouble you're in."

"You know Chit Chat?"

"No."

"It's a social networking thing. Dude hired me to find out the actual identity behind a Chit Chatter named Perseus. Turns out to be a Chinese national named Liu Shaqi. I musta tripped some triggers 'cause they tracked me down in Milwaukee and I had to get the hell outta town."

"Who tracked you down?"

"I got a call from an MPD detective. Harkness. I looked him up. His sister's married to an Oliver Bruning, who's a Chit Chat executive. Lives in Palo Alto."

"You must have had some warning. Look at all the shit you brought."

"That I did. Mama Preston didn't raise no fools. As I was driving away, they was driving up. And it weren't no Chinese. Dudes in suits in a black SUV. You need me to go, just say the word. I just figured, you needed me and you had a spare room."

"It's cool, it's cool. I have to go down to Iowa. You can take care of Fig."

"What's in Iowa?"

"Genghis Khan, I hope."

FAIRFAX

Fitch couldn't return to his apartment. He had to assume that Capadona knew his contact was a narc, which meant Fitch had to get out of town. He had six thousand dollars on him. He could use cash to buy a bus ticket. It would take Tony a while to track that down. But where could he go?

John Duckworth lived in Fairfax, Virginia, far enough that they wouldn't think of looking for him there. Fitch spent the night on the move. He dare not return to his apartment. He rode the MTA to Cambridge Square and back again. He had breakfast at Jack In The Box at six fifteen, right after they opened. Just Fitch and a couple of transit workers coming off their night shift. He killed time sifting through the magazines at an outdoor kiosk at South Station. The proprietor, who looked Indian, finally said, "So are you gonna buy, or what?"

Fitch bought a copy of *High Times*. He waited until

eight before phoning his old friend Duckworth from a public phone.

John sounded sleepy. "Hello."

"John, I hate to bug ya. It's Fabian. I wonder if I could drop by for a few days."

"Oh mannnn, I've been trying to get hold of you! Didn't you hear?"

"Hear what?"

"We went public a couple days ago and the value has shot through the roof! That fifty thou you loaned me? It's now worth one and a half mil!"

Fitch stared at the phone, mouth open. The swish and bustle of traffic, the screech of air brakes in the train station, the back and forth of street vendors, he heard it all. He smelled coal, diesel fuel, a hint of garbage. He had never felt more alive.

"You're shitting me."

"No sir. All of a sudden I'm busier than a tick on a dog. You want to come down, come on down. I'll put you up but I don't know how much time I have to hang out. We're expanding our facilities. I have to get building permits. I have to look at the fucking ordinances. I have to hire people. It's crazy down here. Marie's helping. I don't even know if anyone will be home. I'll leave a key for you under the welcome mat. You know how to find me? You have the address?"

"No, man. Let me grab a pen."

Fitch burrowed through his pockets, found a pen and the sales receipt from the magazine. "Shoot."

"One fifty-one Burroughs Street. We're in the Gardens at Fair Oaks. How you coming?"

"I'm taking the train. I'll grab a cab."

"The train, huh? You okay? What's going on?"

"I'm fine, John. I'll tell you when I get there. It'll probably be sometime tonight. I'll call you when I get to town."

Fitch boarded the train at nine-thirty and took a seat at the rear. He would have to transfer at Washington. The train quickly filled. A heavy woman sat next to him, taking several minutes to arrange two shopping bags filled with clothes on the overhead shelf. She smelled of lilacs, pulled out a paperback novel and read. Fitch sneaked a peak. *Lucky*, by Jackie Collins. Fitch read his *High Times*. He looked at a double-page spread featuring a Daisy Duke type in short shorts posing next to a dazzling bush. The bus rolled through the southern suburbs, past triple deckers, grade schools, freight yards, and freeway.

The reader got off in New York and was replaced by a garrulous young soldier in an Army uniform. He looked at Fitch 's magazine.

"Man, I haven't been high since I got back from Germany last week. What I wouldn't give for a joint."

"Wish I could help you."

"S'all right. I'll be home in a couple hours and my brother will fix me up. Where you headed?"

"Virginia."

"Oh yeah? Me too! My family lives in Richmond."

Great, Fitch thought.

Fitch stood. "Excuse me. Save my seat."

Fitch headed for the restroom at the back of the car, reciting an old song his mother used to sing. "Passengers will please refrain from flushing toilets while the train is standing in the station thank you kindly."

The morning's *Boston Globe* was stuck in a newspaper rack on the wall. He pulled it, held it under his arm while he relieved himself, and returned to his seat. The soldier was napping. Stepping carefully around him, Fitch took his seat and opened the paper. The Sox blew a big lead to lose to the Detroit Tigers, eight to four. Allied Leaders remembered D-Day. Mondale chooses Geraldine Ferraro as running mate. Fitch flipped impatiently through the pages. And there it was on page fourteen, under "Crime Beat."

> Police investigate possible homicide in Charleston. The body of a man believed to be in his thirties was discovered early this morning by sanitation workers lying in an alley off Summer Street, evidently the victim of a hit and run. Police are withholding the victim's name pending notification of his next of kin.

Sweat popped on Fitch's brow. Capadona had to know about this. He knew everything that happened on the street, and he would know that Dallas was an informant, which meant Fitch was too stupid to live. He'd gotten out of town just in time. Few people knew about Fitch's connection to

Duckworth. Certainly, nobody would think to look for him in Virginia.

The train rolled through New Jersey, passing tenements, refineries, and industrial zones. Fitch saw young men play-ing pick-up basketball, baseball, and shooting craps. He saw girls jumping rope and children playing in the spray of a spouting fire hydrant in the hot July heat. The train pulled into Union Station at six p.m. It had been a long, exhaust-ing ride and Fitch hadn't eaten since yesterday. He bought a Philly cheese steak in the station and stood in line at the Greyhound counter to purchase his ticket for Fairfax. The bus left at seven, grinding through the Western suburbs, past red brick row houses and white-pillared mansions, Buz-zard Point, over the river into Arlington, down Highway Fifty until it pulled into the depot in Fairfax at eight-thirty in the evening.

Fitch examined a wall map to determine where his friend lived. He went out front and hailed a cab. The driver let him out at One fifty-one Burroughs Street, a handsome gray contemporary lit from within, two car garage, a new Mercedes in the driveway. Carrying his over nighter, Fitch rang the bell. Kool and the Gang sounded from within.

John opened the door gripping a bottle of champagne, a big grin spreading across his broad, florid face. He wore a shirt with suspenders, his long hair in slight disarray, several guests standing in the living room, two women dancing with one another.

"Brother!" John declared, embracing Fitch. "How the

hell are ya?"

"I'm good, John. Yeah, I'm good."

"Well let me show you to the guest room, then I'll introduce you to the gang."

A week later, Fitch wired Capadona six thousand dollars.

THE ELKHORN TAVERN

Josh set out at eleven Monday morning on his Road King. He would have been more comfortable in the car, but the bike gave him credibility. Gena's brother was a biker. The ride took him through the southwest driftless area of Wisconsin. The glaciers had stopped halfway down the state and their melt carved countless valleys, and most of the roads were paved. Wisconsin was the Dairy State and produce had to get to market. Shunning the interstate, Josh took state highways, reveling in the green beauty, stopping for deer crossing the road. He came around a corner and a combine was backing into a field, blocking the entire road. He'd seen that before.

Instead of taking the straight shot Highway Twenty-Eight, Josh paused at a roadside rest and consulted his road atlas, taking Highway Fifty Two to Oelwein, advancing toward Waterloo like a knight on a chess board. The

Elkhorn was a typical wood frame roadhouse with a broad porch three steps up from the gravel parking lot and a second story where Wayne lived with his girlfriend Tatiana. It was no secret. She was on the Elkhorn's Facebook page, arm in arm with Wayne, who towered over the diminutive woman, holding his arm and smiling. The Elkhorn featured live music on weekends. Fifty Shades of Blue was playing that Friday. Josh wished he could stick around but he was on a mission.

By the time he arrived, there were four chops in the lot and an F-150. A neon Pabst sign glowed in the picture window overlooking the porch. Josh wheeled his bike back to the porch and kicked out. It was two o'clock. The inside smelled like every other roadhouse. Sawdust and beer. Wayne stood behind the bar looking at one of four flat screens on the walls, watching an MMA match, wearing a sweatshirt with the sleeves torn off to show inked biceps. Josh took a seat and looked at the screen. Two women bantamweights. Josh had to admit that a number of women had distinguished themselves. Ten years ago he never would have imagined so many women competing in MMA, but they were true warriors. He particularly liked Joanna Jędrzejczyk although he couldn't pronounce her name. And Rose Namajunas. He subscribed to Fight Club through his cable provider.

Wayne came over. "What'll you have?"

"What's on draft?"

"Pabst, Goliath and Fremont."

"I'll have a Fremont. This is a replay, right?"

"Yeah. I get it on YouTube. That Sammy Wyatt is a real monster."

Josh watched the match while Wayne drew the beer. Wyatt wore black shorts and sports bra, her opponent, an Asian woman named Francine Ngo, a blue one piece. They clinched. Ngo whirled abruptly, planting her hip in Wyatt's, and threw her to ground. Wyatt went with the momentum and rolled out of harm's way, springing to her feet.

Josh took a long drink of the hoppy beer and looked around. Two Nomads played pool in the back. Two Nomads dug into burgers in a booth with two biker old ladies. Too much mascara and plenty of ink. Behind the bar were framed photographs. Wayne and Forrest Griffin. Wayne getting his hand raised in the ring. Gena getting her hand raised in the ring. Wayne cuddling a tiger cub. A framed fight poster headlined by Gena Kropenski. A pair of golden gloves hanging from a hook.

A menu the size of a billboard hung from a sidewall. Burgers. Fries. Buffalo wings. Nachos.

Wyatt was in the mount, raining down blows on Ngo, who tried to shield herself with her hands. The referee leaned in telling her she had to improve her position. Seconds later, it was all over. The ref pushed Wyatt back and waved his arms. Josh finished his beer. Wayne looked down.

"Want another?"

Josh slid the glass toward him. "You fought Golden Gloves?"

"Yeah. I had dreams of turning pro but a rotator cuff

injury took me out of the game. What about you? You look like you can handle yourself."

"I've been in a lot of fights."

"I guess everyone here has."

"You ride?" Josh asked.

"Yeah. Got a '14 Fat Boy."

Josh pointed. "Zat your sister?"

"Yeah. How do you know about her?"

"I follow MMA. Isn't she the woman who was involved in that tiger sanctuary?"

Wayne drew back, antennae quivering. "Yeah. What do you know about that?"

"My name is Josh Pratt. The Wild Animal Initiative hired me to find the missing tiger. That's why I'm here."

"Well why didn't you just say so?"

"I just did."

"Look. I don't know where Gena's at. I didn't have anything to do with that shit show. I told her not to get involved with that guy."

"Do you know where she is?"

Wayne leaned back, squinting. His sidewalls were shaved, thick, twisty black hair on top. "She's my sister, man. You got a problem with her, I got a problem with you."

"I represent the Wild Animal Initiative. Genghis Khan's welfare is their sole interest. If that tiger were to walk in through that door this minute, I'd be outta here, a happy man."

"That ain't likely to happen."

"Have you tried putting out tuna?"

"You're a funny guy, but I'm gonna have to ask you to leave."

Josh placed his card on the counter. "Remember what I said. All I want is the tiger. Before it kills someone."

"I don't know nothin' about a tiger."

"You ever go up there? To the sanctuary?"

Wayne looked around and leaned in. "Look. You don't seem like a bad guy. But Gena's only mistake was hooking up with that lying sack of shit. Why aren't you looking for him?"

"Not my job."

"Look. I can't talk here. Why don't you and me get together later, when we can talk freely."

"We can talk freely now. Nobody's paying any attention. Whatever your sister's done, she'd be better off not dragging that tiger around."

"What happens you find the tiger?"

Josh put his palms up. "I'm done. I'm outta here."

"Well you don't expect to bring it in yourself. What are you gonna do? Throw a leash around it?"

"No sir. I will notify the authorities. It will be sedated and transported to a new home in Colorado."

"Ain't that sweet. I wish somebody would transport me to a new home."

"All we want is the tiger."

"What if it's loose?"

"The police don't have to be involved. Then it would not

be Gena's problem."

"You don't think people won't notice a bunch of kids with pierced tongues and purple hair beating the fields?"

"They're not like that. It's a professional operation."

"Can't help you. Haven't heard from her. Haven't seen her since Christmas."

"There's a reward if he's captured alive."

"How much?"

"Ten thou."

Wayne nodded. "Well I got to think about that."

Josh pulled out his wallet. Wayne waved him off.

"On the house. You want to talk, come by at one. That's when I close."

"See you then."

SIOUX CITY

Gena's first fight was at the Iowa State Fair in 2014, part of the Heartland Headbangers promotion, an amateur event that served as a conduit to the pros. Her opponent, Lethal L'thaqua, was a mean looking featherweight out of St. Louis with a two and oh record.

Austin Bear was her trainer and manager. Hulking and hirsute as his namesake, Austin had boxed professionally in the eighties before opening his gym, and broadening his martial arts skills any way he could. He'd achieved black belts in Brazilian Ju Jitsu, Filipino Arnis, Thai Kickboxing, and Okinawan Karate. Gena's fight was second, in a big tent at the Iowa State Fairgrounds in Des Moines, with a square ring in the center surrounded by several hundred folding chairs. The tent smelled of beer and marijuana. A faint tang of cow manure lingered from a stock show. The temperature was in the low eighties and the concession stands sold beer as fast as they could pour.

Maybe fifty people watched the bout, which started at one-thirty in the afternoon. L'thaqua came out banging, trying to run over her opponent. L'thaqua was built like a fire hydrant. Gena kept her at bay with a piston-like jab as they worked their way around the ring, L'thaqua advancing, keeping Gena on her heels. They closed at the ropes and furiously exchanged. A looping overhand right caught L'thaqua on the jaw and she went down, just as the bell rang.

For the second round, L'thaqua charged like a bull hoping to take Gena down, but Gena sprawled, got L'thaqua in a Thai clinch, and drove her knee into her opponent's chin. L'thaqua went down. Game over. Spectators stood, shouted, and clapped. Austin winked. On the way back to the dressing room he said, "You just improved your marketability about two hundred per cent."

She won three more amateur fights before landing a spot on the undercard of Beatdown Incorporated Fall Fist Fest in Sioux City.

"Listen," Bear said. "You gotta have a name. We need to build some sizzle."

"I have a name."

"Kropenski. I mean a fight name. Like the Natural. Bones Jones. Mr. Perfect. Got any ideas?"

"I always had a thing for tigers."

"Perfect. Queen Tiger. Tiger print fight togs. Marketable. Now all you gotta do is keep winning."

Her opponent was Luana Silva, four and two, from Sao Paulo. Silva was tough. Gena won by split decision. Next three fights, she finished her opponents in the first round. Now she was marketable. There was talk of a title fight. One year later, 2016, she was a featured bout in Beatdown's Winter Whackout, in Omaha. Her opponent, Black Mariah, was a former Bellator champ. They brawled for fifteen minutes, flattening each other's noses and bleeding all over the ring, but in the end, Gena won a unanimous decision.

She was in her dressing room getting stitched up when a man entered with a bouquet of flowers. He was a solid one-eighty with a buzz cut and tiger tats on both forearms.

"Ms. Kropenski? I'm Fabian Fitch. I've followed you since your first pro fight. I just won fifty thousand dollars thanks to you, and I'd like to show my appreciation."

He didn't come on strong. He was good looking and smelled of Paco Rabanne. She'd driven to the event with Bear. She told him to go home without her. Fitch promised her a ride. Bear happily acceded. It wasn't as if she were in any danger. Any man who tried to strong arm her would get a big surprise, when they woke up.

They went to the Regal Room at the top of the hotel, with an expansive view of Sioux City. They sat at a table by the floor to ceiling window looking out at the twinkling lights. "Let me tell you about myself. I'm an investor. When I was in college, I put fifty grand into a friend's speaker company. Maybe you've heard of them. Quack."

"Yeah, I know Quack." She put her hand to her mouth,

made a beak and honked. The more mimosas she had, the more charming Fitch became. She almost let him take her to bed. Almost. But Mama Kropenski didn't raise no fools. They agreed to meet for breakfast.

You had to wonder about a man who'd bed a woman with a flattened nose and a face the color of a mushroom.

Gena, cursed to arrive early, had a window booth at the Sunny Side Up cafe across from the hotel. Fitch entered wearing shades and a wild Hawaiian shirt with Bugs Bunny, Daffy Duck, Lola Bunny, and Beaky Buzzard. He sat down and smiled.

"Forghorn Leghorn's my favorite," Gena said. "I love the way he talks."

"Ah say. Ah say there, sweetheart, how 'bout some gator sausage and grits?"

The waitress brought coffee. They ordered. Fitch folded his hands in front of him on the Formica table showing three enormous rings. On his left hand, a gold ram's head and a topaz the size of a dime. On his right, some kind of platinum club ring with an elaborate symbol.

"I was galvanized the first time I saw you in action. It was on the fight channel, your third amateur bout, I believe."

"What? I didn't know about that. How can they show my image without my permission?"

"Listen. I can help you with that. You may have signed something without looking at it. They take advantage of young people. I'm hip to that jive. Then, when I saw you had chosen Queen Tiger as your fight name, I knew we had to meet. I just bought a tiger."

"Excuse me?"

"Oh yeah. Her name is Tabitha. Used to belong to Mike Tyson. Tyson sold her to an animal act at the Bellagio. I have some land in Wisconsin. I opened a wild animal refuge and rescue animals like Tabitha who have been mistreated."

"I admire that. I love animals. I have a dog back home. Mr. Schermerhorn. My brother's looking out for him right now."

"What kind of dog is Mr. Schermerhorn?"

"He looks like a whippet, but he's too small. He's got ears like a schooner. Wait."

She pulled out her phone and showed him a picture.

"Awww, cute."

The waitress brought their omelets and refilled their coffee. Fitch added half and half and sugar. Fitch insisted on paying the bill.

"It's about eight hours to Des Moines. You ready?"

"I'm checked out. I just have to get my stuff."

"Need any help?"

"I can manage."

They were on the road in fifteen minutes. Fitch drove a ten-year-old, perfectly maintained Mercedes. The radio played soft jazz. "People love big cats. Can't get enough of them. They'll pay a lot of money to play with tiger cubs, have their pictures taken with the big guys."

"How do you do that?"

"We sedate them. One day a week. Photo day. I hope

to have eight tigers soon so we can rotate them. You don't want all your tigers nodding off at once."

"Where do I come in?"

"I can offer you a training camp and priceless publicity. Queen Tiger. I love it."

AFTER HOURS

Josh rented a room at the Keystone Inn, an old clapboard one floor motel that looked like it was built in the fifties. He ate a burger at Wendy's, across the street, asked the night clerk to ring him at midnight, showered, and slept from four until the phone rang. Josh sat up, instantly alert. He put on his jeans, boots, and a black shirt with full length sleeves. He stared at himself in the mirror.

"This is a set-up."

There was a good chance Wayne would have friends, but no more than two. More than that, word got out. Maybe just one. Maybe just Wayne. There was always that chance. Maybe just Wayne. Josh was not allowed to own firearms due to his priors and had brought none. He wore a steel cup. His boots had steel toes. He slipped brass knuckles into the pocket of his cargo jeans.

Quietly leaving the motel, he set off on foot for the tav-

ern, a mile away. Traffic was sparse. The tavern was on Mc-
Cormick Road, perpendicular to the highway. Farm road,
with corn on both sides and a big drainage ditch. Whenever
a vehicle approached, he lay down in the ditch. No one saw
him. The Elkhorn's lights were off, but a soft glow emanated
from upstairs and downstairs. Two chops in the yard. Josh
worked his way around back where there was more gravel
parking lot butting up against another cornfield. Back of
the tavern was dark. Josh crept across the gravel lot without
making a sound. He mounted the three wooden steps and
listened. Faint voices from the front. Opening the screen
door just enough to reach in, he unhooked the spring, entering the tavern silently through the back door.

He was in the kitchen, redolent with the smell of grease.
It was a long room with a horizontal window opening on
the tavern itself, storage and bathroom off to the side, and
a food preparation island with a big sink in the middle. The
tavern had separate men's and women's restrooms up front.
Josh stood by the slot, back to the wall.

"You won't believe who I saw," said a voice Josh recognized.

"Whud?" Wayne said.

Somebody hoovered a line.

"You remember that goth girl, Wilma Gilpin?"

"That girl looked like a corpse?"

Laughter.

"Ran into her in Dubuque last week. She's married to a
cop."

"No way!" Third voice, unknown. Marijuana smoke

drifted over the sill. Josh angled for a better view. It was dark
in the kitchen and he saw them clearly. Wayne, a fireplug
with no neck, and Jeff Gunter, the Hessian from Arena. A
flat mirror rested on the bar with an amber bottle of blow,
several lines, and a cut-up straw. Wayne ran a finger under
his nose. Josh looked around. A cast iron frying pan hung
from a hook. Silently he removed it.

"What cop?"

"Don't know. Some fat old man from Dubuque."

"You're shittin' me. What for?"

Gunter rubbed his fingers together. "What else? In a year
or two, he'll pass away peacefully in his sleep from a heart
attack and she'll move on to the next sucker."

"You just like to talk shit," the fireplug said.

"Yeah, I do."

Laughter.

"When's that motherfucker gonna show?" Gunter said.

"He'll be here."

"I say we jump him soon's he comes in the door."

"No," Wayne said. "Let me talk to him a little. He may
decide to cooperate."

"Not from what I hear," Gunter said.

"You got any soda?" the fireplug said.

"It's in the kitchen."

He could wait for the lights to bong the guy, or he could
bong the guy now. The fireplug entered the kitchen through
a swinging double door.

"Where are the lights?"

BONG.

Setting the frying pan soundlessly on the fireplug's belly, he grabbed him beneath the arms and dragged him into the cooler.

"What the fuck?" Wayne said.

"Harvey! Hey Harvey!"

"Anybody back there, show yourself right now. I got a gun."

Josh stood with his back to the wall next to the kitchen entrance, holding the frying pan over his head in his right hand. Wayne poked the pistol through the plane with both hands. Josh brought the frying pan down on his wrists. Wayne cursed and dropped the pistol. Josh kicked the pistol away from the door and kicked Wayne in the gut with his steel tipped left boot. Wayne deflated like a party balloon and bent over. Josh lowered himself, grabbed the back of Wayne's head in both hands and pivoted, throwing Wayne into the base of the island. Josh round house kicked Wayne in the face, bouncing his head off the island.

Josh scooped up Wayne's pistol, a cocked nine mm. He was lucky it hadn't gone off. Josh crouched in the darkness gripping the gun. The front door opened and seconds later, the sound of an unmuffled Harley shattered the night. Gunter was gone.

Josh checked on Harvey. Out cold, with a gear shift knob rising above his ear. Josh found the lights on the wall and turned them on. Wayne twitched, put a hand to his head. Josh filled a glass with water and threw it in Wayne's face. He tossed Wayne a bar towel. Wayne stayed where he was and wiped his face.

"Let's talk," Josh said.

"Fuuuuck."

"I kinda figured you didn't ask me to meet you at closing time just to talk. If I were a vengeful person, I might take that personally."

"You took it personally enough."

"I have no interest in Gena. I'm looking for the tiger. Now I figure Gena's got the tiger, am I right?"

"I don't know, bro. I talked to her last week. She told me shit was going down and she might have to bug out but she didn't say anything about a tiger."

"I was in Wisconsin last week when they raided the sanctuary. There's a possibility they'll bring charges against her for animal cruelty, among other things. It would be better for her if she contacted the Wild Animal Initiative, those are the people who hired me, and turned the tiger over to them. I'm an MMA fan. I admire your sister. I've watched her fight. I don't know what she's doing with a con artist like Fitch."

"I told Gena there was something about him. A little too slick."

Harvey groaned.

"You might want to call an ambulance. Pretty sure he's got a concussion."

"What did you hit him with?"

Josh picked up the frying pan. Wayne laughed.

"So what was the plan? Beat the shit out of me or what?"

"I wanted to convince you to stop looking for my sister."

"It's what I do. I got a reputation to uphold."

"I'm gonna stand."

"Go ahead."

Wayne got to his feet in stages. He knelt where Harvey lay and ran his finger over the bump. "Holy shit. What am I gonna tell the meds?"

"Tell them he fell on a rock. You have my card, right?"

"Yeah."

"How do you know Gunter?"

"Hessians stop here all the time. This is the biker bar between them and New Orleans."

"Any idea why Gunter would know me?"

"Says you killed a friend of his."

"What friend?"

"Some dude from the Insane Assholes." Wayne laughed. "Gotta love the name."

"I didn't kill anyone from the Insane Assholes. The cops did. In my front yard. You think about what I said. If it makes sense to you, you have my number."

"Let me think about it."

"Where's the girlfriend?"

"Visiting her folks."

"May I have Gena's phone number?"

Wayne sighed and gave it to him.

"Don't think about it too long. The police are liable to file charges."

CHAPTER 19

TIGER MEAT

Having grown up in lower middle class circumstances, Gena thought the main house at the Tiger Sanctuary was just fine. Four bedrooms, three baths, and one of them had a built-in jacuzzi. Fabian was charming and considerate. He showed her around the zoo with pride, pointing out the ligers, the black bears, and a pair of peacocks that strutted the yard shrieking.

"They're better than a watchdog," Fabian said.

Mr. Schermerhorn fit right in. Fabian installed a doggie door in the sliding glass patio door so that Mr. Schermerhorn could come and go as he pleased. Mr. Schermerhorn was a lab/mastiff mix. The peacocks frightened Mr. Schermerhorn so badly, he hid under the bed in Gena's room all day, only emerging to eat. But after a few days, the dog and peacocks worked it out like two rival gangs in prison. The peacocks had the front yard during the morning. Mr.

Schermerhorn had it in the afternoon.

Fabian introduced Gena to Les, Mona, and Gunter.

"What happened to her arm?" Gena asked as they walked away.

"Khan tore it off. Good thing Mona loves animals. She's my best worker."

"Jesus Christ. He tore her arm off and she still works here?"

Fabian shrugged. "It happens. She had no health insurance so I took care of it. Do you have insurance?"

"Yes, I have a policy through Tiger Insurance. They specialize in insurance for martial artists."

"It's a sign."

Gena grinned. "Maybe."

Fabian showed her the barn, floor covered with sawdust on wood planks. A new Mercedes Sprinter sat on the wooden floor with magnetic signs affixed to the sides. A snarling Khan, painted by an expert illustrator, beneath circus style lettering. GENGHIS Khan! Below the tiger's image, TIGER SANCTUARY, Neillsville, WI. "That's my tiger wagon. We use it to fetch the meat and move the animals from enclosure to enclosure."

"Pretty fancy."

"I learned a long time ago not to settle for second best."

"When do I meet Genghis?"

"In a little while. I'll put up a ring in here so you can train."

Gena pointed to the heavy bag hanging from the rafters.

"What's that for?"

"Gunter put it up. He likes to work out. Feel free to use it."

"Can I bring my trainer out?"

"Sure. Invite whoever you like."

They walked from the barn through the compound, past a small pole barn set apart, past mature maple and elm, to a big enclosure in the rear, steel bars sunk into concrete bases surrounding a couple thousand square feet of gently rolling ground covered with weeds. A plastic pond lay between the mounds with softly burbling water, and Genghis lay in the pond.

"There he is. There's my big boy."

Gena gasped. He was magnificent and didn't look emaciated like some of the others.

The great cat leaped to its feet, jaws open revealing scimitar teeth, hair standing on the back of its neck. It hissed.

Fitch took her hand. "Come on. We'll come back when he's in a better mood."

"He seems angry."

"That's just fear. He does that whenever he meets a new person. Needless to say, you can't pet Genghis."

"He's beautiful."

Fitch tugged at her hand. "Come on. Lots to see."

But there really wasn't much left to see and Gena thought Fitch wanted to get away from his star attraction.

That night Gena had one drink and refused the blow. She woke at dawn. Leaving Fitch sawing logs, dressed, crept out of the house and went to Genghis' cage. The big cat lay on a pile of straw, alert, eyeing her with curiosity. She crouched next to the bars and spoke in a low voice.

"What a beautiful boy you are. Who's a good boy? Who's a good boy?"

Genghis yawned and rolled over on his back.

Two days later, Bear called. "You're fighting for the title on November fifteen."

Gena squealed in delight. "Thank you, lawd, thank you! And thank you Bear! How much do I get?"

"Fifty thou with a ten thou bonus if you knock her out."

"Who?

"Cass Byam. We start training in August. When you coming back to town?"

"I'm training here, Bear. At the Tiger Sanctuary."

"What the fuck?"

"Come on out, Bear. You'll dig it. They put up a ring for me and they have all the equipment."

"Are you seeing that slickee boy you met at the fight?"

"His name is Fabian Fitch. He's a genius, Bear. He made a fortune investing in Quack speakers, and this place is pulling in a bundle. Next to The House on the Rock, it's Wisconsin's second biggest tourist attraction."

"What place?"

"The Tiger Sanctuary, duh."

"Do you think this is a good idea? How long have you known this guy?"

"I feel like I've known him all my life."

"Well, everybody's entitled to make their own mistakes, I guess."

"Bear. Come out here. See for yourself."

"Ain't got time. I got a gym to run."

Five miles every morning on the old, paved farm roads surrounding the sanctuary. Back to the gym for more cardio and working the ropes. Bear flew out a week later. He stayed in town. She brought in old friend Estrella Dominguez for a sparring partner. They worked out for a week before Estrella had to return to her home in New Mexico.

One day in December, with six inches of fresh snow on the ground, Gena came out of her bedroom having showered and changed into slacks and a sweatshirt to find Gunter and Fabian bent over a mirror in the living room. Fabian looked up. He held out the straw.

A chill rippled Gena's spine. "No thanks." She marched quickly into the kitchen and poured herself a cup of coffee. Minutes later, the front door opened and closed. Fabian followed her.

"You're not upset, are you?"

Gena stood outside the cage where a tigress named Nubia nurtured two cubs. "I can't be involved in that. I have a fight coming up. My brother was a coke head. He served two years in prison. What the fuck are you thinking?"

"Look, Gena, there are a lot of things about me you don't know. I've turned my life around. I used to be a dealer too. I can handle it. It's not like I'm getting wasted every night. I just like to do a little snort now and then. Helps me get things done."

"I have to undergo a drug test before each fight. You know that."

"That's three months away!"

"I don't care. I like you, Fabian. I may even love you. But being around coke fucks everything up. You know that. I love the tigers. I love this place. Now I have to seriously rethink my commitment to you, and to this place."

"Wow."

Gena stared at him. Fabian looked down. "Wow?"

"Okay. Okay! You're more important to me than getting high. No more coke. I swear."

"How much of that shit do you have sitting around?"

"Not much. I'll get rid of it. Gunter can unload it."

"That guy gives me the creeps."

"Gunter's all right. He loves the tigers."

"Why don't you do something about those cages? Why don't you take out the gravel and replace it with straw? Don't you care about the animals?"

"Of course I care! I love the animals. You know, you're right. I'll tell Gunter to get on it right away. I can buy hay from Johnson across the street."

"I'm going into town."

"What are you going to do?"

"I need something to read. There's nothing to read here."

"Would you mind stopping by Walmart and picking up a few things?"

"Write me a list."

Twenty minutes later, Gena pulled her eight-year-old Forester into the Walmart parking lot at the edge of Neillsville, across the street from Farm & Fleet. She pushed a shopping cart with a recalcitrant wheel down the aisle checking things off her list. Pancake mix. Milk. Eggs. Manager Rod Clark caught up with her.

"Hey Gena. I got forty pounds of meat for you. You wanna pull around to the back of the store we'll get it in your trunk."

"Thanks, Rod." Fitch had worked out a deal to take past due meat in exchange for free passes for Clark and his family. But as the Sanctuary population grew, Walmart couldn't keep up. Fitch was now talking to the Walmarts in Marshfield and Wisconsin Rapids. They had to get corporate approval, but if it came through, the Sanctuary wouldn't have to worry about feeding its tigers ever again. She checked out, stuffed her groceries in the back seat, and drove around to the rear where a butcher in a stained white apron waited with a package the size of a big suitcase wrapped in butcher paper.

Gena popped the lid and got out. She and the butcher deposited the package in her trunk.

"Thanks, Sam."

"You know, you're not the only one trying to feed tigers around here."

"How's that?"

"Guy comes in here once a week and buys pork for his tiger. Pays full retail. I told him he'd be better off going straight to the farm. He didn't come last week so I think he took my advice."

"What guy?"

"Guy named Capadona. Used to be a financier in Boston. Moved out here to get away from it all. Well, he really got away from it all."

"And he's got a tiger?"

Sam shrugged. "People are crazy."

CHAPTER 20

JIGGITY JOG

Josh returned to the motel at two, slept until ten and headed home. He pulled into his driveway at three o'clock in the afternoon. No SUV. He wondered if Ninja had slipped away like smoke. Inside, Fig was gone and there was a note on the counter.

"Found out about a dog park in Verona. Thought I'd take Fig for a walk. Back by five. Let me know if you want me to pick anything up."

Josh called Ray.

"Hi, Josh."

"You still pissed?"

"Is he still there?"

"I'm working on a case. He's helping me."

"Holmes and Watson."

"Has he done anything to upset you?"

"No, I just wish we had a little privacy. That's all."

"Pretend you're in college and you have a roommate."

"Let me know when he's gone."

Click.

Josh showered, went online, and Google earthed the sanctuary. From the sky it was just a collection of rectangles interspersed with trees. The small cages bothered Josh. He couldn't get the image of an old tiger lying listless on its gravel bed, not even moving when one of the veterinarians entered, out of his head. Seeing any animal suffer bothered him. Except for insects and eels and things like that.

He looked up Fabian Fitch.

Fabian Fitch is the founder of the controversial Tiger Sanctuary in Clark County, Wisconsin, infamous for its petting zoos, sale of baby tiger, ligers, tigons, and other tiger hybrids that do not occur in nature. The Tiger Sanctuary boasts the largest tiger in North America, Genghis Khan, weighing seven hundred pounds and measuring ten feet, nose to tail. In 2014, Genghis Khan ripped the arm off a Sanctuary worker who underwent extensive rehabilitation, and later returned to the Sanctuary to resume her duties.

The Sanctuary makes most of its money charging people to take selfies and play with exotic baby animals. Fitch also runs a breeding program catering to celebrities. Heavyweight boxing champion Delbert King purchased a liger from the Sanctuary in

2017. Kim Kardashian purchased a tigon from the Sanctuary in 2019. She has since donated it to the Los Angeles Zoo.

The USDA recently revoked Fitch's license, and the Wisconsin Attorney General filed suit to shut down the entire facility, claiming the animals were living in deplorable conditions. PETA has also filed suit, accusing Fitch of violating the Endangered Species Act. Fitch is notorious for cross-breeding lions and tigers, as well as other species, resulting in a large number of mutant offspring. Many of these animals suffered from genetic malformations. The State Attorney General appointed the Wild Animal Initiative, located in Wallis, Colorado, to seize and place all animals from the sanctuary. There are over one hundred exotic animals at the property, with at least two dozen big cats. The Sanctuary is involved in an intense stand-off with authorities. There are rumors that Sanctuary employees are armed, and that Fitch is prepared to defend his property if necessary. He has characterized the state's actions as an unlawful taking, and that until recently, there had been no complaints.

Fitch points out that it is not illegal to own exotic animals in Wisconsin. Just who is Fabian Fitch? He was born in 1969 in Brookline, MA, the second child of Doctors Cosgrove and Eunice Fitch. He graduated from Boston University in 1993 and clerked for State Supreme Court Justice Harold Swanson. In 1995, he was arrested for possession of cocaine and served seven months at Federal Medical Center, Devens.

His father died in 1997 leaving him a six-figure inheritance which he invested in Quack speakers, created by his childhood friend John Duckworth. When Quack went public, Fitch realized a three thousand per cent return on his investment. It was then that he purchased the land in Clark County.

The front door opened. Fig scrabbled on the hardwood floor and flew into the office, jumping up in Josh's lap, nearly knocking him over.

"We're hommme," Ninja sang falsetto from the living room.

Josh nuzzled Fig. Ninja wore camo trou, a fisherman's vest over a black T, sunglasses, and a Packer cap he'd found in Josh's closet.

"How was the park?"

"Groovy, baby. You should try it. All these dogs running free. And the parade of little dogs. So many little dogs. But big dogs too. Fig was fine. Sniffed a lot of butt, ran around and now we're hungry."

"I got Gena's phone number. I set it on your computer."

"I'll get on it."

Josh pulled a frozen pizza from the freezer.

"Put that back. I got some ribs. Omma grill."

Josh opened a can of Whole Earth Chicken and Turkey recipe and dumped it in Fig's bowl. She ate it in ten seconds. Josh followed Ninja out on the deck where Ninja dumped used coals from the small Weber in a garbage can and put shredded paper in the bottom.

"You find that tiger?"

"No. Her brother tried to scare me off the trail."

"How'd that work out?"

"Not too well."

"I'll bet. So whatcha gonna do now?"

Josh sat in one of the Adirondacks and watched Ninja add coal. "I'd like you to track down every property Fitch owns. There are probably a bunch of dummy corporations and off shore accounts you gotta wade through. I'd like you to try and find Gena via her phone."

"I can do that. You wanna make the salad?"

"What salad?"

"A man's gotta eat."

Josh followed Ninja into the kitchen and unloaded the vegetable drawer. Red leaf lettuce, little peppers that looked like candy corn, fat scallions, tiny tomatoes.

"There's croutons and a can of palm hearts in the cupboard."

Ninja removed a tray of ribs that had been marinating all afternoon. "Where's that fine lady of yours? I got enough for everybody."

"She's not coming."

"Problem?"

Josh didn't know what to say. He needed Ninja to do the job, and booting him out would not help. It wasn't as if he could set up his equipment in a motel room. There was so much of it.

"She's busy."

Josh was eager to wrap it up. You can't hurry love, and you can't hurry an investigation. He'd just have to stick it out. "The sooner I find that tiger, the better."

"I'll get on it tonight, my man."

Josh ran the lettuce through a lettuce spinner Ray had given to him. All his life he'd just been eating the lettuce straight from the shelf. It was a miracle he was still alive. The ribs were good. Ninja carried the dirty dishes inside and rinsed them. They watched *Nobody*, a Bob Odenkirk thriller that ended with Bob and pals mowing down hundreds of nameless, faceless Russian goons. Josh went to bed with Fig at his feet. When he got up to go to the bathroom near midnight, he saw that the lights were still on in the basement.

CHAPTER

21

THE LAST STRAW

Gena found Mona feeding Khan. At two thousand square feet, Khan's cage was the biggest. The ground was covered with straw, not gravel. Mona tossed a raw beef liver through the bars. Khan snatched it out of the air, padded into a corner and went to work.

"Did Fabian do something to Khan?"

"Huh?"

"Yesterday when he brought me back here, Khan suddenly got all pissy, like he wanted to take a chunk out of Fabian."

"I wouldn't know about that. He ripped my arm off but that was my own fault."

"How did it happen?"

"I was feeding him and he was sulking so I stuck my arm through the bars and waved a pork chop around. He was on my arm in a second. I was in the hospital for a week, but it's all good. Fabian paid for rehabilitation and told me I had a job here as long as I liked."

"Who's Capadona?" Gena said.

Mona looked at her. "Huh?"

"The butcher at Walmart said a man named Capadona comes in for meat for his tiger. Don't tell me you're unaware of another tiger in Clark County."

"Oh, Tony! Yeah, he's a friend of Fabian's. He sold him that tiger. Got his own zoo. Nothing like this, of course, but he's got a couple of emus, a honey badger, and that liger Fabian sold him. Fortissimo. Half our money comes from sale of exotic animals. The breeding program isn't just to keep churning out cute little cubbies."

"Where's Capadona keep his tiger?"

"On his farm. Why?"

"Something's not right here. Fabian's still doing blow. Makes him twitchy. Makes me think there's stuff he hasn't told me. I dig your mission. I think it's great that you're helping to preserve these precious animals, but I'd feel better if he'd quit snorting coke."

Mona rolled her eyes. "I know what you mean. I used to do that shit too, but since I lost my arm, the thought of it gives me the heebie jeebies. God knows how much of our revenue goes up his nose. I got a little reefer if you're interested."

"No thanks."

"Ladies!" Fitch called. He stood twenty feet away. "How are we today?"

Gena marched over and stared into his red rimmed eyes. "I warned you." She stomped past.

He ran after. "Wait a minute! Wait a minute! Don't leave me! I'm begging you! Please!"

She turned, hands on hips. "Either the blow goes or I go."

"All right. ALL RIGHT! Follow me."

He hot stepped back to the house. He went into his office, came out with a small zip-lock bag filled with white powder, went into the office bathroom and flushed it down the toilet. Gena threw her arms around him. "Thank you."

They kissed. He cupped her buttocks in his hands. They staggered into the bedroom, ripped each other's clothes off. She pushed him back on the bed and straddled him, her hands on his chest, forcing him to go slow.

"Easy. Easy now."

After that, Gena learned all she could about the sanctuary. She knew each animal by name, their diet, their habits. She brought them food, sometimes paying for it herself when they didn't have enough. She wrote memos to Fitch when she perceived an animal to have health problems.

A week later, she visited the star attraction. She gazed through the bars at Genghis Khan. She cooed to him through the bars. One day, as she came back from a run, not stopping to shower or change her clothes, she went straight to his cage to cool down. "Who's a good boy? Who's a good boy?"

The great cat ambled over and lay on his back next to the

bars. For long seconds she stared at his long, tawny stomach. Tentatively, she put her hand through the bars and held it there. Genghis' tail twitched. She reached out, placed her hand light as a feather on his belly and gently stroked. Genghis purred. He sounded like an idling motor boat. She couldn't believe it. Genghis purred and flicked his tail. She scratched behind his ears.

"What the fuck!" Gunter cried. "Get away from the cage!"

With a roar, Genghis leaped up and lunged at the cage, but not at her. He stood on his hind legs and clawed. Gena rolled back. Gunter picked up a stick and whacked it against the bars.

"Get back! Get back!"

"Stop it!"

Gunter looked at her in astonishment. "What the fuck, Gena! You want to get yourself killed!"

"There's no need for that. You're only making him mad."

"You're outta your fuckin' mind. That's a seven-hundred-pound tiger. It'll rip your arm off, like it did to Mona!"

Gunter whacked the cage again, infuriating the big cat.

"Put that fucking stick down or I'll take it away from you."

Gunter looked at her in astonishment. He looked down. He tossed the stick to the ground and walked away muttering. She went to the office and heard a drawer slam shut as she entered the house. Fabian was behind his desk poring over his computer and making notes in a tablet.

"What's up?"

"Where's the hay you promised?"

Irritation rippled across Fabian's face like heat lightning, replaced by the smooth smile, the warm brown eyes. "You're absolutely right. I've been meaning to do that anyway. Would you like to arrange for a delivery? Can you take care of that? I've got my hands full right now trying to save two bears in a Mexican zoo."

"I didn't even know Mexico had bears."

"They're black bears from Montana. Very popular."

"What happened to the farm across the street?"

"I checked. They don't have any hay."

Gena arranged for Huntington Farms, in Eau Claire County, to deliver two and a half tons of hay. They dumped the hay in the front yard and the entire staff went to work moving animals from cage to cage, removing gravel, spreading the hay. They worked twelve hours, but in the end only had enough hay for half the cages. And Fabian was building more.

There was no on-site veterinarian. Bill Peterson lost his license. Now Fabian used Butte Veterinary in Eau Claire, supplemented with wild animal specialist Dr. Minnie Papadopolous from the Circus World Museum in Baraboo. Dr. Papadopolous visited once a month. As the number of animals grew, she stepped up to twice a week and brought an assistant, veterinary students from the University of Wisconsin.

Malnutrition, parasites, gum disease.

Gena discovered two dead liger cubs in a shallow grave near the sanctuary's burn pile. Donning heavy canvas gloves, she marched into Fabian's office and held them up. Startled, Fabian hurriedly slammed a desk drawer and ran a finger under his nose.

"Did you do this?"

"What? Me? No! Where did you find those?"

"I'm through, you fucking asshole. You've been lying to me the whole time. I'm out of here."

Fabian jumped up from behind his desk. "Wait! Baby please don't go! I'm under a lot of pressure here! These animal rights people are driving me nuts! They're trying to sabotage the sanctuary. They're suing me! I had to hire a lawyer. He's not cheap."

He followed her to the bedroom they shared, where she began throwing her clothes into a suitcase. "I'll sell a tiger! I'll hire a full-time veterinarian! Anything you want!"

Grim lipped, Gena slammed the suitcase shut. "Get out of my way."

She got in her car, drove a mile down the road, and pulled over to phone Bear. "I'll be in Omaha in about eight hours. I'm back to training at the gym."

CHAPTER

22

DOG PARK

Josh got up at six, put on shorts and running shoes and took Fig for a run. She'd healed completely from the gun shot a year ago when Josh had fought his father Duane. Duane was in an Illinois prison serving life without parole for poisoning a family of four.

It was a crisp Monday morning. Josh waved to his neighbors heading into town for work. When he got back to the house, Ninja had made coffee and was frying bacon. Josh showered, fed Fig, grabbed a handful of crisp bacon and stuffed it in his mouth.

Ninja spoke without turning. "Cadaver dogs have found the bodies of at least ten decomposing animals at the sanctuary, including three ligers, two black bears, a tigon, and some wolf cubs."

Josh wiped his mouth with a paper towel. "No people?"

"Not yet. But a search of county records reveals that

Fitch owns twelve acres near Taylor County. They're going to look there next. I'm running a missing persons search through the Wisconsin Bureau of Investigation looking for connections with Fitch, the facility, or big cats in general. The Clark County Sheriff's Department recovered an old computer that had been used for target practice. It is now in the department's evidence room. I would like to take a look at that hard drive."

Josh grabbed another piece of bacon.

"I said, I would like to take a look at that hard drive."

"Okay, okay. I'll look into it."

"Fitch was named a person of interest in the death of police informant Dallas Larson in Boston in 1994. He was questioned about his ties to Casuto crime family lieutenant Tony Capadona, but he had a good lawyer, Muriel Stack, who died in 2014. Then he hit the jackpot with that speaker thing and he stopped dealing coke, as far as we know."

"Where's Capadona now?"

"Working on it."

"What about this dog park?"

"You want to go?"

"Yeah. Let's see it."

Prairie Moraine Dog Park was seventy-nine acres of enclosed pasture and woods with a gravel parking lot, half full when they arrived at ten. Priuses, Lexuses, Subarus, pickup trucks. Josh parked and opened the rear door. Fig leaped out and headed for the front gate barking. Josh grabbed a leash and a bag full of treats and followed. There was an outer gate, a holding area, and an inner gate. A sign said, "Please pick up after your pet." Josh stuffed his pockets with doggie doo bags.

"You only need one," Ninja said.

"I use 'em for all sorts of things. I keep food in them."

Josh let Fig into the park and she took off down the trail until she was out of sight.

"Fig come!" he yelled.

Fig came roaring back with a big grin and sat at his feet. Josh fed her a treat.

"Ah," Ninja said. "So that's how it's done."

They headed down the sloping trail between alder, elm, and cottonwood. Sporadic barking from all over. Fig paused to sniff a collie's butt. They paused at a bench across from another bench. Josh sat and phoned the Clark County sheriff.

"Sir, it's Josh Pratt. You confiscated an old hard drive from the Tiger Sanctuary."

"That's right."

"Sir, I have a man who can reveal the contents of the hard drive, provided it wasn't shot. Can you take a look and tell me if it's still intact?"

"Well I can't now, but I will when I get back to the office. Is this urgent?"

"It would help me locate that missing tiger. A woman on the run with a tiger, that's a potential public menace. The sooner we find her, the better."

"I don't know what you can do that law enforcement

can't. Every lawman in the Upper Midwest is on the lookout for Gena Kropenski. Something like that, you can't stay on the run forever."

"I understand. I would be willing to drive up there to pick up the hard drive. I'll sign whatever forms you like. My sole interest is in locating that tiger. As you know, the Wild Animal Initiative hired me to find it."

"Who's your expert?"

"My expert prefers to remain anonymous. But if you look at my record, you know that I do what I say, and that I support law enforcement."

Pause.

"Can you bring your expert up here so I can meet him?"

"That would sort of defeat the purpose of his anonymity. I will turn over everything he finds. It's a lot faster than waiting for law enforcement to get around to it."

"Okay. I'll see what I can do. I'll call you later."

"Thank you, sir."

Ninja stood with hands in pockets, surveying the rolling hills. Josh gave him the thumbs up. Fig ran up and sat at Josh's feet wagging her tail. A man with his hair done up in a bun wearing shorts and sandals sauntered up with his Bernese mountain dog, his face buried in his phone, and sat on the opposite bench. Josh spread his arms along the back of the bench, happy to just sit there and smell the fields, hints of pine, honeysuckle, and cow manure which he found pleasing in small quantities.

The Bernese squatted and deposited a load in the middle

of the trail. Its owner remained absorbed in his phone. Josh waited a moment. Man absorbed. Josh got up and pulled a doggie bag from his pocket.

"Sir, your dog just took an enormous dump right over there."

The man looked up with a sneer. He reconsidered. He took the doggie bag and stood. "Yeah, thanks, man."

"No problem."

Josh and Ninja continued along the trail.

"No problem!" Ninja hooted. "I love that, man!"

The trail meandered through kettle moraine territory, with occasional glimpses of other dog owners and dogs. By the time they returned to the front gate, forty-five minutes had passed and the lot was full. A Toyota wagon, its tail plastered with bumper stickers. I heart my dog. Corgis rule. Decals in the rear window showing a retriever and five pups. Another Toyota plastered with bumper stickers, including a half-torn Biden For President.

They got home around noon. Leach phoned as they entered the house.

"We normally wouldn't do this, but if your friend can expedite our search for Ms. Kropenski, we're willing to let you look at the hard drive. However, it will have to remain here."

"Well, that's a problem. Let me check with my tech and call you back."

Ninja started shaking his head before Josh finished the sentence. "Sorry. No can do. Last thing I need. Plus which, you got to have specialized equipment to read a hard drive, such as a disk enclosure. I got one downstairs, but I ain't draggin' my ass up to bumfuck."

"Let me try again."

Josh phoned the sheriff.

"Sir, my tech uses specialized equipment to read a hard drive. I'll only need it for twenty-four hours. You can contact Detective Heinz Calloway of the Madison PD as a reference. Otherwise, it's just going to sit around in your locker until the state gets around to it, which could be weeks. You know how busy they are."

"Hang on a minute."

Josh went out on the deck. "Dum de dum dum dum," he hummed. Leach phoned back.

"All right. Twenty-four hours. Come on up."

"I'll be there in three hours."

CHAPTER

23

PINHEIRO

Gena returned to her apartment in Omaha on a Sunday night and showed up at the gym at nine the next morning. Austin Bear was waiting. With his hulking physique and abundance of body hair, he looked like his namesake.

"Glad you come to your senses. I got some videos I want you to watch."

"Byam?"

"That's right. She's twelve and four."

"How much time do I have?"

"Six weeks."

"Well let's watch 'em."

They sat in Bear's office looking out on Blondo Street. Bear brought up the first of several YouTube broadcasts of Byam's fights. The first was with Melissa Souza, a tough Brazilian from the favelas of Rio. Byam wore her war face. It was a Bellator fight in the round ring. At the bell, they came out cautiously circling before Souza tried to run Byam over with flurries and kicks, but Byam bobbed, weaved, changed angles, and came back with a devastating left hook to the head that stunned her opponent.

"See how she moves. She's a runner. You might have to back her into a corner."

They watched two more tapes. Gena got a feel for how Byam moved, went into the gym and replicated those moves. The next step was to bring in sparring partners who could fight like Byam.

It was September twelve. The fight was to take place at Baxter Arena, on the undercard. The headliner was Alaine Philmont versus Yuroslav Dosbeko for the Professional Fighters League welterweight championship. Due to inactivity, Gena's featherweight rating had dropped to number nine. Byam was number three. As they watched Byam's tapes, Gena said, "Why is she taking this fight?"

"You're still a big draw. They're gonna use that spinning heel kick against Silva to fill the seats. Go jump rope. I'll make some calls."

Bear reached out to Dayane Pinheiro, from Sao Paulo, four and two in the Brazilian Fight League, who had moved to Las Vegas to break into the big time. Bear knew her trainer from his competitive years. Bear had fought twice in the UFC at middleweight, and quit with a two and one record. He was twelve and three as an amateur.

Pinheiro flew into Omaha on the fourteenth. Gena and Bear met her at the airport and took her to dinner at V. Mertz. Over a California merlot, Bear asked, "Do you mind staying at the gym? We have some very nice guest rooms. You'll have your own private bath."

"I don't mind," the svelte twenty-four-year-old replied. She had long black hair which she braided before a fight. She'd grown up in a favela and it wasn't until she started training that she ate in a restaurant.

After dinner they went to the gym on Blondo. Bear bought the building twelve years ago and began slowly renovating. He rented the ground floor out to a mattress store. The second floor was the gym, with its heavy bags, kettle bells, ring, and office, and the third floor contained four apartments, including Bear's. He and Gena helped carry Pinheiro's luggage up the stairs, and showed her the two room apartment with a kitchenette and a window looking out on Decatur Plaza. A framed print of Stag at Sharkey's hung on one wall, the iconic black and white photo of Ali standing over a downed Frazier on another. There were beer and sports drinks in the fridge, and bananas on the counter. It had a flat screen TV in the bedroom.

"We get ESPN Plus as well as All Access UFC if you want to watch fights. You familiar with Cassandra Byam?"

"Yes, I am a big fan."

"You familiar with the way she fights?"

"Yes. Since you contact me, I have watched all her fights."

"Good."

In the morning, Gena and Pinheiro put on their sweats and did a five-mile run. They sparred for the first time at ten. Pinheiro started cautiously, implicitly acknowledging Gena as the better fighter, but within the first minute she slipped into Byam mode, rushing her opponent, throwing flurries and reverse spinning kicks. Gena felt a little rusty but after five minutes, she had reverted easily back into combat readiness and confidently deflected Pinheiro's attacks while effortlessly peppering her opponent with light jabs, feinting, setting up round house kicks to the head which landed as softly as a pillow.

On Sunday Gena took Pinheiro to the zoo. They stopped at the tiger exhibit.

"I miss my tigers," Gena said.

Pinheiro looked at her with a half-smile. "What?"

"I was helping this man run a tiger sanctuary in Wisconsin, but he turned out to be a real shit heel. He didn't care about the tigers at all. He was only in it for the money. I'm very concerned that without me there, he's abusing his animals. Not just tigers, but bears, wolves, and other wild animals."

"Let's go beat him up!"

Gena laughed. "That's not a bad idea, but I'm in training now. I wasn't training properly in Wisconsin. There were too many distractions. I can't thank you enough for helping me out."

"Well, you are helping me, too. I have a fight coming up in Brazil in December, a very tough competitor named Dayana Rocha. She is two and oh. This is my first professional fight. If I win, I will devote myself full time to fighting."

"What made you want to be a fighter?"

"Was my brother Eusebio. He fights in the Brazilian

leagues. He's a welterweight. He is three and one."

"My brother got me into it too. He boxed Golden Gloves."

"Does he still box?"

"No. He doesn't have the discipline. He likes to drink and party too much. And he snorts cocaine. I'm very worried about him."

"The cocaine is no good. I have seen the plantations. They rip down all the trees and plant the coca. Where I lived, it was the Family of the North. I had a friend named Berto who joined the gang and was killed in a government raid. If the federales had not shot him, he would have died from doing too much blow."

"Have you ever tried it?"

"No."

"I did. I didn't like the way it made me feel."

"I will pray for you. I will pray that your brother doesn't die from it. Is he a dealer?"

"I'm afraid to ask. He owns a bar in Iowa. He's very proud of me. Has my picture all over the place."

"Oh, I would love to see it."

"It's about five hours away. I don't know if we have time."

"This man you were with. Did you love him?"

"I don't know. I thought I did. He came on real strong, y'know? Maybe I was just in love with the tigers."

CHAPTER 24

SOMETHING ISN'T RIGHT

It was November fifteen. The Baxter Arena was sold out, with a line stretching around the block and young men scalping tickets. The Professional Fighters League Welterweight Championship was on the line. Philmont versus Dosbeko, with a rich undercard including numerous UFC alumni and the highly anticipated Kropenski/Byam fight. When women began participating in pro MMA, the fans were dubious, but soon changed their attitude when the ladies proved they could excite the crowds.

Pioneers like Joanna Jędrzejczyk, Rhonda Rousey, and Cyborg Justino proved they could fight. It was true, most of the women fighters were not Playboy centerfolds, except for Paige Van Zant. Some were mannish with thick legs and muscular shoulders. They were not glamorous. They were there to fight.

The prelims started at four p.m. Gena waited nervously

in her dressing room with Bear, the fights playing silently on a flat screen. She ate a light dinner. Hers was the fifth bout of the evening, in two hours. She sat in a straight-backed chair while Bear massaged her shoulders and spoke soothingly.

"She's gonna charge you at the bell. Don't engage. Get out of her way and let her chase you around until the round's half over. Lotsa head movement. Wait for your opening. Go low, then go high."

A PFL agent stuck his head in the door. "Fifteen minutes."

Gena stood. "Let's go. I can't just sit here."

They stepped into the long corridor lined with lockers and dressing rooms. The Arena was the home of the University of Nebraska and hosted numerous events from hockey to antique car shows. The concrete corridor thrummed with life. Trainers, managers, hangers on, fighters standing in the hall talking to one another, the roar of the crowd from the big room. It was sold out. Eight thousand seats. A fighter with a towel around his shoulders, his face covered in blood, strode by with his trainer murmuring to him in a low voice. Fighters were assigned rooms on opposite sides of the arena to prevent conflict. Gena had never met Byam. She was hyped up, confident, eager to show her skills, but she had nothing against her opponent.

Bear, assistant trainer Ralph Sanchez and Gena hovered just inside the service tunnel, Gena hopping from foot to foot, surrounded by service people, bettors, folks leaving and returning to their seats. Through the narrow framework she could see the ring in the center of the big floor, the referee holding a fighter's hand aloft, the loser applauding in good sportsmanship.

"Winner by split decision, Raucous Ricky Unger!"

A half dozen people stood in the ring. Ricky's trainers and handlers, his opponent's trainers and handlers, an official from the Nebraska Athletic Commission, and Walt Kominsky, president of the Professional Fighters League, a former competitor. The ref used a bucket and towel to clean up blood stains. The ring emptied. The master of ceremonies, a tall man with dyed jet black hair wearing a black tux, spoke in a stentorian voice.

"And now, a featured bout on tonight's undercard, Cassandra "The Mongoose" Byam taking on Gena "Queen Tiger" Kropenski…"

Shouting, cheers. The ref motioned for them to proceed.

Gena in the lead, they trotted down the corridor past fans with their palms out, Bear's hands on her shoulders, a towel around her neck. Gena slapped all the hands she could. They emerged among the bleachers and worked their way through the seats on the floor. Sportscasters at a table flush with the ring base turned in their seats to watch. A video cam hovered on steel wires above the ring. Videographers waited, clutching petite video cams.

Gena climbed up the portable steps to the steel cage, a twenty-five-foot circle with doors on opposite sides. Byam entered opposite. She looked focused. Intense. A man in the first row wearing a blue blazer stood and bellowed through cupped hands, "QUEEN TIGER! QUEEN TIGER! TEAR HER APART! WHOO!"

Gena glanced at him. A dandy in a blue sharkskin suit with curly black hair. She winked. The ref met the fighters in the center and went over the rules. No eye gouging. No fishhooks. "When I say break you break. Touch gloves."

They touched gloves. The ref motioned them back. He turned to Byam. "Are you ready?"

She nodded.

To Gena. "Are you ready? Let's fight!"

Byam charged throwing out a piston-like jab, following Gena around the room, peppering her with jabs, crosses and hooks, finishing with a roundhouse to the head that Gena blocked, ducking, backpedaling. After two minutes the audience started to jeer. Gena's ringside admirer continued to shout her name, and directions. Gena only heard Austin Bear.

"Let it loose!" he called.

Gena planted her feet and when Byam came in punching, Gena ducked low and threw an overhand looping right that connected to the side of Byam's head, staggering her. The audience cheered. Byam recovered and they traded blows in the middle of the ring.

"Back her up!" Bear shouted. "Back her up!"

Gena shuffled forward, hands up, peppering Byam with jabs and hooks, trying to work her into the wall. Byam covered up, threw knees, and coughed. Her eyes went wide and she said "oh." She slowed down. Something was wrong. Gena could feel it. The bell rang and they returned to their corners, Byam moving slowly. She almost slipped off her stool.

Bear crouched in front of Gena while Sanchez squirted water into her mouth and put an ice pack on her head. "Okay. You're backing her up. Keep it up."

"Something's wrong."

"What do you mean?"

"All of a sudden the air just seemed to go out of her. She went from 78 rpm to 33."

"Well take advantage of it. It's not your fault she's gassed out."

"She's never gassed out."

"Seconds out of the ring."

The second round started. Byam moved noticeably slower, shuffling toward the center, throwing one punch at a time. It was child's play for Gena to cover up and avoid any damage. They clinched. Byam's eyes looked unfocused.

"Are you all right?" Gena said around her mouthpiece.

Byam didn't answer, tried to throw a knee. Gena stepped around, took her down with a hip throw and easily slipped into an arm bar. Seconds later, Byam tapped. As the ref raised Gena's hand, Byam looked listless and confused. She stumbled returning to her corner and her handlers leaped into the ring to help her down.

As Gena, Bear and Sanchez walked the corridor back to their dressing room, the man in the sharkskin suit gave her a high five. "Way to go, Gena! I knew you could do it."

Back in the dressing room, Gena turned to Bear. "That wasn't right. That wasn't a legit fight. She looked like she was doped."

CHAPTER
25

HARD DRIVE

Josh arrived at the Neillsville PD at one, Monday afternoon, signed in, signed for the hard drive, and was headed south within a half hour. The hard drive was an old Dell sealed in a plastic evidence bag. It had two bullet holes that went clear through, forty-fives from their size.

Josh stopped at Woodmans and picked up some ribs, greens, and beer. He got home at four-thirty. Ninja's truck was there, but Ninja and Fig were not. Josh carried the hard drive downstairs and left it on Ninja's chair, went back up, put the ribs in a roasting pan and covered them with barbecue sauce. Sherdog said that Austin Bear had been Gena's trainer. He located the gym online and called. A gravelly voice answered, "Bear MMA."

"Mr. Bear, my name is Josh Pratt. I'm a private investigator in Wisconsin. The Wild Animal Initiative has asked me to find Genghis Khan, a Siberian tiger that was taken from the Tiger Sanctuary in Grant County. As you know, Gena Kropenski was at the sanctuary just prior to Khan's disappearance. I have no interest in getting Gena in trouble, but it's important for the sake of the tiger that we locate it as quickly as possible."

"I haven't heard from Gena in five months. Ask her brother."

"Can you tell me why?"

"She went back to that fucking idiot who runs the tiger sanctuary. No wait. She's through with him. Somebody called her from the sanctuary and said her favorite tiger was having problems. Bam. Gone. She was very unhappy with the way the last fight ended. You know the league stripped her of the title when they learned that her opponent had been drugged."

"I did not know that."

"Did you ask her brother?"

"I did, sir. I'm not a police officer. My only interest is in locating the tiger. However, she has broken several laws, if she took the tiger."

"What if she didn't take the tiger?"

"I have no other explanation. Were you unaware of her fascination with tigers?"

Silence.

"I haven't heard from her in five months."

"Sir, if I find her before the police, I will do everything in my power to protect her from prosecution. My focus is entirely on locating Genghis Khan and delivering him to the Wild Animal Initiative. The longer he remains on the run, the greater the danger he poses not only to Gena, but to the public."

"I hear ya. She coulda won that last fight easy. Somebody slipped her opponent a mickey and now her career's down the toilet."

"When was that?"

"Last November. She fought Cassandra Byam. Byam looked woozy, didn't make it out of the second round. The whole thing stunk. Her manager insisted on a blood test and they found xylazine in her blood. It's a horse tranquilizer."

"I did not know that."

"I don't know if it has anything to do with the tiger or not, but maybe if that hadn't happened she wouldn't have gone running back to that shit show in Wisconsin, and she wouldn't be wherever she is now."

"Can put me in touch with her parents?"

"All I know is they live somewhere around here. The father's name is Reggie. The mother is Edie. Good luck."

"What about sparring partners?"

"We brought in Dayane Pinheiro from Brazil. She's ranked down there."

"Would you mind if I contacted her?"

"Why would I mind?"

"Do you have a number for her?"

"Just a minute." Bear returned with a number.

Josh gave Bear his phone number. "If you hear anything, please call me. I don't believe that Gena is in any way involved in the illegal activity that occurred at the Tiger Sanctuary."

"What happened to that prick who ran the place?"

"He's a fugitive from justice."

Josh heard Ninja come in. Seconds later, Fig was in his face, demanding dinner.

"Thanks for talking to me, Mr. Bear."

"No problem."

Josh went into the kitchen where Ninja was looking in the fridge.

"What kind of barbecue sauce you usin'?"

"Arthur Bryant. I hope it meets with your approval."

"Well, I tell ya what. I'm outta here on Friday and you can get back with your woman. Inna meantime, why don't you let me show you my barbecue sauce? Have Ray come over. She'll dig it."

"I'll try. I got the hard drive. It's downstairs on your table."

"When we eatin'?"

"Fig's eating now. Humans at six."

"Then I'll get to it."

"Where'd you go."

"Back to the dog park. She loves that place."

Ninja went downstairs. Josh returned to his computer and looked up Gena's November bout with Byam on Sherdog.

Kropenski win invalidated by Professional

Fighters League after Byam tests positive for horse tranquilizer. Kropenski had been leading on points. Ringside observers sensed something was wrong with the usually hyperactive Byam, who seemed sluggish and unable to get out of the way of Kropenski "Queen Tiger's" fists and feet. Byam's manager insisted on a blood test immediately following the fight. Kropenski's TKO was invalidated. Kropenski's trainer and manager Austin Bear said, "Gena's record speaks for herself. She has never had a whiff of scandal. If Byam was drugged, we had nothing to do with it." Kropenski did not respond to our request for an interview. Her career appears to be in limbo.

Josh found the video online and watched. Byam looked sluggish in the first round. The audience booed. Byam went into a clinch, carrying Gena to the cage wall and the referee had to separate them three times. Byam stumbled on the way back to her corner. There was no question something was wrong with her.

Josh phoned Ray.

"What?"

"Ninja's outta here on Friday. He's making dinner Thursday night. Will you come?"

"*Kung Fu Musical* opens this weekend, Josh. I'm busy every night."

"You gotta eat. He's making his own special barbecue

sauce. Come on, baby. He had nowhere else to go and I need him."

"Why does he have nowhere else to go? Is he in some sort of trouble?"

"Probably, but he won't tell me. He doesn't want to involve me in his shit. Come on. We can go back to your place afterwards. Did you take Sid?"

"Yes, Sid's here with me."

"Sid misses Fig. You know they're tight."

She softened a little. "I'll think about it."

"I'll get everybody I know to come to your show. They'll be lined up around the block."

"We are already sold out for the weekend."

"Then you'd better think about extending the show. What's wrong with that?"

"Okay, I'm thinking."

Josh heard querulous voices in the background. "How am I supposed to do this step?"

"Gotta go, baby. The cast is getting restless."

"Love you."

She called him baby. She threw him a lifeline. Josh went outside, added the coals and lit the grill. He went to the basement door.

"When we gonna eat?"

"Hang on," Ninja called. "I've got something."

Josh went downstairs where Ninja had the computer in pieces, the hard drive hooked up to his own machine. "What?"

"Email exchange from two years ago. 'Hell yeah, bro. I'll take one of those cats off your hands. I got my own zoo goin'. Come on over. We'll have a blast. TC."

"TC?"

"Yeah. I don't know who that is, but I'll find out."

"Keep at it. I'll put the ribs on."

"I also found a video you're not gonna like."

"What?"

"Come down here."

Ninja cued up the video which had been stored on the hard drive. Amateur stuff, swinging around until it focused on the wolf enclosure, two adult wolves, ribs poking, staring through the bars. The camera swung to a box filled with five puppies.

"Let's do it," a voice said.

A hand reached into the box, grabbed one of the pups by the scruff of its neck, and hurled it over the bars into the enclosure. The two wolves pounced, tearing the tiny body apart until another puppy sailed over the bars.

PRIVATE ZOO

Josh woke at six, Fig looking up expectantly from where she slept at the bottom of the mattress.

"Yeah, let's run."

They hit the road ten minutes later. Fig loped easily at Josh's side, one step behind. Josh carried a plastic garbage bag and filled it with litter. He thought about putting up a sign. "This Section of Ptarmigan Road Maintained By Josh Pratt."

They reached the mini-mall where Ptarmigan met McKenna, stuffed the bag in the trash, bought a twenty-ounce sports drink, drained it, and headed back. It was six forty-five by the time he emerged from the shower. Rap pounded faintly through the floor. Pulling on jeans and a shirt, Josh went into the basement where Ninja danced among his gear and tables, white AirPods contrasting with his black skin.

He had two monitors set up at an angle. One was filled

with scrolling figures. The other showed a Google Earth aerial photograph of a rural property. All Josh saw were a series of rectangles among trees.

"What's going on?" he said.

Ninja danced. Josh cupped his hands.

"EARTH TO NINJA!"

Ninja whirled in a karate stance, straightened up, turned off the feed and took out the AirPods.

"Shit! Don't scare me like that!"

Josh stared into Ninja's blood shot eyes, noticed a bundle of white paper on the table.

"Have you been up all night?"

"What time is it?"

"It's almost seven."

"Holy shit. You won't believe what I found out."

"What."

"You know Fitch split Boston. The night before, he was present when some Paddy boys killed a police informant named Dallas Larson."

"I knew that."

"Did you know that a week later, the police arrested Mick O'Hern and Pete Hegseth, two members of the Paddy O's?"

"How'd they find 'em?"

"They had surveillance video from a camera attached to an Ace Hardware. It shows a car stopping to confront Fitch. Fuckers almost hit him. Ten minutes later, camera on the alley. Here. You can see Fitch talking to someone."

Josh watched the grainy video. Fitch was identifiable from the previous video. Car lights filled the darkness. Fitch leaped behind a dumpster. The car barreled into the other man who flew over the roof. The car backed over him. The Paddy boys piled out. One socked Fitch in the gut and retrieved a Tupperware container that fell out of his jacket.

"The footage was good enough to identify their vehicle, a 1980 Chevy Impala. Picked it up two nights later with a stolen license plate. The Paddy O's dealt blow in Southie."

"They never questioned Fitch?"

"No. He disappeared that night. The next day, a gang tried to take down a Brinks armored car and there was a shootout downtown. All hands on deck. Later, when Fitch resurfaced, the Paddies had confessed."

"Are you doing blow?"

"Hey, man. You want results, you got to fuel the machine."

"I don't care. Just be discreet. For Chrissake don't let Ray find out."

Ninja spread his hands. He wore a purple velour jumpsuit with gold stripes. "I'm discreet."

Josh pointed to the Google Earth. "What's that?"

Ninja grinned ear to ear. "That, my man, is the personal zoo of one Anthony Capadona, formerly of Boston."

"What's the significance?"

"Anthony Capadona. Tony Capadona. TC."

"Ninja, you're a genius! What's it show?"

"Pull up a chair."

They faced the monitor. Ninja worked the mouse. The view changed to from the street, a rural highway made of crumbling blacktop, a gated drive that ran between clusters of cottonwoods, an old farmhouse partially visible. The view jumped to overhead, a series of what looked like concrete enclosures with open tops.

"Capadona was a captain in the Casuto Family, that controlled drugs in the North End, downtown Boston, Framingham, Back Bay, Brookline, and Cambridge. He curiously absconded about a week after your boy Fitch. He covered his tracks pretty well. Disappeared for twenty-five years. Three years ago, he shows up in Milwaukee looking to buy farmland. At some point I'm assuming he got in touch with Fitch …"

"Wait wait wait. Why would he get in touch with Fitch?"

"Cuz Tony was Fitch's coke connection."

"How do you know that?"

"DUH. Cuz the cops said so!"

"Oh. Okay. Proceed."

"So now he's legit, all right? He's a professional gambler who bet heavily on bit-coins and made out like a bandit. Bets online. Was in Vegas numerous times up until three years ago. He sold a Degas for six and a half mil. He's an art collector too."

"What are we looking at?"

"It's a zoo."

"Excuse me?"

"It's his personal zoo. Like Pablo Escobar. It's in Trempealeau County."

"Only drug dealers have private zoos."

"Tell me about it!"

"How did you find it?"

"You'll love this. I had to crack into the FBI database. They have a file on the guy including financial transactions. In 2012, he put most of his money in the Caribbean National Bank which created three offshore holding companies on his behalf. The property in Trempealeau County is owned by the IDC Corporation, with headquarters in Trinidad."

"So why isn't the DEA crawling up his ass?"

"Well believe it or not, there's no evidence of TC having anything to do with drugs since 2002. That's when he made the decision to go straight."

"And hook up with his old pal Fabian."

"Exactomundo."

"So why haven't the cops raided this place? You know they found a meth lab at the sanctuary."

"They don't know about it. I figured you'd want to take a look. That meth lab might not be Capadona. It could be Gunter. You should ask them about fingerprints."

"Ninja, you're a genius. Where's Capadona now?"

"He's in the wind. Someone shut off the utilities in March."

"What about Kropenski's parents? Can you find them? Mother's name is Reggie. Mother Edie."

Ninja wrote it down in a note pad. "Also, he was re-searching tracking devices online."

"Holy shit. What for?"

"Don't know. But he's too smart to order one online. If he got one, he bought it in person and paid cash."

"Lemme see."

Ninja stroked up the online destinations Fitch had visited. Amazon. Bellabeat. Linxup. Samsung.

"I'm heading up to Trempealeau. You want to come?"

Ninja waved his hands. "I got too much work to do. You go. I'll take Fig to the dog park later."

Josh hadn't brought Ninja onboard to risk his life. He would have to go alone. He thought about taking a firearm, of which he had several, but he was a convicted felon and forbidden to possess arms. One of the reasons he hoped Ray would move in with him was so he could put all the guns in her name. As if. Ray was all for confiscating private weapons. She had no idea what Josh had in his safe. It was better to leave them where they were.

"Can you watch it in real time?"

"That's what we're doin', bro."

"Have you seen any sign of life?"

"No. Only death."

"What death?"

"You ain't gonna like this, man."

"Show me."

The image hovered over a particular rectangle and zoomed in. At first, Josh couldn't make out what he was seeing. It looked like a jumble of sticks in the corner. Then he saw the skull and the animal's skeleton snapped into focus.

"What is it?"

"A zebra. Look. You can see its hide."

Josh took the Chrysler. He stopped at a mini-mart to buy a six-pack of Gator Ade and some rubber gloves. Everything else he needed was in the trunk.

CHAPTER

27

BUSTER

Trempealeau County had a grip on the Mississippi, but most of it was glacial drift, myriad wooded valleys through which snaked winding blacktops, like most of Southwest Wisconsin. Josh loved the land. He could ride endlessly through those coulees over hill and dale, sucking up the green. It was the greatest natural high. He got off the interstate at Tomah and lowered the windows, inhaling the rich scent of late summer. TC's zoo lay northwest of Whitehall, in a broad swatch of forested hills interspersed with farms, at the end of a winding dirt road. McCawber Road. Since leaving Elk Creek, he hadn't seen another person.

The entrance to the property was a locked aluminum gate with a NO TRESPASSING sign. The fact that it had not been seized by the state for back taxes indicated that someone still took an interest in the property. Josh knew from the aerial view that there was another way in, a dirt road that entered from the west, off a state forest road. He circled the property clockwise until he came to the access road, drove the big Chrysler a mile in and found the rutted dirt trail that emerged from a barbed wire fence. A simple padlocked chain ran across the opening. Josh used the bolt cutters from the trunk to cut the padlock, drove through, replaced the chain, and continued over several ridges and dips until at the top of the third ridge, he saw the compound across a fallow field. Working the car into a thick stand of gorse, he pulled binoculars from his trunk, lay in the brush, and studied the property for five minutes. Aside from birds and woodland animals, there was no sign of life. It wasn't good farmland. It wasn't flat. He hefted the heavy backpack filled with tools and headed down slope, reaching a six-foot chain-link fence surrounding the property within minutes.

Josh put on leather gloves, tossed his backpack over the fence and scrambled after. A field of weeds lay between him and a concrete enclosure. The concrete cell was ten by twenty, with a concrete floor and an aluminum bowl filled with dust. Josh snapped a picture. He moved on to the next enclosure. It was the one with the bones. Someone had simply abandoned the zebra to die. What kind of mind had a private zoo? Criminals and narcissists. In Josh's experience, many criminals were narcissists. Working toward the front, he passed six empty enclosures, and what appeared to be a mass grave, a mound of dirt and rocks overgrown with weeds, tracks from a front loader still visible. It had been there long enough for small trees to take root.

Crouching behind a shed, Josh examined the main house, a simple ranch-style with faded yellow siding. A once red barn had been blasted colorless by the weather. The barn doors were closed and padlocked. Josh used a crowbar to bust the lock and pulled open one side with a hair-raising shriek. Inside, beams of sunlight shone through gaps in the ceiling. Pigeons flew from beam to beam. The sawdust-covered wood plank floor was splattered with bird shit. Cattle stalls stood open. It had once been a dairy farm. A tarp covered an old John Deere front loader.

Josh checked the stalls. All but the last were empty. Inside the last stall were cans of paint thinner, hydrochloric acid, a crate of Diamond box matches, brake fluid and lye. It was a meth lab. It was not out of the question. From the dust on the supplies, it hadn't been used in some time. But why would a canny dude like Capadona, who'd operated under the tightly controlled auspices of the Casuto crime family, turn to making meth? That was hillbilly stuff. Loser redneck stuff.

Unless the lab wasn't Capadona's. Maybe somebody had remained when Tony moved on. Maybe Capadona knew Gunter. Josh took photographs of the stall. He busted a kitchen window in the back of the house to get in. The house felt like it had been sealed for a long time. It smelled of dust, Pine-Sol, and a faint undercurrent of rot. The kitchen cupboards still contained mismatched dinnerware, the silverware drawer was filled with packets of plastic utensils from drive throughs. Under the sink lay cleanser, a bottle of

Pine-Sol, and a mousetrap holding a desiccated gray mouse. One cupboard contained a nearly empty bottle of Johnny Walker Black. Using gloves, Josh picked it up delicately by the rim, put it in a plastic bag and put it in his backpack.

Josh opened the refrigerator, reeled back from the stench. It had been unplugged and still contained leftovers. An open box of baking soda did little to dispel the smell. Three cans of Old Milwaukee in a plastic yoke. The freezer yielded two long spoiled once-frozen pizzas. An old poster taped to the wall advertised a tractor pull in Eau Claire.

The living room had a once beige rug covered with stains and cigarette burns. A threadbare sofa sat beneath a framed Currier & Ives print. A cheap coffee table still held a couple mugs, brown at the bottom where the coffee had evaporated. A pale rectangle on the wall opposite indicated where a flat screen had once been. There was a brick fireplace with dead coals and a several 4H trophies on the mantle for Best Hog, Best Sheep, and Best Pumpkin. The dates were 1984 to 1986.

Down the hall to the master bedroom, queen-sized bed in an old painted wood frame with a headboard, bed stand with a goose neck lamp. He pulled open the drawer. Hard core porn. *I Like Big Butts. Anal Antics. Three Ways the Right Way.* Old packs of rubbers. Either Capadona didn't care what people thought or he figured no one would ever look, which meant he still held title to the property and all taxes were up to date. Josh would ask Ninja about that. Who was paying the taxes? A bank in the Bahamas?

More importantly, why had Capadona come here in the first place? Why would a rising lieutenant in one of the most powerful crime families in the Northeast suddenly pull up stakes and move to Bumfuck, Wisconsin? The dresser was nice. Mahogany. Josh went through the drawers and found several pair of silk socks that had never been worn, as well as silk briefs, colorful silk shirts, clothes that went well with a self-obsessed pretty boy.

The bathroom cabinets were empty. The water had been turned off. One bedroom had been converted into an office, with a gun metal gray desk and a sprung wooden office chair that looked like it had survived the forties. A Rigid Tools girlie calendar on the wall was turned to June, 2017.

That left the basement. He opened the door off the kitchen and automatically flipped the switch, but there was no power. Dim light entered the basement through ground level windows. He descended the creaking wood stairs to a concrete room running the length of the house, water heater and furnace in one corner, a pile of cardboard boxes, and what he at first took to be a pile of rags. As he approached, he saw the chain connected to a collar, the other end fastened to a pipe. The dead pitbull looked like a deflated toy, its water bowl long since dried up. Someone had left it down here to die.

Gingerly, Josh detached the dog tag. Buster. Trempealeau County Humane Society, along with serial and telephone numbers.

He took pictures. He took the dog tag. He opened a

cardboard box. Inside were several shoe boxes. The first one contained arrowheads, the kind you saw in museums or rock stores. Another contained belt buckles, some of them silver, bucking broncos, steers, bas relief six-shooters, adorned with turquoise and other semi-precious stones. Whoever put them there was either a collector or a dealer. A third contained old American coins including Morgan silver dollars and coins dating back to colonial days. Josh was no expert, but he recognized valuable collectibles. There was a small fortune here for someone willing to go through the trouble of selling them. eBay or antique stores. A fourth contained old magazines, including a *Sports Illustrated* with Gena on the cover.

At the back of the pile, surrounded on all sides and on top by cardboard boxes, stood a Gateway hard drive.

CHAPTER

28

CAPADONA

The Trempealeau County Humane Society lay on Highway Fifty-Three in the middle of nowhere. Josh parked in front of the one-story ranch style office. Dogs barked from somewhere in back. The door jingled as he entered and a young woman with glasses looked up from behind her desk.

"Good morning. What can I do for you?"

Josh put Buster's tags on the counter. "These tags belonged to a dog that died. He appeared to have died a long time ago. I'd like to inform the owner that I found the remains of his pet."

The woman stood and picked up the tags. "I'm so sorry to hear that. Where did you find these?"

"In rural Trempealeau County. I'm a dog owner myself. I think the owner would like to know. I'd hate to think that he or she is still grieving, wondering what happened to their pet."

"Well let me take a look." The young woman sat at a computer and ran the tags. "Ah. Here we are. Before I give you this information, would you mind providing some identification? We appreciate what you're trying to do, but we'd like to know who you are."

"Certainly." Josh produced his driver's license.

"From Madison, huh? They have an excellent humane society. This dog was registered four years ago by Anthony Capadona of Rural Route Twelve, Trempealeau County. Is that near where you found them?"

"Yes, it is, ma'am. Do you have a phone number?"

"I'll write it down for you. Thank you for doing this."

"Thank you, ma'am. If my dog disappeared I hope that someone would do the same for me."

It was four p.m. by the time Josh got home. Fig and Ninja were gone. That dog was getting a lot of park time. Josh flopped onto the sofa and phoned Capadona's number.

"Hello. You have reached Anthony Capadona. I'm sorry I can't come to the phone right now. Please leave your name, a detailed explanation of why you called and your phone number and I'll get back to you as soon as I can."

"Mr. Capadona, my name is Josh Pratt. I'm interested in purchasing your property in Trempealeau County." He left his phone number.

The front door opened. Fig attacked with a fusillade of tongue and barking. Ninja wore Dockers and a crew-neck cotton sweater. He looked almost normal.

"Well, that's it, big guy. Omma pack my shit and hit the

road."

"Wait. I found a hard drive at Capadona's place in Trempealeau. I need you to take a look."

"Bro, if I stay one more day your old lady ain't gonna be happy."

"Her show opens tonight. I gotta be there. I'll hang around and we'll go back to her place. I need to know what's on that hard drive. You gotta stick around."

"Bro, I already made arrangements. I got a hot date in Milwaukee. What am I supposed to tell her?"

"What's it worth to you?"

"Come on, man. You know I don't like charging friends."

"You don't like it, but you do it. How about five thou to pry it open? I don't care how long it takes. I'll put you up in a motel and pay expenses."

Ninja spread his hands. "How can I refuse."

"I also got Capadona's phone number."

Ninja raised his eyebrows.

"I got it from the Trempealeau County Humane Society. Can you find him? Here's the number."

Josh wrote it down in a tablet.

"I'll give it a shot."

"Thank you."

Josh was restless. He knew he couldn't sleep. Graham Central Station boomed from the basement. "We've been waiting...for so long. To sing and play for you...some of our songs." At least Ninja mixed it up. A steady diet of rap was enough to drive one mad. Like ninety-nine per cent of all bikers, Josh loved the blues. He loved a lot of other music too, especially jazz, which his friend Bobby Hines played. Chaplain Dorgan had introduced Josh to jazz in Waupun, as he had introduced Josh to so many things. Chaplain Dorgan was old school. Everything up to and including bebop. No time for the free jazz movement. Dorgan called it "bug music." Music for bugs. No forms, no set patterns, like spilling colors all over the floor.

He scrolled through Facebook. Sensing his unrest, Fig laid her snout on his thigh.

"All right, let's go for a run."

Fig at his side, Josh veered into White Oaks and ran through the upscale neighborhood, passing one mini-manse after another. At least Phil Bass hadn't insisted on architectural conformity. He passed red brick Georgians, Mies Van der Rohe houses that looked like they came from Ikea, all horizontal lines and glass walls, one-level prairie styles made from native stone and tucked into the landscape, and one hilariously out of place Spanish style hacienda. Fig squatted for a dump. Josh fished a plastic bag from his sweat pants, bagged it and turned around.

Back at the house he showered, fed Fig, and stuffed some deli meat and a cheese stick in his mouth. The Beastie Boys blasted from below. Clarity set in. He skipped down the basement steps where Ninja sat at his boards, hands flying.

"Yo," Josh said.

Ninja held up a finger. He swiveled, grinning. "Capadona's at the South Point in Las Vegas."

CHAPTER 29

GENGHIS PERKS UP

Two months before the State of Wisconsin filed suit to shut down the Tiger Sanctuary, Gena was still living in the apartment at Bear's Gym. Bear hired her to teach mixed martial arts, afternoons and evenings, five days a week. A cloud had settled over her career after the Byam bout, even though she had nothing to do with it. The Nebraska Athletic Commission launched an investigation but had yet to determine who had put the dope in Byam's drink. It may have been put in the Kill Cliff Ignites she was constantly chugging, but the empty cans had gone to a landfill the day following the fight and by the time investigators got around to it, had been covered with more trash.

Investigators reviewed video footage, including cameras set in the corridors. They ran the footage through face recognition software, looking for matches with known gamblers, bookmakers, and felons. The few matches were dead ends.

Fights had always attracted felons. They interviewed Byam, her trainer, her manager, and her friends. They interviewed Gena and Bear. Nada.

It was two o'clock in the afternoon, May 15, and Gena had just finished teaching her class to six students ranging in age from fourteen to sixty-seven. She went up the stairs to the roof where Bear had put out a picnic table with an umbrella. It was a clear, brisk day, temperature in the seventies as Gena rested her arms on the steel rail and looked toward downtown, toward the First National Bank tower, when her cell phone chirped. She didn't recognize the number, but it had a Wisconsin area code.

"Hello."

"Gena, this is Mona Davis."

"Mona, how are you doing? What's going on?"

"Listen, I hate to bother you with this, but Fabian's in all sorts of trouble. The state has shut down the facility and they're threatening to raid. Fabian took off last night and left us here holding the bag. Matt, Jeff and I are the only ones left and we just can't keep up with the animals' needs. Is there any chance you can come back here and help us manage the place until the state shits or gets off the pot?"

"How's Genghis?"

"He's losing weight. He's been sad since you left. I've tried to work with him, but he doesn't trust anyone but you. I don't want to just turn him over to the state, or one of those animal rescue places. They don't understand him like you do."

"I'll be there tomorrow."

Gena found Bear in his office filling out racing forms. "Bear, I gotta go."

"Where?"

Gena told him about the phone call. Bear folded his forms and leaned back in his old wooden captain's chair with a creak. "You can do what you like, but this doesn't mean you're through with fighting. Nobody's gonna blame you for what happened to Byam."

"Well, I wish that were true, but there are comments on Twitter saying that I'm a crook, ever since I hooked up with Fitch."

"That's guilt by association. It'll blow over. But like I said, do what you gotta do. I just hate to see you throw a promising career down the toilet. What is it with you and that tiger?"

"It's hard to explain. I felt a connection the first time I laid eyes on him. You know I've always been fascinated with tigers."

"I know."

Gena packed her 2013 Forester and left the next morning. She took the Interstate to Iowa City and cut north on Thirty to Dubuque. The brakes started squealing and pulsing. Another hassle she didn't need. Crossing the bridge into Wisconsin, she felt a great weight lifting from her shoulders. The fight game was exhausting. Training. Politics. Watching what she ate. Nebraska was mostly prairie. Wisconsin was hilly and green. She headed north on Sixty-One, crossing the river at Boscobel. It was just after three when she arrived at the Sanctuary's front gate, now locked. She phoned Mona. The Native American woman came out and opened the gate, closed it after, and trotted up to the car, embracing Gena with her one arm.

"Thank you for coming. We've been so worried. He isn't eating. He just lies there, flicking his tail at the flies."

"Give me a minute to go potty."

Ten minutes later, Gena followed Mona past cages holding bears and wolves.

"What happened to the straw?"

"Fabian had it all taken out. He said it was breeding disease. He left Genghis alone."

"Did he ever abuse Genghis?"

Mona stared at the ground. "He used an electric cattle prod through the fence."

"Why? Why would he do that?"

"Because Genghis refused to breed."

The star attraction's enclosure was set off from the others, approachable via a flagstone path that the employees had spent a full day installing. No other animal had such a grand entrance. The big cat's cage was larger than any of the others, but miniscule compared to the habitat at non-commercial facilities dedicated to preserving wild animals. The Wild Animal Initiative had been on their case for years. Out of curiosity, Gena had looked them up and taken a virtual tour. The Wild Animal Initiative's Colorado facility, the one which provided visitors with a fifty-foot skyway, enclosed over eight hundred acres, divided into separate habitats for various species.

Genghis lay sleeping on his side, back toward the front.

"Genghis," Gena said. The big cat didn't move.

"Genghis, it's me, Gena."

The tiger rippled, raised its head, and rolled over. At the sight of Gena it sat up roaring, and with a piteous mewling sound, rushed over and licked Gena's hand through the bars. Mona instinctively stepped back.

"Wow. I don't fucking believe it. Anybody else, he would have ripped their arm off."

"Oh come on."

Mona turned her armless shoulder to Gena.

Gena reached through the bars and ruffled the big cat's ears. "Why didn't you tell me that before?"

"I didn't think it was important. It's what tigers do."

"And yet you stayed here taking care of him?"

"Before I came here, I was a mess. Failed marriage. I was addicted to heroin. I was an alcoholic." She laughed mirthlessly. "I was a caricature of the reservation Indian. I grew up on Pine Ridge in South Dakota. It's the poorest Indian reservation in the nation. No casino for us."

"When's the last time the vet checked Genghis?"

"Months. We can't afford to pay them. Two of the ligers have ear infections. I was gonna call that zoo in Madison and see if they could send anyone, but we've just been overwhelmed taking care of these animals…"

"What happened to Jennifer?"

"She split. She got a job offer from the Cincinnati zoo."

"Okay. I'll find a vet. I'll pay for it. Let's make the rounds. Show me who's left." She reached through the bars and caressed the big cat's cheek. "I'll be back."

The black bears were flea infested. The wolves needed dentals. Fourteen exotic animals remained, all in need of medical care. Gena called six area veterinarians before she found someone willing to come out. Dr. Erica Sodaro wanted cash up front.

"Sorry to have to do it, but we've all heard about Fitch stiffing people."

"Do you take credit cards?"

"Yes, I do."

"How much."

"I'll need five thousand dollars. That will barely cover my time and expenses, assuming I'm treating these animals for parasites and infections." Sodaro agreed to come down Friday from her practice in Wausau. She had experience from treating exotic animals at the Baraboo Circus World Museum.

Gena moved back into her old bedroom in the main building, the one she'd shared with Fabian. Her car would have to wait until the morning.

CHAPTER
30

SOUTH POINT

Josh rode to the Dane County Airport and parked in the garage. He strapped on a mask and went inside. At this hour, the airport was moribund. Southwest had a non-stop leaving at ten. Putting his shoes, wallet, cell phone, belt, and keys in a plastic bin, he passed through security. "No luggage?" an agent asked.

"No sir."

"Wait here one minute." Josh stood by the kiosk as the TSA agent looked him up on his computer. "Okay, I'm going to pat you down. I'm going to feel up your butt cheeks with the back of my hand and around your waist."

"Go ahead."

The agent pulled on blue nitrile gloves and did his thing. "Okay, you're free to go." The plane was boarding as he reached the gate. Josh snagged an aisle seat near the back. He slept most of the way. The flight to Vegas was two hours, but due to the time zone change, Josh landed at eleven and took an Uber directly to the South Point. Josh grabbed a blue face mask from a box near the main entrance. You could never have too many. Ahead and on both sides spread the epilepsy-inducing casino, clanging, flashing, buzzing. In his biker jeans and boots, tatted arms descending from his sleeveless sweatshirt, Josh fit right in. A banner to his right declared, "THIRD ANNUAL LAS VEGAS SPORTS MEMORABILIA AND COLLECTIBLES." Standing, because there were no chairs, he downloaded a Mac Jones Panini and a Tom Brady Bowman chrome.

He got a room on the eleventh floor, showing his driver's license and paying cash.

He studied a map near the front desk and located the poker room to his left, next to the Grandview Lounge. Stopping at a booth to purchase five hundred dollars' worth of chips, Josh walked through the aisles of slot machines where grizzled military veterans, morbidly obese cigarette smokers, and coke-blitzed kids compulsively pulled the lever, like pigeons trained to peck a button in exchange for a kernel of corn. Josh sat at the Grandview bar and watched Wes Winters regale the blue hairs with "What's New Pussycat."

Josh had a shot of Jack and a beer chaser. Following years of hard drinking, that was his limit, and had hardly any effect on him. He sauntered to the poker room and looked around. At one o'clock in the morning, the joint was jumping, with every table busy. Texas Hold 'Em was inside a no limit corral on a raised dais. There were five circular tables. It took Josh five seconds to locate Capadona, seated next to an Asian man in a tuxedo. Capadona had aged well, with a smooth roundish face topped with close-cropped curly hair dyed black. He wore a blue sharkskin suit, a blindingly white shirt open at the collar to reveal several gold chains.

There were five players at Capadona's table, the dealer a young Latina in a blue vest with a bolo tie. As he approached, a middle-aged man with a bad comb-over threw his cards down, picked up his chips and stood. "I'm out."

Josh swooped on the chair, carefully placing his chips in front of him. He glanced to his left where Capadona had a small castle going, surrounded by a barricade of arms. The button dealt out five sets of hole cards, then the flop. A wiry blue-collar type with tatted arms and an Adam's apple the size of a toilet float pushed a hundred bucks into the pot at the flop, two of Spades, Jack of Hearts, and Jack of Spades. Capadona matched it. An Asian man wearing horn-rimmed glasses and a tan sports jacket pushed a hundred into the pot. Josh peeked at his hole cards. An Ace of Hearts and a Four of Clubs. He'd played poker with the Bedouins, but he hadn't played in years. He wasn't interested in winning. He raised the pot by fifty.

Possible flush. Josh's hand was going nowhere. The twin was the Ten of Diamonds. The river was the Eight of Clubs. Capadona shoved two hundred into the pot. The redneck matched it. The Asian raised another two hundred. The middle-aged blue hair folded.

"I'm out."

"Me too," Josh said. He parlayed his five hundred into ninety minutes until the final hand. Capadona was up by several thousand. Josh cursed under his breath. "I'm out."

The hand ended. Josh said, "I need to up my bank. Anybody here interested in a Mac Jones trading card? It's worth a cool thou."

"You're not permitted to parlay at the table," the dealer said.

Josh pushed back and stood. "Fuck it."

"Wait a minute," Capadona said. "Can you show me the card?"

Josh sat down again and poked at his phone.

"Not here," the dealer said. "You have private business, do it in private."

"Let's go to the Grandview," Josh said. Capadona grabbed his chips.

They took stools at the bar, looking past the bar to the stage where Wes Winters was on his knees, serenading a laughing middle-aged woman with corn-rows, singing "Fly Me to the Moon."

Josh ordered a whiskey. Capadona ordered cognac and insisted on paying.

Josh showed the picture of the Mac Jones card he'd downloaded.

"You here for the sports memorabilia convention?" Capadona said.

"Yup. I made some lucky trades last year. My old man got me into it. He had a baseball bat signed by Babe Ruth. Unfortunately, he sold it when I was fifteen. You collect?"

Capadona leaned back and showed his teeth. "Only Beantown. I love the Patriots, the Celtics, and the Sox. I got

season tickets to Foxborough. I rarely miss a game. I have a
Deion Branch jersey signed and framed in my den. I must
have a couple thousand trading cards by now. I mean, I'll
buy anything if it's rare and I like that guy, but Beantown's
my thing. Do you have the card with you?"

"It's in the safe in my room, along with a bunch of other
stuff."

"What else you got?"

Josh leaned back and pursed his lips. "Okay. I got a 2000
Bowman chrome Tom Brady that's worth thirty-five thousand dollars."

"Seriously?"

"Want to see it?"

"Would you be willing to barter? Save you a lot of time."

"I was hoping to get top dollar for it."

"Let me take a look. I'm pretty savvy about this shit."

Josh waited a beat. "I guess it can't hurt."

Setting their glasses on the bartop they strolled through
the clanging, flashing, beeping casino. It only lacked for
smoke. They took the elevator to the eleventh floor. Josh
had never been in the room. He swiped his card and pushed
the door open, leading the way. Capadona followed. Josh
flicked the light switch illuminating a standard hotel room
with two queen size beds facing a big flat screen. Capadona
looked around. A crease of anxiety pierced his brow.

Josh turned and punched Capadona in the gut, folding
him over. Capadona fell to his knees.

CHAPTER
31

NO DEAL

As Capadona struggled for breath, Josh went through his pockets, lifting his wallet and phone from inside jacket pockets, finding a gravity knife with a four-inch blade in the pants. Capadona rolled on his ass and crabbed backward until he hit the bed.

"What do you want?"

"You remember Buster?"

Confusion clouded Capadona's face, replaced by the harsh glare of understanding. "What the fuck?!"

"You left Buster to die of thirst in the basement."

"Wait a minute. Wait a minute. How the fuck do you even know that?"

"I visited your zoo, Tony. Not much left. That zebra you left to die. God knows how many other animals. Why would a smart guy like you even have a zoo? Who do you think you are? Pablo Escobar?"

"Who sent you? PETA?"

Josh laughed. "I'm your worst nightmare, Tony. I'm not here about Buster. Well maybe I am. I'm here about a tiger. Genghis Khan. Maybe you've heard of him."

"That's not mine! That's Fitch's! What the fuck? I don't know anything about Genghis Khan!"

"You know Gena Kropenski, don't you?"

Confusion and fear on Capadona's face.

"But you were there, right? At the Baxter Arena. And you bet on her. How did you spike her opponent's drink? That can't have been easy. Did you go backstage posing as a fan?"

Capadona turned red. "I don't know what you're talking about."

"Sure you do. I'll be you're on the security camera. They save those for a couple years, you know."

"What did you say your name was?"

"Josh Pratt."

"Listen, Pratt, I don't know what the hell you're talking about, and you apparently know very little about me or you wouldn't try to muscle me."

"I know all about you, Tony. You're tied in with the Casutos. They're currently dealing with several federal indictments. I don't think they have the time or inclination to pull your sorry ass out of this shitpile, and they probably wouldn't appreciate you dragging them in. Doping fighters and dealing meth, that's not their game."

"What meth?"

Josh shook his head. "Tony, Tony, Tony. The police

found a meth lab at the Tiger Sanctuary. Don't tell me that genius Fabian Fitch set it up. It has your fingerprints all over it."

"Bullshit."

"Fitch left a hard drive at the sanctuary. They're tough to recycle. We found a video of you and Fitch throwing puppies to the tigers. You're not really a dog lover, are you?"

Capadona blanched. "May I get up?"

"No, you keep your ass on the floor. I'm not really interested in you, except that you're a shit human being. Anybody who would treat animals like you did doesn't deserve to live."

Capadona swallowed. A bead of sweat appeared on his brow. "Listen. I've got twenty thou on my right now. It's yours if you just forget this shit and walk out. I don't know nothin' about nothin'. If that crazy bitch took that tiger, that's on her. What kind of crazy bitch runs off with a tiger anyhow? They can't be hard to find."

"You'd be surprised. Think. Think hard. Where's Fitch?"

"I don't know. We were never close."

"Bullshit. You bought land in Clark County and you bought a tiger from him."

"I had to get out of town. It seemed as good a place as any."

"Who keeps up the taxes?"

"I have an accountant."

Josh grabbed the note pad and pen off the desk and tossed them in Capadona's lap. Capadona stared at them.

"That's none of your business."

Josh kicked him in the nuts. Capadona went sideways, curling like a carpet worm. Gradually he uncoiled enough to write in the pad. Josh picked it up and looked at it. He sat on the bed, pulled out his phone and poked. The name was real.

"They found dead animals at the Sanctuary. What do you think they'll find on your property?"

"I don't know what you're talking about."

"I think I can make a strong case you doped Gena's opponent in that fight, given your history. I'll be looking at video from the Baxter next week. That could open up a whole can of worms."

Capadona crawled to the desk and grabbed his wallet. He pulled it open showing a fat wad of cash. "Twenty thou. Take it. Just leave me alone."

"I don't want your twenty thou. I don't want you to go near dogs. If you're walking down the street and a pretty woman is approaching with a Labradoodle on a leash, cross the road. Don't think about coming after me. Better people than you have tried and they're dead. You can have the little plastic toiletries in the bathroom."

Josh tossed his card on the floor. "You know where to find me. Help me find that tiger and I'll forget all about you, Gena, and the Baxter."

Josh left. He hailed a taxi in front of the hotel. "Airport, please."

The driver, whose name was Ali Khouri, handed him a

box of blue face masks. "Would you please put one of these on, sir?"

Josh put the mask on. At the airport, he booked the next direct flight to Madison, which left at eight in the morning. Security pulled him aside. A bored agent who looked like a howitzer shell said, "Sir, I'm going to feel inside your waistband, up and down your legs, and up your buttock cheeks with the backs of my hand."

"Okay."

He fell asleep in a chair at his gate. The next thing he knew a Southwest gate agent gently rocking his shoulder. It was seven forty-five.

"Sir, we're closing the door in five minutes."

"Right, right. Thanks for waking me."

Haggard and bleary, Josh made his way on the plane and took the last empty seat at the back in front of the restrooms. He was asleep before the plane took off.

CHAPTER

32

GOD BLESS

In 2020, the Tiger Sanctuary hit a dry patch. The pandemic caused people to huddle in their homes, afraid to go out, afraid of their family. Business was bad. One blustery day in March, Mona entered Fitch's office and plopped into a chair. Fitch looked up from his computer, where he'd been tracking his offshore holdings.

"What?"

"We don't have enough food to feed the tigers."

"What about Walmart? Did you get the weekly shipment?"

"Yeah, but their business is down too. We only got two hundred and fifty pounds, and some of that was too far gone even for the wolves. I could probably pick up enough dog food, but that's gonna cost several hundred, at least, and that's only for the wolves. Bears and cats won't eat that shit."

"Well, shit."

"What should I do, boss? I could put out an appeal on the message boards."

"No way. We're not gonna go around begging like some homeless shit bum. The Tiger Sanctuary breeds success. People won't come out of pity."

"I got a couple thou in the bank."

Fitch waved his hand. "No way. I'm not having my employees pay me. I know I'm behind on salaries, and I want to thank you and everyone else who's sticking it out."

"What else I got to do?"

"How much do we have on hand?"

"Enough for two more days. I could call the Wild Animal Initiative."

"Fuck that shit! I wouldn't give them the satisfaction. They've been on my ass since I opened. They're the ones making all these complaints to the state!"

"You know me, boss. I got nowhere else to go. I'll stick it out 'til the end. I'm just sayin', we have to find some food in the next forty-eight hours or we're gonna have to farm some of these animals out."

"Okay. Okay. I get it. I got a few ideas. I'll take care of it. Listen. You haven't had a day off in months. Go see your folks. They must be worried sick about you." He reached for his wallet. "Here's a hundred bucks for gas money and incidentals."

Mona stared at the crisp Benjamin. "You sure? Don't you need this for food?"

"What's a hundred bucks? I need to scrape up a couple

thou at least, and I know some people who might be willing to kick in. Animal lovers. You leave it to me?"

"Man, I hate to take off at a time like this."

"Mona, you're my most loyal employee. You deserve a breather. Go. Don't come back for at least twenty-four hours. Me and the boys can handle it."

She stuffed the bill into her tight jeans. "Well, if you're sure."

Fitch pointed at the door. "Go. Give my regards to your parents."

"Thanks, boss." Mona left.

Fitch told everyone to go but Gunter. Only Fitch would hire the ex-con whose surly demeanor made him largely unemployable. They'd made a few bucks brewing meth, but ever since that bitch Vukelov sicced the cops on him, they'd had to lay low. The last thing he needed was a meth bust. By seven-thirty it was dark. Fitch went into his bathroom and took down an amber bottle of barbiturates.

"Jeff, I got to run an errand. I may not be back until after midnight. Can you keep an eye on things?"

"Yeah, but you know, we got no food for the big cats or the bears. We're gonna have to do something."

"Don't you worry about it. I'll take care of it. I got some rich donors I can tap."

Fitch left the compound in his Sprint, which he referred to as the Meat Wagon. He'd learned from Tony Capadona that a class guy always went first class. He could have purchased any number of used delivery vans, but he was flush at the time, and Tony had impressed upon him that a class guy bought Mercedes. Besides being both a luxury ride and a reliable workhorse, the Mercedes served other functions. He drove to Eau Claire, an hour away. Eau Claire was a city of about seventy thousand noted for its museums and the University of Wisconsin. The Chippewa River ran through town. At this time of year, the forests had not yet bloomed. The fields lay fallow and mounds of snow hunkered in mall parking lots. Like most cities in Wisconsin, the residents bet on which snow mound would last the longest. Some snow mounds remained into June. Snow lay in the ditches and the fields.

Fitch took twelve to the city, where it turned into East Clairemont, passing the familiar icons. McDonald's, Wendy's, Taco Bell, Taco John, Panda Express, Arby's, Big O Tires, Bed, Bath, and Beyond, mini malls with liquor stores, laundromats, and karate studios. He entered Oakwood with its Scheels, Five Guys, Ulta and Maurices. He drove around the parking lot until he spotted the beggar standing near the exit, dressed in a pea coat and knit cap pulled low over his grizzled face, holding a cardboard sign. "Veteran. Anything helps. God Bless."

Fitch pulled to the side of the road and lowered the passenger window. The man appeared at the window. He had a face that looked like it had been left in the sun too long, his brown eyes crouching like ferrets beneath an occipital brow, face covered with silver stubble. Even through the open window in March Fitch caught a whiff of cheap booze.

"Thank you, brother," the man said before Fitch offered anything.

"You look like you could use a meal. Get in. We'll drive through Five Guys."

The man didn't hesitate. "God bless you, brother." The rank smell of body odor permeated the truck.

"What branch of the service were you in?"

"I was in the Army. I can't get benefits because the motherfuckers gave me a dishonorable discharge, cuz I fucked up some camel jockey who was beating a dog. Can you believe that shit?"

"I'm an animal lover myself. Name's Randy."

"Burt. You believe this shit? I'm livin' in a tent down by the river. They won't let me into the shelter 'cuz I refuse to wear a mask. Fuck that shit. I already had the covid. I was flat on my ass for a week and then I was fine."

"Did you get tested?"

"No, but I know I had it. What else can it be?"

Fitch reached into his door pocket and pulled out a bottle of Jack Daniels. "You want a snort?"

"Don't mind if I do. Ain't tasted the stuff for weeks. Can't afford it."

Yeah, right.

So desperate was Burt for a drink, he never thought to think that it was an odd coincidence a Samaritan would pick him up and offer him a drink. He unscrewed the cap. His Adam's apple bobbed up and down. He drank half the pint. By the time they got to Five Guys, he was nodding off.

Fitch couldn't back up because there were cars behind him. When he got to the window, he ordered a cheeseburger. He ate it on the drive back to the sanctuary. Once inside, he drove straight back to Khan's cage, where he unloaded a cattle prod from the rear, went to the gate, zapping sparks.

Snarling, Khan backed off. The big cat knew from experience not to get near the prod.

Fitch helped the barely conscious Burt from the driver's side. "Here, man, put your arm over my shoulder. I got a nice bed for you."

The homeless man muttered unintelligibly and staggered with Fitch to the gate. Fitch leaned Burt carefully against the gate and wrapped the veteran's fingers around the bars. "Hang here for one sec and I'll get you inside. Nice comfy bed."

Burt drooled on the bars. Fitch unlocked the gate, helped Burt over the threshold, and let him fall on his face. Quickly, Fitch shut and locked the gate. He backed off.

"Come and get it, kitty. Don't say I never did nothin' for ya."

Several hours later, Fitch returned. Khan lay supine in a stupor from the drugs in his system. Fitch put on heavy leather gloves, took the cattle prod, and gathered Burt's remains. He threw the odd bits and pieces through the bars, carried everything in the van out back near one of the burn piles, took out a shovel, and dug.

CHAPTER 33

KUNG FU MUSICAL

The line outside Rise Up stretched around the block. Half the attendees wore masks and edged away from the maskless. A woman with short purple hair stood outside the door. "No backpacks! No containers with fluid in them! You can leave them outside or empty them out. Only empty containers will be allowed!"

Josh walked down the alley separating the dance studio from a food coop and entered through the back door. Inside, actors, musicians and techies adjusted their costumes, checked their sheet music or fiddled with their sound systems. Josh found Ray onstage behind the closed curtain, checking the tape on the floor. Red Xs for people to stand. Blue arrows indicating direction. She had her arm around a young man named Ralph, the star of the show, playing Russel, who cruises into town on his one wheeled skateboard determined to start his own martial arts school and runs into a group of kung fu guys who follow the Way of the Snake. If he wants to teach, he has to fight all the kung fu guys! At the skateboard park! On skateboards!

Ray looked up and winked, then turned Russel around and spoke to him softly and intensely. Russel, who had a mop of lank brown hair, wore pegged trousers and a muscle shirt and carried his one-wheeled skateboard under his arm, nodded. She smacked his ass and turned toward Josh, smiling broadly.

"There you are!"

"Here I am."

"Your seat is in the front row. It has your name on it. You're seated next to the mayor."

"Groovy, baby."

"Fifteen minutes!" a stagehand called.

Ray hugged him and shoved. "Go."

Josh made his way from backstage down the short stairs to the orchestra where the front row had been cordoned off with a blue ribbon. Sheets of blue foolscap on each seat had a name. Josh sat down next to Mayor For Life Saul Brogden, a short man with a beard whom Josh had met at his neighbors the Lowrys. Every seat was taken with about a dozen people standing against the back wall. The theater held about two hundred. Social distancing was out the window.

"Hello, Mr. Mayor."

The mayor wore a tweed jacket over blue jeans and Beatle boots. "How do you rate?"

"I know the director."

The mayor's wife Gwen leaned forward, a gregarious woman in her fifties with straight bronze hair. "We met them at the Lowrys, dear. Hello, Josh."

The orchestra filed out. Electric guitar, electric bass, keyboard, drums. Josh recognized members of the Wickershams and Side Effects. With a mighty *kerrang* that filled the hall, the band dove into a vampy groove, quoting Carl Douglas' "Everybody Was Kung Fu Fighting."

The curtain rose as the fanfare ended showing a lively street scene, painted backboards with Del's Records, Badger Kung Fu, Snoid's Comics, and Skateboard and Son. Three boys and a girl stunted on their boards on a staircase with pipe rails, that could be wheeled on and off the stage. As one boy slid down the rail, flipped his board and nailed the landing, the other three broke into "Bouncing Off the Walls," a mid-tempo rocker about the joys of skating.

"Enter the Dragon got my tail waggin'," she sang in a clear tenor. "Then Jackie Chan, the man with the plan! Bouncing off walls, Jackie's got balls! He trained for years with Biggie Smalls!"

Ninety minutes later, it was over and the audience stood clapping, whistling, screaming. The cast skated out and took their bows. The applause went on and on. The mayor and his wife yelled themselves hoarse.

Well-wishers rushed backstage for the after-party. Booze flowed and the smell of marijuana was thick. Even the mayor took a puff. No one wore a mask. The crowd thinned around nine-thirty. Josh pulled Ray into a corner.

"Let's blow this popsicle stand."

"Where?"

"Your place."

"Is Ninja still there?"

"He's almost gone."

She threw her arms around his neck. "I wish I didn't love you so much."

"I know. It's a drag."

CHAPTER 34

THE GETAWAY

It was late July. Two of the ligers had canine distemper. "There's nothing I can do for them," Dr. Sodaro said. "They're too far gone. I'm sorry."

"Can you euthanize them?"

"Yes."

"Do you need help?"

"No. I can tranquilize them through the bars. I brought an air pistol."

"Do you mind if I leave you alone?"

"No. I understand."

Gena returned to the office and performed triage on the bills. Mona hadn't been paid in six months. She had nowhere else to go. Nothing to do. Radcliff Fencing was still owed twelve thousand dollars for repairing several enclosures going back two years. The electric company threatened to turn off the power. The electric bill hadn't been paid in two months. Gena used her credit card to pay the electric and gas bills. She thought about setting up a GoFundMe, but she didn't know how to do that. She called Bear.

"Bear, do you know how to set up a go fund me?"

"No. How you doin' out there? Any sign of that bum?"

"No. I'm very worried. These animals are in poor condition and need a lot of help. I've half a mind to just call the Wild Animal Initiative and turn them all over, but I don't have the authority to do that. Only Fabian can do that and nobody knows where he is."

"When it comes to online shit, I don't know nothin'. You're an Einstein compared to me. Just go online and watch a tutorial."

"The problem is, the Tiger Sanctuary is no longer viable. It has been forever tainted by Fabian's behavior. There are a number of actions pending. The state has revoked his license and they're threatening to seize the property. The only thing holding them back is they have no idea how to deal with these animals. Neither do I, frankly. There's a veterinarian here now who has to euthanize two of the ligers. She hasn't even got to the bears and wolves."

"It's not your problem."

"It is my problem. I can't save them all, but maybe I can save Genghis."

"You're gonna what? How much does that tiger weigh?"

"Seven hundred pounds."

"Don't be stupid. Call those wild animal people. They'll take care of him. You're closed down. I saw it on the news.

Just hand it over or they're going to put you in jail."

"I have a little time before that court order comes through. It's in the works, but I don't know how long it will take."

"Listen. I think you're making a big mistake turning your back on your career. This Byam thing, it's just a setback. No reasonable person thinks you had anything to do with it."

"Any news on that subject?"

"The State Athletic Commission is investigating. They move about as fast as a glacier. I'll let you know. Listen. I got to run. I'm supposed to be training Bill Hobart. He's got a bout next week.'

"All right. Thanks for listening."

"Sweetheart, I'm there for you. You know that. But when it comes to wild animals, that just ain't my thing."

"I understand."

She called her brother.

"Sis, I don't know what to tell you. I can't just leave the tavern. My life is here. I can loan you some money. I got maybe ten thou saved up."

"Thanks, Wayne. I'll let you know."

Dr. Sodaro found her in the office. "I've done what I can. I euthanized the tigers. I'm going to have to return tomorrow and examine the rest. I'll have to bring an assistant."

"What do I do with the bodies?"

"I don't know. I saw a backhoe out behind the barn. Does anyone here know how to use a backhoe?"

"I do."

"Then I suggest you bury them."

"Thanks, Doc. See you tomorrow."

The next day, she fired up the backhoe and used it to dig a six foot pit in the field that lay between the enclosures and the hurricane fence surrounding the property. Using the little tractor from the barn, Mona and Matt helped drag the carcasses into the backhoe. They worked all morning and finished around one in the afternoon. They were exhausted.

Matt made a run to Walmart and returned with one hundred and fifty pounds of past due pork and beef which they fed to the bears, wolves, and Genghis Khan.

"It's eerie how he lets you pet him," Matt said.

"I guess."

"You know, he wanted to kill Fitch. I don't know what went on between those two, but every time Fitch appeared Genghis would go crazy, roaring and trying to get at him."

"He's probably a pretty good judge of character. Thank you for your help. I know you haven't been paid in months."

"What else I got to do?" Matt said.

"I feel this is my calling now," Mona said.

"What did you do when Genghis ripped off your arm? Did you report it?"

"Well I had to report it to the hospital. They saved my life. Then the police came out and Fabian told them he'd already euthanized Beemis."

"Beemis?"

"Beemis was old and had severe arthritis."

"Did he?"

"Yeah. Fabian buried him over there." She pointed to a mound covered with dandelions. "There are a lot of animals buried over there."

Gena lay in bed staring at the ceiling, unable to sleep. She got up around midnight, put on some clothes and went to where the big cat sprawled in his cage. She sat down outside the bars. Genghis appeared to be sleeping, but as soon as she sat, he opened his eyes and ambled over, lying down just on the other side of the bars. She reached inside and stroked his muzzle. Genghis Khan rolled over so she could stroke his belly. He purred. Like a subway car rolling underneath.

"I can't save you all," she murmured. "But I can save you."

Taking a flashlight, Gena prowled the property, finding what she needed in the barn that housed wheeled cages, a small tractor, and several large freezers used to store food, empty since the power had been cut off. There was the Sanctuary's workhorse, a Mercedes Benz Sprinter, with magnetic signs of a ferocious Khan sandwiched between a circus style GENGHIS Khan! on top, and TIGER SANCTUARY, Neillsville, WI, below, like a biker's patch. It was big enough to transport a single tiger if she didn't spend too much time on the road. But where could she go? Where do you hide a seven-hundred-pound tiger? The Wild Animal Initiative would take him, but that would be a big deal with cameras rolling. She had no legal right to turn Genghis Khan over to anyone. If she wanted to save him, she had to do it herself.

She spent the rest of the night planning their escape. In

the morning, she checked out the truck, made sure the tires were properly inflated, the gas tank full, and the cargo bay filled with hay and blankets. It had its own air conditioning unit. She peeled off the signs and tossed them aside, wrapped her phone in aluminum foil, pulled out an old atlas of the United States and planned her route.

Just before dawn, she backed the Sprinter up to Genghis's cage and shut off the engine. She talked to the big cat soothingly, opened the Sprinter's tail gate and showed him the raw meat spread out on butcher paper.

"Come on, big guy. We're getting out of here."

The tiger regarded her with great yellow eyes. When she opened the cage, he padded silently into the back of the truck and settled down.

THINGS THAT ARE BURIED

Josh woke in Ray's apartment with Sid Vicious sitting on his chest, purring.

"The world turned upside-down," he muttered. He heard the shower running. A few minutes later Ray emerged from the bathroom wearing a terry cloth robe, her hair wrapped in a towel. Even without makeup she looked great. Josh pointed to the purring cat.

"He likes you!"

"Does this mean he'll stop pissing on my shirts?"

"I think so. It's a breakthrough. All that therapy was worthwhile." She ran her hands over his stubble. "Careful there, big boy. People will think you're a hippy."

When Josh came out of the shower Ray was still in her bathrobe, seated at the kitchen table with the *State Journal's* Arts section open.

"Ray McRaney's *Kung Fu Musical* is a blast, the type

of old-fashioned musical Hollywood used to make with a modern, hip-hop soundtrack. Echoes of *West Side Story* are intentional, but the treatment is more lighthearted and the songs are memorable. Kudos to Mark Wiley and Tommy Jasmin who scored the soundtrack. Smart Studios already has plans to release the soundtrack on disc, and if an entertainment reporter from *Variety* is any indication, *Kung Fu Musical* may have legs."

Ray looked up, beaming. "We're going to have to add more shows."

Her phone rang. She answered, put up a finger, and went into the living room. Josh helped himself to coffee and cereal. Ray returned, face lit up.

"What?"

"That was some Hollywood agent who saw a clip of the show. He wants to talk to me about the rights."

"Holy shit! Where did he see a clip of the show?"

"Apparently, some people were live streaming last night, and one of them is a Facebook friend of his."

When Josh arrived home at eight-thirty, Ninja's van was in the driveway.

Fig barked Josh through the door. Ninja was asleep in the basement. Fig capered about, barking Josh into the kitchen where Josh decanted a can of Purina into her bowl. Fig snapped the whole thing up in ten seconds.

"You really should savor your food. I'd take you for a run but I just showered." Josh left a note for Ninja on tracking Fitch via his phone. "We'll go to the dog park."

At ten, the dog park parking lot was half full. Dogs bugled over the hills. Josh grabbed a handful of doggie disposal bags. Once in the gate, Fig took off like a rocket. Soon he was back with a dog that looked like a bottle brush. They sniffed each other's butts and took off again. Josh picked up dog shit as he walked, depositing them in trash cans.

When he got home, Ninja was up, blasting rap in the basement. Josh went downstairs. Ninja killed the sounds. "I found your note."

"Can you find him?"

"If the phone is still active. The phone company has the records. If the phone is a smart phone or even an old flip phone it will have an integrated GPS chip recording its location every time it moves more than X number of meters. Most people don't know how to turn it off.

"All cell phones have to talk to cell towers and those towers have a limited range. The phone company knows what number is talking to what tower. The towers have limited range. Even with no GPS a phone company stores the data of what number is talking to what tower and when, with a range of four kilometers."

"So where is he?"

"What's his phone number?"

"Didn't you get his phone number off the hard drive?"

"No."

"Shit. Hang on."

Josh phoned the Clark County Sheriff's Department. Leach was busy but would call him back.

"How'd things go last night at the show?"

"Big hit. Hollywood agent wants to talk to Ray."

Ninja held his hand up for a high five. "Get me the number. I'll see what I can do."

"I thought you had to hit the road."

"My plans got delayed."

"Is this some chick?"

Ninja laughed. "Chick? I'm trying to get in touch with my brother."

"I didn't know you even had a brother."

"Haven't seen him in years. He was overseas. He was supposed to be in Milwaukee yesterday but his flight got delayed."

"Where was he?"

"Germany. He was in the Air Force. He refused to get the shot and they're booting him out."

"That sucks. Did you get the shot?"

"No way. You?"

"Nah. I just don't believe a goddamn word they say, you know?"

"Same here. I found a Reginald Kropenski in Fremont. Here's the number." Ninja handed Josh a slip of paper.

Josh went into his office and called the number. "Hello," a woman answered.

"Ma'am, I'm looking for Reginald or Edie Kropenski."

"What's this about?"

"My name is Josh Pratt. I'm a private investigator. The Wild Animal Initiative has hired me to find a missing tiger,

Genghis Khan, who was an attraction at the Tiger Sanctuary in Wisconsin."

The woman sighed. "Yes, we know all about the Tiger
Sanctuary. I'm sorry our daughter ever hooked up with that
grifter. We haven't heard from Gena in over a week. We're
worried sick about her."

"I think she took the tiger. I don't have to tell you what
a dangerous course of action that is. Do you have any idea
where she might be? She would need a secluded property
with some kind of enclosure or fence to prevent the tiger
from escaping."

"Well, I don't know. Some farm somewhere."

"Does she know anyone who has a farm?"

"Reggie's folks had a farm in Iowa, but they sold it when
she was twelve. They're no longer around."

"I don't suppose you have the address?"

"I'd have to look around. It was so long ago."

"What were their names?"

"I'd rather not say."

"Ma'am, I have nothing but respect for your daughter.
I don't want to get her in any trouble. All I want is to find
that tiger and turn it over to the Wild Animal Initiative. If
you think of anything, will you give me a call?"

"I'm sorry, Mr. Pratt, but I don't really know you."

"I can provide references, if you like."

"Let me think about it."

"Thank you."

Josh saw that Mandy Palmer had called while he was on

the phone. He called her back.

"I haven't heard from you in several days."

"I talked to Tony Capadona." He told her about the abandoned dog and the cell phone. There was silence.

"He left the dog to die of dehydration?"

"Looks that way."

"I'm not a violent person, Josh. But I can't help what I'm thinking."

"I have a dog. I'm thinking the same thing. Capadona was not helpful. I doubt very much Fitch took Genghis. He doesn't care about the animals. All he cares about is himself. I do think that Kropenski cares about the animals. I'm just trying to figure out how a one hundred and forty-five pound woman escapes with a seven-hundred-pound tiger, and why she can't be found. I talked to her brother in Iowa. I talked to her parents. They want to help, but they have no clue. We are now focusing our efforts on where she might stash Genghis. Obviously, this would have to be some rural area. It beats me why she doesn't just call you and offer you the tiger."

"We've wondered about that too."

"If I catch up with her, I'll ask. I don't suppose you have her phone number."

"Just a minute."

A few minutes later she gave him the number.

"Thank you, ma'am."

"Thank you, Josh. The police brought in cadaver dogs and uncovered a burial pit containing three ligers and other animals. It looks like Fitch euthanized them either because they were too sick, or he couldn't monetize them. He had to keep breeding big cats because most of the money comes from the cubs. Part of our mission is educating the public about these places. Unfortunately, there are few left. Two in Florida. One in Indiana."

"I'll let you know as soon as I find something."

"Thank you."

This is to inform you that the headquarters offices are here to announce that your name and email was found among of the lucky winners of late overdue payment which you suppose to receive for a very long time due to false control promises.

Your instructed to contact (Mr. Charlie Mock) who is responsible to take care of all outstanding payments and your name and email is among of the lucky winners so congratulation one more time, The announcement was made earlier this morning and the compensation prize is ($3.450,000.00 USD only) so you're now advice to contact Mr. Charlie Mock so he will inform you how to receive your compensation prize within your Country and it will expire on January 15. 2022.

And for your information do not release your ticket number to anyone until you ask for it by Mr. Charlie Mock who is in charge of all outstanding payments,

> Ticket number (008abd3)
> Approval Code (9041480)

So you're instructed to contact (Mr. Charlie Mock) who is in-charge of this transaction before the announcement reach the expiring limit which clock on January 15, 2022, Sorry if you may receive this message in your Spam due to the poor network failure.

Office In-charge Mr. Charlie Mock
> *E-mail: charliemock07@zohomail.com*
> *+1(571-389-6456)*

Thank you,
> *UN Report Center*
> *Mrs. Mary Jackson*

Josh deleted it.

Dear Friend!
I have E-mailed you earlier a week ago and no response from you, I hope all is well with you?

    Once again, I am Marc Fernandez, from France. I have something very important I want to discuss with you privately after my due deliberation base on my decision to relocate to your Country after my retirement, which is the reason why I am writing to you and you will have a good reward.

Unfortunately, I will soon be permanently go for my retirement this year, and I am the Chief of Internal Audit in accounting Department here in my bank. I have the sum of €8. 500, 000.00, Eight Million Five Hundred Thousand Euros, I kept in my bank since 14 years now. I received this money from the Foreign Independent Contractors, that I assisted them to participate in the contracts that was awarded to them here in France. I am the only person who is aware of the Deposit in my bank, and my bank is not aware.

For this reason, I cannot personally manage the funds here in France, because of the sensitive nature of my job and the certain restriction in our office. All the details relating to this funds are in my position. So, I want you to apply for it, to help me receive the money before the time of my retirement, and we invest it into any good business of your choice in your Country.

I appreciate your quick response and further discussions.

Yours Sincerely,

Marc Fernandez.

Josh deleted it. He went downstairs and slapped the number in front of Ninja. "That belongs to Gena Kropenski. If anybody has the tiger, it's her. See what you can find."

"Aye aye, captain."

Josh made coffee, took a mug out on the rear deck from where he could see a six thousand

square foot mini-mansion through the trees. Phil Bass, the developer who built White Oaks and who was on the HOA, hadn't bugged him about buying his place in over six months. Phil had been remarkably quiet since shooting con man and cult leader Scipio last fall.

Josh's phone rang. Sheriff Leach. "What's up, Sheriff?"

"Want to give you a head's up. We found human remains yesterday at the Tiger Sanctuary."

CHAPTER
36

ON THE ROAD

"Do you know who it is?" Josh said.

"We won't know for a while, if ever. The county coroner is going to attempt to match their teeth to dental records. They appear to be two men. We're poring over reports of missing men. The coroner estimates they lay in the ground for at least two years. The Sanctuary was founded eight years ago. We're also looking at Fitch's known associates. We're treating this as a homicide. How are you doing on the tiger hunt?"

"Talked to Kropenski's brother and trainer. Today I'm going to reach out to her sparring partner, who's in Brazil, on the off chance Kropenski said something to her. Her last fight was nine months ago. The Professional Fighters League abrogated her victory because her opponent was doped."

"How doped?"

"Xylazine. It's a horse tranquilizer. It was Tony Capadona."

"How do you know that?"

"I talked to him."

"Where?"

"In Vegas."

"And he told you he doped that fighter?"

"Not in so many words, but there's no doubt in my mind. Pretty sure he has no lead on Kropenski or Genghis Khan. Pretty sure they're out of the state by now. I'll know more after I talk to the sparring partner, Dayane Pinheiro, from Sao Paulo. I reached out to Kropenski's parents but they were not helpful."

"Well, that's fine but we're more concerned with finding Fitch. Once we establish the identity of those cadavers, we'll name him as a person of interest. We're gonna need that hard drive back."

"I'll bring it back tomorrow."

"See you then."

Josh phoned the Baxter Arena and asked for security.

"Baxter security," a man answered.

"Sir, my name is Josh Pratt. I'm a private investigator from Wisconsin. I'm inquiring about a bout that took place last year on October 25 between Gena Kropenski and Cassandra Byam."

"Oh yeah. The dope a rope. What about it?"

"Do you still have video footage of the crowd ringside? I'm trying to locate the party that slipped Byam a mickey."

"I'd have to check, but probably. We hang on to the

video for at least a year."

"If I came down there, could I take a look?"

"Who'd you say you were?"

"Josh Pratt. I can provide references. Who's this?"

"Arn Williams, head of security."

"Were you there that night?"

"I was. Right now we're preparing for a hockey game. Mavericks versus Lake Superior State."

"Did the police examine that footage?"

"No. It kinda got lost in the shuffle. I don't see a problem if you want to take a look. I'll have to verify who you are, of course."

"I can come down Tuesday. Will you be there?"

"Yes. Come to the front gate. I'll let them know you're coming and they'll direct you."

"Thank you, Mr. Williams."

Josh called Dayane Pinheiro with the number Bear had given him. The recorded message was in Portuguese. Bear had told him that Pinheiro spoke English.

"Miss Pinheiro, my name is Josh Pratt. I'm a private investigator in Wisconsin. I've been hired by the Wild Animal Initiative to locate a seven-hundred-pound Siberian tiger named Genghis Khan. We have reason to believe that Gena Kropenski has taken the tiger out of state, which is a felony. We have no interest in causing Miss Kropenski any trouble. Our only interest is in recovering the tiger. If you can help, if you know of any place she might have taken the tiger, please call me. It will save Miss Kropenski a lot of trouble.

My phone number is... Thank you."

Josh checked the weather. Rain throughout the Upper Midwest.

He left home at seven the following morning under threatening skies. He took the Chrysler so he would stay dry and could listen to tunes. He took the Interstate to Black River Falls and cut north on Ninety-Five to Neillsville. Pulling on a rain proof parka, he parked on a side street and carried the plastic-wrapped bullet-riddled hard drive to the Sheriff's Department on Court Street, a two-story blond brick building with a street level entrance. Inside, the reception area smelled of coffee. A plexiglass shield rose from the counter behind which a middle-aged woman with glasses looked up.

"Can I help you?"

"Josh Pratt to see Sheriff Leach. He's expecting me."

"Have a seat. Help yourself to coffee."

Josh stared at the Keurig. He sat, holding the hard drive in his lap. Moments later, the sheriff emerged from a back office, unlatched the gate from the inside and motioned Josh back. They walked down a tiled corridor with doors on both sides to the sheriff's office in the back, looking out on the parking lot. There was a photo on the wall of a much younger Leach wearing combat fatigues in the desert with four other soldiers. A framed photograph on his desk showed a smiling, plump wife and two smiling kids in their preteens. Certificates of merit and degrees hung on the wall. Leach sat behind a gun metal gray desk. Josh set the hard drive in front of him.

"What did you find?"

"Fitch sold a tiger to Capadona, of Boston, who is or was a member of the Casuto crime family, which has been dealing cocaine and meth up and down the New England coast. They have ties to a Columbian cartel. As far as I have been able to ascertain, Capadona has kept his nose clean for the last ten years, but my resources are limited. Several years ago he bought a farm in Trempealeau County not far from the Tiger Initiative. I visited the farm and found the remains of several neglected animals, including a dog he left to die of thirst in the basement."

Leach's mouth was a slot. "Would you like some coffee?"

"No thank you, sir. I can't drink that Keurig slop."

"I keep a pitcher of the real stuff in the break room. Let's go in there."

Leaving the laptop on the desk, they went to the break room with a window looking out on Parsons Street. The room was empty. Rain drenched the sidewalks and cars. Josh helped himself to a cup of coffee and sat down opposite the sheriff at a Formica topped table. Framed Green Bay Packer and Neillsville High varsity football posters.

"Where is Capadona now?"

"Last I saw him, at the South Point Casino in Las Vegas."

"You mentioned that."

"We had a frank and honest discussion."

"You should have notified me immediately. How did you get onto the farm?"

"I came across a field behind the main house. I didn't break anything."

"Damn it, Pratt."

"Sir, I know you're understaffed and it's my goal to assist you in this investigation. Tell me how long it would have taken you to recover that information from a punctured hard drive."

The sheriff pursed his lips. "I'm familiar with your record and inclined to overlook your indiscretions. I spoke with Detective Calloway and a few other people. These are difficult times and we'll take any help we can get. But I don't want you running around beating people up."

Josh shrugged. "Have there been any complaints?"

"No. But that was in Nevada."

"I'm heading down to Omaha tomorrow to look at video from Kropenski's last fight, to see if I can identify the person who spiked her opponent's drink."

"You said Capadona confessed."

"Not in so many words."

"Then why go?"

"To bring it to the attention of the Omaha Police. He shouldn't be walking around."

"I don't see how this is germane to our current investigation. We have reason to believe Fitch may have murdered some people. But we don't know why. A warrant has been issued for the arrest of Miss Kropenski."

"If I knew where Kropenski was, that's what I'd be doing. But I don't, so I do shit to keep busy until I do."

Josh drove south, the metronomic beat of the windshield wipers lulling him into a fugue state. When a blue Prius abruptly entered his lane from a feeder, he snapped out of it, turned on the radio, and found WMSE in Milwaukee playing Lightnin' Hopkins. Josh adjusted the wipers so they matched the deep beat bass of the blues.

He pulled into his driveway at four. Ninja's Denali was still there. He had mixed feelings. He loved Ninja like a brother, and needed his help. But the man was messing with his love life. Josh folded his hands and bowed his head on the wheel.

"Dear Lord…" He didn't know what to say. It seemed selfish to pray for his own happiness. "Never mind."

ON THE ROAD AGAIN

Gena crossed into Minnesota at noon. She had an old high school friend who lived in Fergus Falls. She dare not use her cell phone, and was thinking of ditching it altogether. She'd wrapped it in aluminum foil so she couldn't be tracked. She pulled off the Interstate near Alexandria and found a public phone outside a Loaf & Jug. Fitch had installed a chain link barrier behind the seats to prevent animals from getting out through the passenger doors. Gena parked at the back of the lot and turned around. Khan was right there, muzzle at the fence, staring at her.

"Hang tight, big boy. I'll get you something to eat."

The public phone wasn't working. Gena retrieved her smart phone from the car and took it out of the aluminum foil. She called the Fergus Falls directory and got Cal Hammond's phone number. She'd kept in touch with her high school friend via Facebook, and Hammond had been an enthusiastic supporter, although he preferred football.

The phone rang.

"Cal Hammond."

"Cal, it's Gena Kropenski."

"Gena! Well, this is a surprise. What can I do for you?"

"I'm on my way to North Dakota and I wonder if you'd put me and my tiger up for the night."

"Yeah, right. You always were a kidder."

"Cal, I'm serious. You know about the Tiger Sanctuary."

"Yeah, I been meaning to get down there one of these days, then it was all over the news with your friend Fitch in the wind and cops all over the place. What the heck's goin' on?"

"Cal, you know me. I would never mistreat an animal. Fitch lied to me. All this time I thought he was some kind of animal savior when he was just exploiting them for money. I couldn't believe some of the things he's done. The state took his license and ordered him to turn the animals over to the Wild Life Initiative. By the time they arrived, we'd lost several to disease and malnutrition. He really let conditions slide. I wasn't there the whole time or I wouldn't have let it happen. I came back because of Genghis. He was already gone. Now they say they found a meth lab. I would never touch that stuff. I wouldn't even smoke marijuana!"

"I know that. Sure, Gena. Come on by. I've got a spare room. We can catch up on old times. You know I've followed your career."

"Thank you, Cal. It's not just me. Do you have a barn,

some big space where I could keep a tiger overnight?"

Cal laughed. "I thought you didn't go in for that wacky tabacky!"

"Cal, I'm not joking. Genghis Khan responds to me. He is a wonderful animal and I don't want him locked up in captivity for the rest of his life."

"Whoa. Whoa. Are you telling me you're traveling with a tiger? How is that even possible?"

"I have a special truck. He won't hurt me. I can control him. We need a place to hole up for the night before we head to Canada."

"Canada? What's in Canada?"

"Canada is what we have to go through to get to Alaska. Tigers live in the wild up there."

"Gena, this just sounds crazy."

Gena giggled inappropriately. "I can't explain it. You know I've always had a thing about tigers. Genghis was their star attraction. He's the biggest tiger in captivity, maybe in the world. We bonded."

"Yeah, I got a barn. I just sold my last heifer. I wasn't cut out to be a dairy farmer. Things were okay when Linda and me were together, but she died last winter. Cancer."

"Oh Cal. I'm so sorry. I never got to meet her."

"You two gals would have got along just fine. She used to watch you fight. She was a bigger fight fan than I was."

"Got any kids?"

"Got a boy, Rick, master sergeant in the Army. Been in five years."

"You must be proud."

"You bet I am. Well, you come on by. I'll lock up my dog and we'll figure out what to feed you and your friend for dinner."

"That's not your responsibility, Cal. I'm going to try and rustle something up on the way."

"I ain't even gonna ask." He gave her directions to his farm, northeast of town.

Carefully wrapping her phone in aluminum foil, Gena entered the Loaf & Jug, bought a jumbo Gatorade, nuked a burrito, went to the counter.

An obese young man with acne rang her up behind the plastic shield.

"Do you have any meat you're throwing out?"

He looked up. "Huh?"

"I'm headed toward a wolf sanctuary. They'll eat anything. Any meat that's past due."

"Yeah, I think I tossed some franks this morning. They were like two weeks old."

"Could I have them?"

"I guess. They're in the dumpster out back. Been sitting out there all day."

"Thank you."

She paid the clerk and went around back. The dumpster stank. A circus of flies circled overhead. She opened the lid with a clang and breathing shallowly through her mouth, picked through the garbage until she found ten pounds of Werner's Weiners inside a plastic bag. They didn't look too bad. Ten pounds was just a snack, but every little bit helped. She returned to the van.

Inside, it stank of tiger shit. Khan eyed her with interest. She unwrapped the franks and pushed them through the fence. The plastic bucket strapped to the wall was half full of water. Khan had arranged the hay in a comfy nest, and seemed content as long as he could see Gena. They hit the road.

It was just past five as Gena pulled into Cal's driveway, leading to an old, two-story white clapboard farm house with a veranda, and a red barn behind. An old hound came out from under the porch barking.

Cal came out of the house, a fit man with a swatch of straw-colored hair wearing coveralls. "Yodel! Come! Yodel!"

The dog circled the van barking. In the back, Khan arched and hissed.

"Wait a minute!" Cal called, went back in the house, and returned a minute later shaking a cellophane package of dog treats. Yodel did a quick one eighty and within seconds was back in the house. Gena got out. Cal went to meet her and they embraced. Cal smelled of straw and Axe body lotion.

"You look great, girl! You look like you're ready to go for the world title!"

"I wish. I don't know if I'm ever going to fight again."

"Let me see this beast."

"Okay, but go slow. Don't say anything. Just look." She opened the passenger door and motioned Cal over. Cautiously, he leaned into the van. For long seconds he hung there, just looking. Gena went around to the driver's side, her appearance calming the big cat.

Cal got out and quietly shut the door. "Holy shit. You weren't kidding. How are you going to get him into the barn without him walking all over you?"

"Don't worry about that. Better make sure it's escape proof, though. We don't want him taking a powder."

"I did a run through this afternoon. At first I thought you were joking. Then I remembered, you weren't much for telling stories. I doubt even that tiger can get out. We'll bar the door from the outside. It was built strong enough to contain bulls. I filled the trough with water and there's fresh hay. Why don't you put your pal in the barn and come inside? I'm frying pork chops for dinner."

CHAPTER

38

DIRECTION

The week following Fitch's flight from the Sanctuary were a blur. Fitch checked into The Palms, a weekly motel in St. Paul. The only palms to be found were two artificial plastic palms surrounding the pool, and the neon palm on the sign by the highway. He had a satellite phone. He had twenty-five gees in cash and an ounce of coke. It was too much and he knew it. He thought about selling some in the Twin Cities, but that was just an invitation to disaster. He didn't know anybody there. What the hell, he'd do it all himself. He'd need it.

He spent the last forty-eight hours drinking vodka, snorting coke, having sex with a hooker and making an enemies list. That bitch Kropenski was at the top. He wondered if he ever really loved her, or was it because she was a celebrity? Or because she was beautiful? He didn't turn on the television or listen to the radio in his banged-up Subaru.

The Porsches and Corvettes would have to wait until he got back on his feet. On July 26, he picked up a black hooker named Syreeta and they partied for twenty-four hours, first at the Tic Tac Lounge then at the Palms. At one point, he said, "Let's get some grub in here! I'm gonna call room service. What do you want?"

Syreeta laughed and laughed. "Room service! You are hilarious. Let me order. Grubhub will drop it off."

She pulled out her phone wrapped in a hard plastic leopard spot bumper. "Yeah, is this Ginzo? Yeah, I'd like to order some fried clams, linguini, and two dinner salads."

Paranoia made Fitch gasp. The bitch was signaling her pimp! They were gonna clean him out! He dove for the phone, wrestled it out of her grasp.

"What the fuck?" Syreeta said. "What the fuck is the matter with you?"

"Never mind. I ain't hungry. Get your shit together. I'm dropping you off."

"What the fuck you mean you're dropping me off? You told me you were gonna take me out! You told me you were gonna treat me special!"

"That was before you called your fuckin' pimp Ginzo, or whatever the hell his name is. You think I'm stupid?"

She goggled, mouth open. "Ginzo's is an Italian restaurant, you stupid wop! I'd think you'd like Italian food!"

"Is that how it's gonna be? You call me a stupid wop? How about I call you a nigger bitch?"

Fitch regretted his comment immediately. Syreeta's eyes

leveled to slits and she reached into her big, gaudy, plum colored hand bag and came out with a balisong which she flipped open in a practiced move. Fitch grabbed the cheap wood desk chair. He felt like a lion tamer as they squared off.

"Just get the fuck out. Look. Hang on. Omma give you five hundred dollars to forget you ever saw me."

Fitch could see the wheels spinning. Syreeta flipped the balisong closed and held out her hand. "Then you drop me off on Carnahan Street and I don't ever want to see your sorry ass again."

Keeping one eye on Syreeta, Fitch retrieved his wallet from between box spring and frame, peeled off five crisp Benjamins and tossed them on the bed. Syreeta swooped, stuffing them into her bosom.

"Let's go, big spender."

He threw his few personal possessions into an overnighter he'd bought in Mexico, stitched together with different color leather.

"Where to, big spender?"

"I'm going back to Milwaukee. Even Milwaukee is better than this shit hole." He left the lights on. He kept a loaded automatic in the glove compartment, but he'd locked the glove compartment. He hoped he wouldn't need it. He ran through various scenarios should she pull the knife. There was always slam on the brakes and send her through the windshield. Or hit something, let the air bags deploy, and fight his way out before she did. One place he was not going was Milwaukee. That was just to throw her off.

They exited the Palms onto Minnehaha, once a splendid avenue, now decrepit with pot holes and orange cones, framed by fast food outlets. McDonald's. Wendy's. Arby's. Burger King. Culver's. A&W. Taco John. Taco Bell. Olive Garden. Auto Parts. Mattresses. A Stop'n'Go with four black teenagers smoking dope outside. Through the smeared window, Fitch glimpsed the Indian proprietor. Welcome to America.

"Turn here," Syreeta said, pointing at the next light, the intersection with Sebastian Boulevard, notorious for drug deals and street walkers. Hookers gathered beneath overhangs to smoke and talk smack, their pimps seated in nice cars up and down the block. A half block down a neon sign flashed Sylvester's.

"Let me out there."

Fitch pulled up in front. A half dozen men huddled outside, one wearing a gold lame track suit, another a full-length fur coat. In July. As soon as the door opened, Syreeta screamed.

"Somebody get this motherfucker off me! He's trying to kill me!"

The men uncoiled, reaching for their waists. Fitch hit the gas and the car lurched forward, door slamming shut. He nearly hit a double-parked Cadillac as he rabbited down the street.

Christ I'm high. He should have thought this through. Fitch had a rare moment of insight. *I'm an impulsive moth-*

erfucker. I'm always looking for immediate gratification. No the fuck wonder I'm ears deep in shit. No. That can't be true. He'd put together the Tiger Sanctuary and run it for years. He'd made a good living and socked it away. It was just bad luck. Bad luck to fall in love with a treacherous bitch who loved animals more than she loved him.

He hadn't had time to raid the van. The money was still there, if he could get to it. Fuck! The GPS! He'd forgotten all about it! Had he downloaded the program? He couldn't remember! There was nothing he could do about it while driving. He had to get someplace safe where he could lay low for a bit and figure out where he was. Chances were, the Sprinter was right where he'd left it, in the barn. It had been a week since he'd split. There was a good chance that Clark County had moved on. Why leave personnel watch a washed-out wreck of farm with the stink of death?

Christ, he hadn't tuned into the news for a week. He didn't want to know. But maybe he'd better take a look. At least help him choose a direction. He looked at his speedo. Fuck, he was doing twenty over. He took his foot off the gas and let the car slow down by itself. His heart was pounding like a marching band. He pulled into the parking lot of a church and shut off the engine. He felt like he was having a heart attack, but he knew it was just the coke.

No history of heart trouble in his family. He turned on accessories and twirled around the dial until he came to a 24/7 news channel. California had ordered everybody to stay at home and wear masks. Gas hit a new high. The price of beef was skyrocketing. Sheriff's deputies had found human remains at the Tiger Sanctuary.

"Fuck me!" Fitch burst. All right. Calm down. Breathe deeply. Make a plan. He still had close to twenty gees, the gun, and the blow. But first, he had to know if the Sprinter was where he'd left it. To do that, he needed internet access. He pulled out his *State Farm Road Atlas of the United States*. He headed for St. Cloud. They'd have internet in St. Cloud.

GENGHIS' NEW QUARTERS

Yodel at his heels, Hammond did a walk through to see if there were any way Genghis Khan could get out of the barn. No way. Not unless it tried to claw through the door, and tigers didn't think that way. He went up in the loft and pitched piles of hay onto the main floor, which he put in one of the stables, a foot thick. He gave Gena a tour of the barn, including his twelve-year-old John Deere.

"Sold most everything else. Got the farm listed. Agent tells me I should clear a half mil, long enough to last me until I figure out what I want to do with the rest of my life."

"You're done farming?"

"I was never really cut out for it. Just because my dad was a farmer, I just assumed I would be a farmer too."

"What do you want to do?"

"Buy a truck and drive."

"Really?"

"In case you hadn't noticed, there's a severe shortage of truckers. Goods can't get to market. I'll drive anywhere. I've always wanted to see the country. Everywhere but California."

Gena squinted. "I can see it. Breaker breaker. This here's the Rubber Ducky."

Cal laughed. "I can't believe you've seen that movie."

"Wayne made me watch. He has the complete Peckinpah collection. I like that one, and *Ride the High Country*. The rest are too gruesome."

"Yeah, how's he doing?"

"He bought a tavern in Waterloo. The Elkhorn."

"I remember the Elkhorn."

"How the hell did you end up in Minnesota?"

Hammond laughed. "I keep asking myself that. I fell in love with Linda at Shimer. She majored in animal husbandry and sold me on her dream of operating a dairy farm. My folks did it. How hard can it be? She was all for locally sourced and all that shit, said there was a co-op out here that paid fair market prices. I was head over heels. I would have become a gravedigger if that's what she wanted."

"What co-op?"

"The peoples' store. Went belly up five years ago, so I started selling my milk to the Branford Dairy. Ended up selling them my cows."

"I need to get Genghis some food. Is there a Walmart in town?"

"Yeah, there's a Super Center out on the highway. How

much does he eat?"

"Forty to sixty pounds."

"You got the money to buy that?"

"What I'm going to do is ask the manager if they have any past-due produce I can take. That's how we fed them at the Sanctuary."

"I'll come with you. I know the manager."

"You think this barn is secure?"

"Let's do a walk-through."

Hammond shut the doors from inside and placed a four by four on the interior slats. He kicked it. It didn't give an inch. "You try it."

Gena laughed. "Cal, what do you weigh?"

"One eighty-five."

"Genghis weighs seven hundred pounds."

"You think he's smart enough to hurl himself at these doors? I don't think he could break through. I'm going to bar it on the outside too."

"How are we going to get in?"

Hammond pointed to a door at the back. "That's solid oak. He's not going to get through that either."

They walked to the back. Gena stopped at the sight of an empty cardboard box in one of the stalls. "What was in there?"

"My riding mower. I don't know why I kept it. It's just, like, a really good box."

"Let's move that into Genghis' stall and fill it with hay."

"All right."

They carried the box into the stall with the hay and dumped armloads of hay in the box until it, too, was a foot thick. Hammond filled a corrugated steel pail with water from a hose.

"All right. Let's move Genghis into his temporary quarters."

They unlatched the front door opening one half, Hammond carrying the four by four out with him. Yodel crouched at the rear of the van barking.

"Yodel! Stop that! Come here."

With a backward glance, Yodel came over and sat at Hammond's feet, tongue lolling.

"That's a well-trained dog."

"I have nothing else to do." He snapped a leash on Yodel and took him in the house.

Gena backed the van up so that it was almost flush with the door frame. Hammond came back, hands on hips.

"You want any help?"

"I don't think there's anything you can do, and I don't think Genghis can squeeze between the back of the van and the frame. I'm going to squeeze in, let him out, and get out. I'll stand behind the open van hatch so he can't get at me. Just in case."

Hammond picked up the pitchfork. "Go on."

Gena squeezed between the van and the barn door frame. "Good boy!" she cooed, opening the rear door. "Come on out, Genghis. Come on."

For a moment, Genghis crouched near the front of the

van. Gena watched him through the crack between the van door and body. In one smooth, motion, Genghis uncurled and leaped into the barn, stood there for a minute, then began exploring, going from stall to stall sniffing. Gena was tempted to go up to him and pet him, but who knows what kind of mood the big cat was in. She wouldn't be happy if she'd been locked in the back of a van for twelve hours.

She squeezed out, got in the van and pulled ahead, Hammond shutting the door behind her and placing the bar in the slots.

Gena got out of the van. "Is there any way to feed him without opening the barn door?"

"Well, I suppose you could climb up the outside to the loft and throw the food from there, but there's a ladder inside too. Can that cat climb a ladder?"

"What if I get up there and pull the ladder up?"

"That would do it. It's kinda heavy."

Gena made a bicep. "Wanna arm wrestle?"

Hammond laughed. "No thanks. I thought I'd never live down that time you beat me back in high school."

"And I've been working out ever since."

"What are you going to tell the manager?"

"I'm working with a new animal sanctuary. Wolves."

They drove to the Walmart on the highway. They put on complimentary blue cloth masks in the entry. Gena followed Hammond to produce, where he approached a stocky bald man wearing an apron and a mask.

"Gene," Hammond said.

The manager's eyes lit up. "Cal. How the hell are ya?"

"Gene, this is my friend Gena."

"How you?" Gena said. They bopped elbows.

"What can I do you for, Cal?"

"Gene, do you have any past due meat we can have?"

"It's for the wolves," Gena said.

"What wolves?"

"I'm working with a wolf sanctuary outside of town. Since they legalized hunting, the population has declined precipitously. We're hoping to preserve this magnificent animal. After all, they were here first."

"Well come on back. Let's take a look."

They headed back to the farm with a hundred pounds of past due hamburger, chicken, and pork. They pulled into the yard and parked near the barn.

"That's funny," Hammond said.

"What?"

"I don't hear Yodel."

CHAPTER

40

TONY AT THE FIGHT

Josh took One Fifty One to Dubuque and drove south to the Interstate, west on Eighty. Rain began to fall in Iowa and drummed steadily throughout the day. Josh drove with both hands on the wheel, windshield wipers and headlights on, listening to the Butterfield Blues Band. He reached Omaha at three-thirty, drove directly to the Baxter Arena, and parked in the visitor's lot on South Sixty-Seventh. The Baxter was a big modern clear glass box crouching under a mattress. Hunching into a hoodie, Josh went through the main entrance and up to the ticket counter where a fresh-faced college kid looked up with a grin.

"How can I help you?"

"My name is Josh Pratt. I'm looking for Arn Williams. He's in security."

"Let me make a call."

Minutes later, Williams strode into the big foyer. He was

a heavyset man with fading hair wearing gray suit pants and a white shirt. They shook hands.

"Thank you for seeing me, Mr. Williams."

"Come on back, we'll get you set up."

Josh followed Williams down a service corridor to an elevator. They went up five levels to another service corridor with one side opening up on sky boxes, offices on the other. The security center was a big windowless room with a half dozen desks, two facing a wall of monitors which showed black and white views of empty corridors, Zambonis polishing the arena floor, one person in front of a computer typing. Williams walked to a table facing two desk-mounted monitors at an angle.

"Let me just cue up those dates and show you how to scroll through them. We have six monitors covering the hall. A and B are mounted in the center of the ceiling and are used to look outward at the audience. Those are the ones you want." He sat down. "You can toggle clockwise or counter-clockwise."

He demonstrated. "This key freezes the frame, and this key magnifies the view. I'm assuming that whoever you're looking for was ringside during the Kropenski/Byam bout, so I've earmarked the footage from ten minutes prior to ten minutes after."

"You were there that night."

"Yeah. I was trying to watch football too, on my phone." He laughed.

"What game?"

"Bears vs. Pack."

"Are you a Bears fan?"

"Hell no. Go Pack."

"That's good. Me, too."

"Well, I'll leave you to it. Come see me before you leave."

"Thank you, sir."

Josh sat and brought up the monitor that faced the main entrance from above the ring. The video quality was excellent and he was able to zoom in on faces. It would have been simpler to run the video through face recognition software, but that was beyond his capabilities. Fight fans streamed down the corridor clutching plastic containers of beer. Three corridors led from the main entrance, six other corridors arranged radially. He had been at it for an hour and twenty minutes when Capadona appeared, unmistakable in a blue blazer, carrying a plastic cup of beer, grinning and talking to everyone around him. Josh tracked him to ringside and checked the time. It was ten minutes before the main bout.

Josh backed up, froze the image, and sent it to himself and Sheriff Leach.

"Sir. This is Anthony Capadona at the Kropenski/Byam fight last October, which was declared a no-contest following the discovery that Byam had been doped."

Josh found Williams in his office on the same floor. "Mr. Williams, I found what I want, video of Anthony Capadona entering the arena. I would like your permission to show that video to law enforcement agencies."

"This the guy was supposed to have doped Byam?"

"Yes, sir. I have no proof, but the fact that he was there will be of interest. Mr. Capadona is a known gambler, sometime coke dealer, and has ties to the Casuto crime family in Boston."

"Yeah, sure, tell me what you need and I'll forward the footage. Who you doing this for?"

"It's ancillary to my investigation. Mr. Capadona abuses animals. I won't go into details, but they'd gag a dog off a gut wagon."

"What animals? I'm a big boy. I can take it."

"Well, for starters, he left his own dog chained in a basement to die of dehydration."

Williams' face turned into a mask. "Anything I can do. I have dogs."

"Me, too."

Williams pulled out his phone and brought up a photo of two Labradors. "Morris and Chloe."

Josh showed him a picture of Fig.

"Are you getting paid for this?"

"Not this part. Think of it as a lagniappe."

Williams laughed. "Okay, Mr. Pratt. Let me know if you need anything else."

Josh gave Williams his card.

It was six when he got back on the Interstate. He shuffled through his disc player. Butterfield. Electric Flag. Old stuff he learned from Dorgan. What else was there to do on the Interstate? Why did they have to die so young?

Mike Bloomfield was found dead in his car, all four

doors locked, in San Francisco, 1981, age thirty-eight. They found an empty bottle of valium, but no drugs were found in his system. Butterfield never touched heroin until the end. He started shooting smack to relieve intestinal pain from peritonitis. In 1987, they found him dead in his North Hollywood apartment from an overdose, age forty-four. Josh considered the first Electric Flag album a masterpiece. He considered several of Butter's albums masterpieces. He wished he could have been there, Newport Folk Festival, 1965, when Butterfield scandalized and electrified the audience with his electric blues, which until that moment, had been considered an abortion. After he had listened to *The Resurrection of Pigboy Crabshaw* and *Long Time Comin'*, he switched over to a jazz station out of Omaha.

It was one when he pulled into his driveway behind the battered Denali. Lights gleamed in the basement. Fig greeted him with kisses. Bass thumped through the floor. Josh went downstairs where Ninja was hunched over his keyboard, wearing a knit cap and head phones. Josh tapped him on the shoulder. Ninja leaped up and whirled, coming down in a karate stance. Josh laughed.

Ninja took off the phones and killed the sound. "Don't sneak up on me like that!"

Josh laughed. "Who's the ninja?"

"Guess what. Your gal's on the move. I got a reading on her cell phone from two days ago, Alexandria, Minnesota. Since then, nada."

"Minnesota?"

"Yah, hey."

"All right. Thanks, man. I gotta crash. I been driving all day."

"Find anything?"

"Tony Capadona ringside at the Kropenski/Byam fight."

"Beautimous."

CHAPTER
41

NORTHWEST PASSAGE

Josh was conked out when Ninja stormed into his bedroom and raised the blinds. Sunshine struck like a hammer. Josh turned over and groaned.

"Josh. Get up. Fitch planted a transmitter in that van and now it's on the move."

Josh sat up. "Huh?"

"Yeah. I found encryption software. From there it was just a matter of running the numbers. Since there were several billion possibilities, I tapped into the NSA's main frame in Fort Meade and crunched 'em there. I copied the program to a dedicated computer. Your gal's in Fergus Falls, Minnesota.

Josh got up, threw on some clothes. "Can you copy that program to my phone so I can catch up with her?"

"I can do better than that. I copied the program to a burner!" Ninja held out a plain black notepad. "Keep it plugged in 'cuz she's gonna take off."

"Where's she going?"

"I don't know. That's your department."

"Thanks, Ninja! Is she still in Fergus Falls?"

"Yeah. Her first reading was yesterday afternoon. She's still there, unless she left the vehicle behind."

"What's she driving?"

"Omma work on that. Gonna have to use whatever cameras are available. I can track her to within three meters and if she stops, but I only got the one reading. I can search the surrounding area for CCTV and get some images. If I had the license, I could use traffic cameras."

"You keep on it," Josh said, heading for the garage. He checked the tires. He'd have to gas up. He threw a yoke of Killcliff energy drinks in a cooler along with a package of beef sticks, cheese sticks, apples and bananas. He carried a change of clothes in the trunk. He loaded the disc player with Son Seals, Tower of Power, and Scott Miller. He mounted the notepad in a Weathertec CupFone and plugged it in. The screen showed a red dot off a rural road in Fergus Falls. Ninja and Fig came out to watch.

"Take care of Fig, will ya?"

"Yeah, but don't be surprised if you come back and me and Fig are gone! We're getting mighty close."

Josh flipped him the bird and backed out of the driveway. He stopped at the 7/11 at the crossroads, gassed up, and headed for Minnesota. He crossed the Mississippi shortly after noon. One thought nagged him. "Did you know there are Siberian tigers in Alaska? They swam across the Bering

Strait."

That was a long drive. Anything could happen along the way. Why didn't she just turn Genghis over to the Wild Life Initiative? Alaska was over three thousand miles. Who knew what she thought? Josh felt a keen sense of anticipation. He wanted to meet her. He admired her guts, determination, and skill in the ring. He'd never met anyone like her, to his knowledge. He liked his women feminine.

Why had Fitch planted a transmitter in the van? There had to be some reason and Josh didn't believe it was because Fitch was concerned with theft. No one would steal such a distinctive and specialized vehicle. How long could she keep a tiger in the back of a van? Palmer had showed him pictures of tigers who had been kept in small cages for years. They were sick, their hair falling out, ribs showing. Tigers did not commit suicide. Perhaps if they were self-aware. By all accounts, Gena loved the tiger. Why else run away with it?

It was three p.m. when Josh pulled into an A&W in Saint Cloud. A sign at the entrance said DRIVE THROUGH SERVICE ONLY. He went through the drive through, got a double burger and a Coke and pulled into a parking space to eat. The tiger van was on the move. It had left Fergus Falls heading north on the interstate. If she planned to cross over into Canada, there were plenty of places east along the Minnesota/Manitoba border. She would drive the speed limit. She couldn't risk being pulled over.

How could she get the tiger into Canada?

Josh pulled out his road atlas. He could ask the fucking computer to give him a route where he could drive fast, but then it would live forever in the ether. Josh had always preferred maps. He would visualize his destination and very rarely made a wrong turn. He decided to leave the interstate and take Highway Nine north, relying on his radar detector to avoid being pulled over. He had to get ahead of her.

He considered her behavior. The GPS showed that she had spent the night at a private farm on State Highway Eighteen, east of town. She'd been there for twelve hours. Forwarding the GPS' findings to Ninja, Josh wrote, "Can you find the owner of this property?"

Ninja phoned him back on the burner as he was about to pull out.

"The property belongs to Cal Hammond, age twenty-nine, dairy farmer. He is married to Linda, age twenty-eight."

"Any connection with Gena?"

"They went to the same high school in Nebraska. Hans Rotenberry High."

"How's Fig?"

"She can't get enough of these frosted doughnuts."

"You're not feeding her frosted doughnuts."

Ninja laughed. "Still looking for Fitch. Have fun."

An hour later, Josh turned east onto Highway Eighteen, in Fergus Falls. Lush fields of corn stood waist high, punctuated by fields of bright green soybean. Josh rode with the windows down, inhaling the rich scent of farmland. He passed a hog farm. It smelled like shit. The GPS indicated Hammond's farm lay a half mile ahead on the north side of the road. Josh turned off the highway onto a dirt road, passing a rural mailbox on a stout beam anchored in concrete, and stopped in front of the old two-story farmhouse with its red barn a half step back.

A man sat in a rocker on the front porch wearing coveralls. He didn't get up as Josh approached the house.

"Mr. Hammond?"

"Yes. You looking for Gena? She left several hours ago."

"Mr. Hammond, I'm Josh Pratt. I'm a private investigator. The Wild Animal Initiative hired me to bring back their tiger. Do you know where I might find it?"

Hammond rocked and stared into the distance. "I just finished burying my dog."

"I'm sorry."

"I don't know how he got in the barn, maybe wiggled in through the back door. There was nothing left but his tail."

"I'm very sorry, sir. I have a dog myself. I don't want to get Gena into any trouble, at least no more than she's already in. My sole interest is in locating the tiger and returning it to the Wild Animal Initiative."

"How you gonna do that? You think that tiger's gonna fit in the back of your car?"

"I don't know yet."

Hammond laughed. "You want a glass of cider?"

"I wouldn't mind. But I can't stay long."

Hammond heaved himself out of the chair. "Yeah, you got a tiger to catch."

CHAPTER 42

CROSSING THE BORDER

Josh headed west, turning north on Nine an hour out of Fergus. The sparsely traveled state road swept past farms and swampland. Big rigs passed him going the other way delivering grain or lumber. He caught up with a Mayflower moving van, waited for a slight rise where he could see the plumb line straight highway a mile ahead, and swooped around it. A sign said BORUP FIVE MILES. Approaching the tiny town, his fuzzbuster squealed. He slowed way down, passing through at twenty-five miles an hour, noting the Smoky lurking behind a Renk Seed billboard.

The tiny red dot on his screen showed that Gena had crossed into North Dakota at Grand Forks and headed north on Eighty-One. Josh was five hours behind. Once out of town, the highway stretched straight to the horizon. Fuzzbuster turned to the max Josh put the pedal to the metal. He cruised at one hundred and twenty. The 300 had another forty miles per hour in reserve but he didn't want to do anything stupid. It wasn't the cops that worried him, it was some animal crossing the highway. Something wandered onto the highway at the fringe of visibility. Josh slowed down, approaching at fifty. A cow. Some cow had got loose from its enclosure and stood in the middle of the highway looking stupidly around.

Josh stopped ten feet away and watched. The cow chewed something. Josh put the car in gear and cruised slowly around, tires on the shoulder. With the cow in his rear view, he accelerated. He went through the Wendy's drive-through in Borup, wolfed down a double as he drove through town. By five pm, he was sixty miles past Crookston approaching the Canadian border. He pulled into a roadside rest station, a wood fence surrounding a half acre of gravel with a picnic table and a trash barrel. He took his phone. He was in a dead zone, except for the GPS, which was fed by satellite. Gena headed west on State Highway Two Eight-One, passing the Turtle Mountain Indian Reservation. Josh got back in the car and booked.

He put the radio on autotune. Nothing but farm reports and Come To Jesus shows. He punched up Tower of Power. The driving rhythm and blues was at odds with the pastoral, nearly deserted landscape. Gena obviously intended to sneak into Canada on some back road. So long as the GPS worked, Josh was fine doing it legally. There was a checkpoint entry on Highway Eighty-Three.

As he neared Grafton, his phone chirped with texts and

calls. He ignored it. He had been driving for ten hours. The sun lowered itself in the west. Time to hole up for the evening. In Grafton, he checked into the Grandview, a one-story row of twelve rooms with a grand view of the cow pasture across the highway. The marquee advertised FREE WI-FI AND HBO.

Josh took a shower and flopped on the bed, returning phone calls.

"Hi, baby," Ray answered. "Where are you?"

"I'm in North Dakota. Tomorrow I cross into Canada."

"How do you know where to go?"

"Fitch planted a transmitter in his van. Ninja cracked the code and I'm following Genghis Khan via GPS."

"Why is she taking that tiger to Canada?"

"She plans to release it in Alaska. Apparently, there are other Siberian tigers there. They swam across the Bering Strait."

"Are you serious?"

"That's what Roth Eisely told me. I'm hoping to catch up with her while the tiger's still in the van. I'd hate to have to shoot it."

"How'd you like me to suck your cock?"

"Oh please, baby. Don't start with that. I have to get some sleep."

"Just thought I'd throw it out there."

"Hold that thought. I'll be home as soon as I can. How'd it go with the producer?"

"Wild. His name is Ainsley Cruikshank and he produced

the *Monster In A Can* series. He's putting together a video presentation to sell it to the majors."

"I don't know what that means."

"Fat city, baby!"

They smacked each other over the phone. Josh called Ninja.

"The number you are calling is no longer in service."

Ninja called back five minutes later. "Yo."

"You are not alone."

"Couldn't wait for you to clear out so I could ask my girlfriends over."

"THERE CAN BE ONLY ONE!" the woman yelled.

Syreeta sang in the background and a woman cooed, "Come back here."

"You are not alone."

"Only when I want to be."

"Any luck with Fitch?"

"Nada. If he had a phone, he ditched it. But a word to the wise. He didn't install that tracking program to ignore it."

"You think he's on the trail?"

"It's a possibility. Just sayin'."

"I thought of that too. I'm going into Canada in the morning."

"Have you got your vaccine passport and Covid test results?"

"Shit."

"Yeah."

"Well, we'll see. I got the vax. Ray wouldn't let up."

"Good luck, my friend."

"Ninja, come over here."

"Gotta go."

Josh had a hard time falling asleep. He turned the cheap digital clock to the walk and concentrated on his breathing. Nelson Ferreira had taught him how to relax starting with his toes. Just let the toes relax completely. Up to the calves. He unhooked his muscles stage by stage all the way to the top of his head and finally fell asleep.

He woke to a truck's air horns, sun shining through the window. It was eight o'clock. He'd overslept. Ten minutes later he was on the road, listening to Dexys Midnight Runners. He was a sucker for any band with horns.

It was ten when he passed Saint John and turned north on Highway Ten, one of the less frequented points of entry. There were six vehicles ahead of him at the open air station, a roof over the highway with kiosks for agents in the middle. GPS indicated that Gena had crossed over into Canada in Kittson County and was heading northwest on Manitoba Highway Twelve.

A Mazda M5 with Iowa plates, stuffed like a Christmas turkey was in front of him. The rear facade was a cavalcade of bumper stickers. They loved their dog. Family of five, not counting dogs. They loved skiing. They loved sailing. Their son was an honor student. They were tolerant. Josh cruised the web on his burner phone. A mass demonstration in Melbourne. The Duke and Duchess of Essex landed a reality show. Josh dialed up the custom bike competition in Las Vegas.

A burp of horn jolted him. The way ahead was clear. He drove up to the kiosk, where a plump ginger Canadian customs officer, wearing a mask, hair tied in a bun, held her hand out the window.

"May I see your passport please."

Josh handed it over. She saw stamps from Brazil and Paraguay.

"May I see proof of vaccination?"

He handed over the card.

"What is the purpose of your visit?"

"I'm on my way to Alaska."

She peered at him with pursed lips. "Are you carrying any contraband, illegal drugs or weapons?"

"No ma'am."

"Pull ahead and park on the right."

Josh pulled to the side. He'd been arrested numerous times and knew how to act. He prepared his driver's license, title, and proof of insurance. They brought out a dog. The dog went crazy barking under the front passenger seat until a customs officer reached under and pulled out a dog biscuit, which the dog ate. Josh watched with bemused detachment.

They ran a mirror under the chassis. They went through the trunk examining his spare tire, jack, and air pump. An hour later they threw everything back together and the customs officer stamped his passport.

"Enjoy your visit, Mr. Pratt."

CHAPTER

43

BREAKFAST

Gena pulled over outside Humboldt. Saskatchewan looked a lot like North Dakota, with lots of open space, herds of cattle placidly munching, fields of peas, lentils, durum wheat and oats. She passed corporate farms and family farms, lakes and creeks. It was past nine when she finally stopped at Norman Coates Regional Park, closed with a chain across the entrance, and a sign explaining that due to the pandemic, no was allowed in. Gena had crossed from Manitoba into Saskatchewan through a little-known fire road. Due to the pandemic, travel between regions was severely restricted. She was twenty-five hundred miles from her destination. It would take her at four days to drive that distance, stopping eight hours a day, looking for food, cleaning out the van.

She sang to Genghis Khan while driving. Sometimes she played the radio. She talked to the big cat. "Sit tight, big guy, we're headed toward the promised land. Soon you'll be romping with grizzly bears, and maybe finding an old lady, if you're lucky. She will be a very refined and cultured lady tiger, and perhaps she will recite poetry. You will have many children. I hope you don't eat them."

Genghis had been remarkably laid back about the whole thing, lounging in the hey, stretching and yawning. She got in there once a day, opening a gate between the front and the back, crawling through to clean up his scat, pour more water, and relax against his warm, rumbling skin as she tickled his ears and talked baby talk. She wondered how long she could keep him cooped up like this, then remembered that Fitch had kept big cats in enclosures almost as small for years. It had broken their spirits. She vowed that wouldn't happen to Genghis.

"I love you, Genghis. I really love you. Not like that shit heel Fitch. I thought I loved him, but I was really in love with the idea of having some high profile celebrity boyfriend. What a laugh that was."

Genghis yawned. She touched one of his incisors. It was three inches long. And yet she felt in no danger. Ever since the first time they'd met, Gena felt that Genghis had understood her as few humans could.

"I'm going insane," she hissed. "Too many hits to the head. I'm shacked up with a tiger in the middle of Canada."

Genghis dragged his sandpaper tongue across Gena's face. He smelled of meat and deep, primordial forces. Gena wondered if she would attract attention by ordering fifty Big Macs. Genghis had wolfed down the food she brought and she couldn't help but wonder if she ran out of food whether he'd start looking at her differently.

Gena slept curled up Genghis' warm embrace. She wondered if it had ever happened before. She knew that ninety-eight per cent of big cats died within two years of captivity. Genghis was going on four. She knew that tigers routinely escaped their enclosures and killed people, with whom they associated with food. She knew that male tigers routinely roamed twenty miles a day, marking their territory with urine and feces. Genghis could turn on her at any minute and eat her. It had happened a thousand times.

She woke in the morning, Genghis still sleeping, fore paw heavy on her. She slipped out of the van, quietly shutting the door behind her and went into the forest to relieve herself. Wiping herself off with a tissue, she buckled up and looked around. The forest in which she'd parked was not unlike many forests in Wisconsin and her native Nebraska. Tree squirrels scolded. She wondered how many squirrels it would take to satiate Genghis. A deer appeared fleetingly. She wished she'd brought a rifle. She'd learned to shoot on her grandparents' farm, along with Wayne. They hunted pheasant in the fall. Wayne hunted deer. Her grandfather would butcher the deer himself and they'd eat venison for weeks.

Tires crunched on gravel. Hell. Who could be driving around at this hour in the morning? Cautiously she made her way through the trees to the edge of the clearing where two men had emerged from a beat-up old Pontiac and were approaching the Transit.

"Help you gentlemen?" Gena called out.

The men stopped. Big hairy men, one in a red plaid wool jacket and Elmer Fudd cap, the other in a black leather jacket belted at the waist.

"Hello!" Fudd called. "Is this your van?"

She walked toward them, stopping ten feet away. "Yes. Is there a problem?"

"Nobody's supposed to be using this park due to the covid restrictions," he answered. He had a five-day stubble. The other one was clean shaven with a weak chin. Gena eyed their piece-of-shit car.

"What are you doing here?"

They looked at each other with big, shit-eating grins.

"We kinda patrol the area on behalf of the locals," Fudd said.

"We're volunteers," the other said.

"I volunteer too," Gena said. "Okay now?"

"Y'know, you're kind of lippy for a woman alone in the woods," Fudd said.

"Good looking woman," the other said. "Kinda big, but no fat."

"Thanks for the head's up. I'll leave."

Fudd stepped toward her. "Not so fast. You could earn the right to stay here by performing a small service for us."

"That's right," the other said. "You got a mattress in there?"

"Not exactly."

"Doesn't matter. How about you take your clothes off."

Gena grinned. "Why don't you come over here and help."

They looked. They grinned.

"Well, all right," Fudd said. "Don't mind if I do."

The spinning reverse heel kick is difficult to use successfully in the ring, because experienced fighters know to look for it. Gena waited until he was at four feet and closing before spinning clockwise and planting her foot center chest, knocking him on his ass. The other one pulled a black automatic from his jacket and ratcheted a round into the chamber.

"George, you all right?"

George lay on his back staring up at the trees. "Just give me a minute. I did not see that coming."

"You must be some kind of warrior woman. I always wanted to fuck a warrior woman. So here's what we're gonna do. Unless you can outrun this here bullet, take off those clothes."

Only Gena noticed the van shifting.

"Please don't hurt me. I'll do whatever you ask. May I put in my diaphragm?"

Leather turned. "George?"

"What the hell. Don't let nobody say we aren't gentlemen. Put in your diaphragm."

Head meekly bowed, Gena walked in defeated posture to the rear of the van and pulled the door open. Genghis sprang ten feet through the air carrying leather jacket to the

ground and ripped out his throat. George got to his knees
and tried to run. Genghis was on him instantly, massive
incisors cutting through the thigh and piercing the femoral
artery. The man bled out in minutes.

Genghis went to work. By the time he was finished, only
their heads, belt buckles, and scraps of clothing were left.
She grabbed the automatic. She could always ditch it before
entering Alaska.

"Good boy," Gena cooed. "Come on, Genghis. We've
got to get out of here."

She motioned for him to get back in the van. Genghis
squatted, defecated, urinated on the men's remains, and
jumped back into the van.

CHAPTER

44

KOA

Fitch took a room at the Reynolds Motel on Minnehaha Avenue. FREE WIFI. HBO. Paid cash. Children whooped and splashed in the rectangular pool surrounded by hurricane fencing within sight of the highway. It was eight o'clock at night and the temperature was near ninety. Fitch turned the AC to the max, took a shower, and ordered a pizza via Grubhub. He flopped on the thin mattress and tuned into CNN showing an in-store video of thirty masked and armed robbers invading a Louis Vuitton store and making off with over a hundred thousand dollars' worth of merchandise.

"Thus," the news reader solemnly intoned, "these traditionally marginalized people have struck a bold blow for equity and redress of historic wrongs. Louis Vuitton has decided to close the store."

He laid a line on the bathroom counter, snorted up, swigged from a pocket flask of Jack Daniels, balanced his laptop on his gut and went to work. Twenty minutes spent looking at big bottomed girls exposing their vaginas. Twenty minutes trying to masturbate with the complimentary bottle of skin lotion. Took a shower. Wiped himself off. Back to work. Holy shit! Gena had crossed into Canada! That bitch. He never should have left the keys in his desk drawer.

He didn't give a shit about the van. He wanted to teach that bitch a lesson. He wanted the two hundred thousand dollars in gold Pandas concealed in the chassis. He'd cleaned up on the Byam fight. Capadona told him about the deal ahead of time. After all he'd done for her, made her a partner in the Sanctuary, converted the barn to a training camp, bought her nice clothes and dinners, this was how she repaid him. He would have killed that tiger rather than turn it over to the tree huggers.

Well hell. He knew he wasn't going to get any sleep, not with those kids raising a racket and all that blow. The room only cost eighty-nine dollars. The old Subaru wouldn't cut it. By now they would know what he was driving. He'd have to switch cars. He threw his things in a leather bag, got in his car and drove to the St. Paul Downtown Airport, hard by the Mississippi. He donned a black watch cap, sunglasses, and a mask. He was now immune from facial recognition technology.

He entered long-term parking, taking the tag from the machine and drove down to the lowest level, which was at fifty percent. He opened the spare tire bay and jammed the

Colt 45 in the back of his belt. Grabbing his overnighter, he went from car to car peering at the dashboards. He found what he was looking for, a 2019 Toyota Rav4 with a ticket from that morning. He removed the Grainger tool kit from his bag, selected the slim metal bar and popped the door open. He slipped inside, shut the door, placed his bag in the passenger well, hunkered down and shined a pen light on the underside of the dash. As a teenager in Boston, stealing cars had been a popular past time. They'd usually leave the cars at Logan and take the train back in. The dash looked good, but underneath it was just cheap plastic. He pried loose the panel on the underside of the steering column and pulled out the wire bundle, all different colors. The battery wire was red, the others green, blue and black. He'd have to use trial and error to discover which was the ignition wire. He used a pen knife to cut the insulation from the wires, made sure the vehicle was in park. Two tries and the engine turned over. He used black electrician's tape to bind the two wires together. He eased into the driver's seat, gripped the wheel and broke the lock with a savage twist.

He transferred things, putting the satellite phone on the front seat next to him.

He followed the exit signs to the automatic kiosk and used a stolen credit card to pay the tab. Twelve fifty. Not bad. Minutes later he was across the bridge and headed north on Thirty-Five. Now he had to sneak into Canada. The smuggling routes were not available on the internet. Between highways Fifty-nine and Eighty-nine lay the Roseau

River State Wildlife Management Area, an impenetrable evergreen forest with a handful of rugged logging trails. It could be done, the question was, could the Rav4 do it? Or was he better off heading to the far more rugged Montana/ Manitoba border?

Fitch took the Interstate north almost to Duluth, turning west on Highway Two. The Rav4 had a fuzzbuster. He pulled into a rest stop with decent reception and tracked the traitorous bitch. She was in Saskatchewan headed west. Where the fuck was she going? Fitch thought he could make better time skirting the roof, so he headed west. By the time he reached Grand Forks he'd been up for twenty hours and was feeling crashy. He found a KOA just west of Grand Forks, pulled in, and registered with a pimply teen aged boy who gave a cursory glance at his fake driver's license and assigned him a spot at the far end of the camp.

Fitch got out, took a whiz in the concrete outhouse, and opened the Rav4's tailgate. It was filled with camping gear. The air mattress had its own foot-powered pump, and there was a down-filled sleeping bag. A sealed plastic ditty bag contained beef jerky, dried apricots, dried mangoes, and trail mix. A backpack contained insect repellent, a toothbrush, toothpaste, aspirin, sunglasses, and a sewing kit. Fitch filled a gallon thermos with water from the communal pump, lowered the rear seat backs, spread the sleeping bag on the mattress, crawled in and tried to sleep. It was only seven-thirty and still light.

Some kids played in a sand-filled playground containing

a jungle gym and swing set, shrieking and laughing. Fitch conked out. He dreamed about women he'd known, women he'd had, women over whom he'd lusted. He did not dream about Gena. When he woke, it was dark out. He looked at his watch. Ten-thirty. He felt fully rested.

He pulled out his satellite phone and activated the program. The transmitter showed that Gena was stationary outside Red Deer, Alberta. He wondered if she'd made a stupid mistake and Genghis escaped. He wondered if Genghis had enough pussy-footing around and killed her. He hoped so. He could always find that truck. He wouldn't know until the red dot started moving again. In any case, he had no choice. Shaking out a line on his hand, he snorkled up and hit the road. At least he had the coke to keep him going.

CHAPTER

45

NORDIC RAIDERS

Josh pulled into a motel in Moose Jaw. He'd been on the road for twelve hours, stopping only for potty breaks and to study the map. Reception faded in and out depending on where he was. He was lucky to get one bar. If he lost the internet, he'd have to rely on Ninja. He'd have to stop at public phones, wait for Ninja to boot up the program, and give him a real time update.

Reception at the Lamplighter was shit. He'd passed a roadhouse with a half dozen chops outside. Said best hamburgers in town, not that great an achievement with a small town that had only a McDonald's and a Dairy Queen. He put on a Packers sweatshirt and walked the hundred yards to the Karakahl down the street. Made of logs with a copper roof, it had a front porch that extended the length of the building. It was just past nine, Stray Cats booming from a juke box. Up three steps and through the screen door, the peaked roof was open, criss-crossed with timbers and ducts. A moose head glowered from above the bar, with six booths on the right and a pool table in the back. Three massive bikers sat at the bar, their backs resembling caissons. It took a minute for Josh to register their colors. The Nordic Raiders, Minnesota chapter. He looked at them in the mirror. The man nearest the door had a beard that Rasputin would envy and a shaved skull that gleamed in the bar lights. Josh went up to him.

"Lars Larsen?"

The Raider swiveled showing his President patch. His denim vest was covered with patches. MIA/POW. 1%ers. WE EAT LUTEFISK. He squinted. He weighed three hundred pounds and was six feet five inches in his socks. Lars glowered. Josh grinned. Lars' mouth opened in hesitation.

"Do I know you?"

"Sturgis, six years ago. You saved my ass from a beating. The Mastodons!"

Lars stood. "Josh Pratt! How the hell are ya?" He crushed Josh to him like an anaconda. "Man, you're a fucking legend! You're the man who killed Hitler and then the Bigfoot!"

Josh laughed. "No one's supposed to know that."

"You remember Sven and Steve! Look here, boys!"

The two other Raiders swiveled. Sven wore the same Packer jersey. He made a fist. "Go Pack!"

They bopped fists. Lars insisted Josh join them for dinner, so they snagged a booth, barely large enough to contain them. The waitress wore a plaid shirt and denim skirt.

"What'll it be, boys?" she said in a world-weary voice.

"How 'bout your phone number, honey?" Sven said, eliciting a wan smile.

"What else?"

Everyone ordered double cheeseburgers but Josh, who ordered a single. They ordered four drafts.

"What are you doing here?" Lars and Josh said. They looked at each other and burst out laughing.

"You first," Josh said.

"We're on our way home. One day we decided we'd ride to Alaska. So we did! Took twelve days to get there, taking our time, and half that time we had to wear rain gear."

"We was visiting his mom," Sven said.

"My mother lives in Juneau. She's seventy-five."

"How's she doing?"

Lars turned his hand like a toy airplane. "Some days better than others. Still lives by herself, although the neighbors look in on her. She's got a malamute named Sitka. Sit, Sitka! Sit!"

"Those fuckin' moose are big," said the third Raider, whose patch identified him as Archie.

"Yeah, don't fuck with the moose," Lars said. "Now we're on our way back. Last year, we went to Baja. Brought back a shitload of Baja Bad! Did you know they grew reefer down there?"

"How'd you bring it back?"

Lars grinned slyly. "Did you know I'm an honorary Papago Indian?"

"I never heard of them."

"Oh yeah. They got a res that straddles the Arizona/Mexico border. It's its own little nation."

"I see. What's up here? Alaskan Thunderfuck?"

Lars brayed and sprayed. "I haven't heard that phrase since I was in college! Well, you know, we'd been thinking about it for years, and we realized what the hell, we weren't getting any younger."

"Are you glad you went?"

"Fuck an A! What are you doing here?"

"You ever hear of Queen Tiger?"

"Isn't she that MMA broad who gave it up to go live with the tigers?" Sven said.

"That's right. The state shut the Tiger Sanctuary down so Miss Kropenski absconded with Genghis Khan, their star attraction. The Wild Animal Initiative hired me to find Khan and bring him back."

The Raiders stared at Josh. Sven burst out laughing.

"You're good."

"It's the truth. She's headed for Alaska to turn that tiger loose."

"Whaaat?" Sven said.

"Miss Kropenski is an animal lover. Let me amend that. She loves that tiger, and will do anything to prevent Genghis from falling into the wrong hands, and her opinion, the Wild Animal Initiative is the wrong hands. I hope to catch up with her and convince her that Genghis would be better off on the Initiative's eight-hundred-acre retreat in

Colorado."

"And then she's what? Gonna turn around and drive back? How is she even traveling with a tiger?"

"She's got a big van. I assume Genghis is in the back. As to the logistics of meals and relieving himself, I just pray he doesn't get away. If he gets away, it may be impossible to save his life."

"How big is he?" Archie said.

"At seven hundred pounds, Genghis Khan is one of the biggest Siberian tigers ever."

"Jayzus."

"So how you gonna find this cat?" Lars said.

"The vehicle she's driving has a transmitter. Holy shit! That's why I came here!" Josh pulled out his pad. Three bars. He was in business. The red blip was stationary in Norman Coates Regional Park. They were in the same province. She was less than two hundred and fifty miles away. If he left, he could be there in four hours. At this hour, she was likely down for the evening. Should he take a chance and leave immediately, or have a burger with the boys and catch a few hours sleep?

Josh was famished.

"Well?" Lars said.

"She's close. She's not going anywhere at this hour."

"What if she drives by night so as to be less noticeable?"

"Hmmm. I hadn't thought of that."

Josh reviewed what he knew about Gena. Sensible woman by all accounts. She would travel by day. That would be less noticeable. Sven and Archie had already consumed their burgers and signaled for more beer. Lars got his in a two-fisted grip and went to work.

"Pass the ketchup," Josh said.

When they were finished, Lars grabbed the bill. "I'd go with ya, but I have to get back to work."

"'Preciate it, Lars. I think I can handle this."

The Raiders looked dubious. Josh returned to his room, slept fitfully for six hours, until the first rays of dawn penetrated the room.

NOT HERE

Gena left the park immediately, heading toward Edmonton on Highway Fourteen. The land changed from Midwestern prairie to rolling hills with snow-capped peaks in the distance. Lakes and fir trees everywhere. It reminded her of Northern Minnesota. Every now and then she'd pass a farm. Wheat, barley, hay, canola, rye and flax. She passed the Van Der Gun Dairy. She'd learned from her grandparents that each cow needed one point eight acres. Twenty acres could support eleven cows. She passed Rack Red Angus and Severtson Land and Cattle. The van jounced and shifted every time Genghis rearranged himself.

It was almost as if the big cat understood the purpose of their mission. She was no veterinarian, but she ran her hands over his body and stared at his red gums and saber teeth when he yawned, which was often. She wondered about his next meal. Canada wasn't like the United States where a Walmart manager would let her burrow through the bins. Genghis' feast would satisfy him for three days. Then he would need another meal. She pictured herself driving through a fast-food restaurant and ordering two hundred quarter pounders. She pulled into Kinsella to fill the tank. A gallon of premium at Petro Canada was less than three Canadian dollars. They had the oil fields, refineries and pipelines.

The land was beautiful, but this was August. Gena was not a winter person. She didn't ski, snowmobile, or play hockey. She mused about buying a remote farm and surrounding it with eight-foot hurricane fencing topped with barbed wire. She and Genghis could live out their days in solitude. She had the money. She wondered if she were going insane. She'd had boyfriends, none worth marrying. For a while, she thought she was in love with Fitch. He showered her with gifts and attention, but that didn't last. Once she moved to the refuge, he began treating her just another employee, except when he wanted sex. She knew he cheated on her. She'd looked at his phone.

Perhaps she was too cynical for marriage.

She'd never been one of the go-to cute girls in high school. She was too big for that. She'd always been shapely but she was big. She was intimidating even when she didn't try.

She entered the foothills of Jasper National Park, pulling out to pass a truck pulling a motor home. The Sprinter's diesel V6 was powerful enough to pass slow moving traffic, but insufficient to joust with sports cars. A group of twenty cyclists roared past heading toward Edmonton. She drove up Highway Forty-Three, the only paved road through the park. Dirt roads with signs like Philbert's Crag and Asmundsen Peak jutted off the main drive. She wondered how far up one of those trails she could coax the big machine. The signs also marked various campsites, but at this time of year they would be filled with vacationers. She couldn't take a chance parking among them. It was doubtful she would get out of the mountains that day. She'd have to find a secluded place to hole up for the night.

Several car lengths ahead traffic slowed and appeared to be making its way around a hazard in the right lane. When she finally pulled abreast, she saw a dead deer lying in the road with a puddle of black blood extending from its muzzle. As she pulled away, a vehicle behind her pulled onto the shoulder behind the carcass. A man got out and dragged the carcass out of the road.

Damn, she thought. *I could have used that.*

Six hours later, as the sun dipped below the horizon, she knew it was time to pull over. She waited until there was no traffic before or behind and turned north onto a rutted dirt road studded with boulders and potholes. The big Mercedes bounced and wallowed but pulled strong as the road led up a slight incline and then dipped precipitously. Headlights revealed a clear path and Gena let the vehicle lunge. A flicker of movement caught her eye an instant before a deer leaped directly in her path. The Transit caught the hapless creature dead on, killing it instantly. Gena immediately stopped and shut off the engine.

Shaking, she got out and bent over, hands on knees, breathing deeply. That was too close for comfort. She'd always been an animal lover and the thought of killing a deer made her sick. As a child, Wayne and her father had gone deer hunting every fall and Wayne would tease her, trying to get her to go along. They hung their trophies in the garage and butchered them. Gena did not refuse the meat.

In the headlights, the deer lay on its side, one eye staring sightlessly at the sky, tongue protruding. There was no blood. From inside the vehicle, Khan roared. The chassis rocked.

Well hell. She went to the back of the van and opened the door. Genghis sprang out and ran to the front as if he knew, seized the carcass in his massive jaws, and ran into the woods. Gena was in shock, frozen.

"Not here," she said. "Not here!"

She didn't know whether to run after him or get in the van and go. But this was not the place. These mountains were filled with hikers, skiers, fishermen. It was only a matter of time before Genghis was spotted and then they'd bring in the hunters and sharpshooters. She was paralyzed. She hesitantly stepped toward the woods. Genghis was still a wild animal. What would his reaction be if she interrupted his meal? She had always been the meat bringer. She knew all about supposedly domesticated wild animals turning on their owners and ripping them apart. Maybe this was it.

Maybe this was the end of the ride. She had a couple thou with her. She could just keep on going. Go to Alaska. She was an American citizen. She could always find work.

She was all alone. She had no future. She had that thug's automatic. She wondered if the truth ever came out, if she could be found liable for their deaths. She went to the front of the van and pulled the automatic from beneath the passenger seat. It was a CZ nine. She sat for a long time on the rear deck with the pistol in her lap, smelling Genghis' scat. She picked it up and ratcheted a shell into the chamber.

Genghis emerged from the trees, sauntered over, and laid his head in her lap.

CHAPTER
47

FIVE STARS

On August 1, Chadwick Productions flew Ray from Madison to Burbank, where a chauffeur driven limousine drove her Chadwick's headquarters, A two story white stucco on Victory Boulevard. The receptionist directed her to the elevator.

"Go on up. They're waiting for you."

The meeting room was directly opposite the elevator, looking out on Victory. There were flat screens at both ends of the long rectangle, with a long mahogany table in the middle around which sat two men and a woman. They all rose as Ray entered. Ainsley Cruikshank, with whom she'd spoken on a Zoom call, shook her hand.

"Thank you so much for coming. Ray, this is Shawn Chadwick, and Melanie Hofstetter, who oversees production."

Ray shook hands smiling. "Thank you for having me.

This is all very exciting."

Cruikshank held a chair out facing the window. "Please sit. Would you like coffee? A cruller?"

Ray went to the sideboard. "I'll mix my own coffee because people don't believe how much sugar I use."

"One would never know it looking at you," Hofstetter said.

They all sat.

"We've all watched the musical," Chadwick said. "It's delightful, and such a fresh take on the modern musical. It's a wonder nobody has thought of it before."

"Thank you. I've written five musicals for Rise Up, but this is the most successful. We had to add five shows, then cast members had other commitments, so we're going to stage it again this winter."

"Ainsley tells us you don't have a written agreement."

"Well, that's one of the reasons I'm out here."

"Of course. Everything we discuss in here is just hypothetical, but I must assure you that Chadwick is very interested in making a film of *Kung Fu Musical*. We're a small studio, but we punch above our weight. *Edgerton* was nominated for nine Academy Awards."

"I saw it. Great movie."

"Who wrote your music?"

"Mark Wiley and Tommy Jasmin."

"We would like to add to it," Hofstetter said. "As it is, the entire show times in at eight-five minutes. We would like to add additional material that would make it more interesting to an international market. Of course we would ask you to write this additional material."

Ray looked around with a goofy grin. "I can do that."

"How would you feel if Russel were a lesbian of color?"

Ray chuckled. She realized they weren't kidding. "Well, of course I support greater representation of traditionally marginalized groups. Did you have anyone in mind?"

"As a matter of fact, pop diva Griselda is looking for her first feature film. Needless to say, with her international following it will be a smash hit."

"Oh I love Griselda!"

"It's just an idea."

"Would you use any of the original cast members?"

"It's a possibility," Hofstetter said. "I understand you dance, sing and act as well."

"Well, I have to. We're a tiny theater. We all wear many hats."

"We watched you on YouTube. *Kiss Me Kate.* What inspired you to stage that?"

"I like the music. And the first time I saw it, you know that Ann Miller number. 'It's Too Darn Hot.' I had to do it."

"And you did it well. In addition to being a producer, you could be a performer in a supporting role."

"Wow."

"This is just an informal meeting to see if you're interested. We are very encouraged. Now before we proceed, you and Ainsley have to come to an understanding."

"Would you be free for dinner?" Chadwick asked. He was a hearty Midwestern type, a college athlete gone to seed, but built like a bull in the neck and shoulders."

"Of course!"

"Excellent. My driver will pick you up at seven in front of the hotel. Now if you'll excuse me, I have to see what Cody Cosgrove wants before he starts screaming and waving that gun around."

Hofstetter excused herself with a shake and a smile. Ray spent the next two hours in the room with Cruikshank, as he outlined the contract, his role, her role. It was four o'clock when they stopped.

"I'll drop you off at the hotel. Meet me out front."

Cruikshank was a freckled ginger, cute in a British invasion kind of way. He pulled up in a gleaming blue Corvette. Ray got in and shut the door.

"Wow. I can't believe this is happening."

"Well, it has to happen or there wouldn't be any movies, would there?"

Cruikshank bent the law driving Ray back to the hotel, pulling under the portico where a liveried doorman held the door for her.

"Good luck tonight!" Cruikshank sang, chirping his tires.

Ray wondered what he meant by that. She spent the next couple of hours going over her notes for her next production, *Canary in the Canyon*, a singing cowboy show with dancing cattle. She showered and put on a strapless emerald green evening dress, did her makeup, applied the perfume, admiring herself in the bathroom mirror. Batting her eyelashes, she said, "I'd kiss you, darling, but I just washed my hair."

She was in the lobby at six forty-five. She sat at the bar, treating herself to a sherry. As she sipped, looking at the main entrance in the mirror, the bartender, a man with a comb over and a potato nose, refilled her glass.

"Compliments of the gentleman at the end of the bar."

Ray looked. The man smiled and waved. With his wide lapel suit and Homburg on the bar, he looked like a gangster. Chadwick walked through the automatic doors and was halfway across the floor before being intercepted by a slim black man in a suit. They shook hands, talked a little, and Cruikshank proceeded. Ten feet from the bar, a busty young woman with glossy black hair approached. Ray heard her say, "Shawn?"

Chadwick's face became a mask. He took the young woman by the elbow and walked her toward a booth. He looked at Ray, winked, and held up a finger. They talked intensely for a few minutes before the woman got up and marched out, fists clenched. Cruikshank appeared.

"Ready?"

"You bet. You're a popular man."

"Not with everybody. One of the hazards of being known in this town is that you can't go anywhere without someone coming up with an idea, a suggestion, a pathetic appeal, or a threat."

"I should think you'd have a bodyguard."

"Don't need one. These people know better than to mess with me. I boxed in college. Once, I laid a producer out cold with one punch. He wanted me to dump Bill Wiist and replace him with some unknown. He was drunk and belligerent. I gave him every chance to walk away until he became physically abusive. That's a famous story."

"I never knew."

They went outside where Chadwick's Aston Martin was parked. The doorman opened the door for Ray, Chadwick slipped him a bill and got in the driver's seat. Ray had never been to Los Angeles and was unfamiliar with its landmarks, but when the car ascended into the Hollywood Hills, she said, "Where are we going?"

"I thought we'd go to my place. I have a five star chef who is cooking us dinner."

"O-kay."

CHAPTER
48

UBER ALLES

As Ray white-knuckled the grip bar, Chadwick strafed apexes on Mulholland Drive. He turned into Mulholland Estates where a uniformed guard waved him through. Chadwick's house was on Clarendon, with a startling view of downtown Los Angeles. He keyed the gate and drove up the red brick driveway to the front of an ultramodern glass box. The gate clicked shut behind them. Chadwick ran around the car to open her door.

"Come on in. Let me show you around."

A dark hued woman in a blue linen jacket and white pants held the door for them.

"Ray, this is Isadora. She's from Honduras. What would you like to drink?"

The sherry she'd consumed had no effect on her. "I'll have a vodka gimlet."

Chadwick ushered her into the massive living room with

furniture clusters, glass walls facing west and north. A rectangular swimming pool gleamed in the late afternoon sun, several cabanas standing nearby. There was a guest house on the other side. Chadwick pointed to a framed landscape over the stainless steel fireplace.

"That's an original Les Dorscheid. Every painting in here is an original."

Ray was drawn to a painting of a heroic woman standing on a crag. Something out of Ayn Rand or Soviet art of the sixties. "What's this?"

"That's Steve Rude. Being a movie man, I like representational art. I have no use for abstracts. That's his original painting for my production of *Hildegard, a Norse Myth*."

"Is that a movie?"

Chadwick's mouth twitched. "Yes. We grossed six hundred million worldwide, and that was six years ago, before the fucking plague."

"Is that good?"

Chadwick laughed. "You are delightfully Hollywood free. Do you like movies?"

"I adore movies. I watch at least two a week. I make my boyfriend watch."

"You have a boyfriend?"

"He's a private detective."

"Oh come on." Chadwick gestured for her to join him on a curving leather sofa facing out.

"Seriously. He's kind of a rough and tumble type. He used to be a biker."

"I ride. I have a Harley Softail."

"Well, I shouldn't say he used to be. He used to be in a gang. He still rides, but now he's a law-abiding citizen."

"Good to know."

Isadora delivered their drinks in heavy glass tumblers. Chadwick held his up. "Here's to making movies."

They clinked. They sipped.

"Would you like a tour of the gardens? We should go while the light is good."

"Of course."

Exiting through a sliding glass door, they circled the pool and looked down at Los Angeles spread before them. A layer of smog hung over the city like a dirty halo. Chadwick caressed a marble statue of a nymph holding a vase, pouring water into a circular pond. Carp gleamed gold in the slanting evening light. "This is a genuine Comstock, one of the most original and innovative or our modern sculptors."

"It's beautiful." It looked more to Ray like the Renaissance, like something Michelangelo might sculpt. She liked that he gave his money to living artists. Maybe he would give some of it to her. Wasn't that why she came? Chadwick showed her the herb garden.

"Isadora keeps this. She raises the most fabulous plants. You'll taste some of them tonight."

"What are we having?"

"Breast of pheasant Magdalena, baby carrots glazed in chive butter, Belgic white asparagus with mace butter, and Belgic endive, romaine and beets in Campania dressing."

Ray laughed. "You sound like a maître d."

"Like everybody else, I started out working in restaurants. I was a cook. I was never a very good cook, which is why I have Isadora."

There were other sculptures, a topiary, and an eight-car garage. He showed her his Lamborghini Ursa, the Bentley, the new Ford Bronco, and his motorcycles.

"I keep a place at Bear Lake. I have a thirty-foot Mastercraft Pro Star at Big Bear. I'd like to show it to you. Do you water ski?"

"As a matter of fact I do."

"We could go up there tonight, after dinner."

"I have a nine o'clock flight tomorrow morning."

"Ah well. Some other time. Are you hungry?"

"Famished."

They entered the main house through a sliding glass door on the patio near the pool. The dining room was one glass wall, the others zebra wood. A white linen tablecloth covered the round table in the middle, gleaming with china and silverware. A bottle of Dom Perignon shivered in a wine cooler. Chadwick held Ray's chair, sat opposite, and picked up a sterling silver bell.

Isadora responded immediately, replacing their drinks.

"Isadora, you may begin."

The chef returned rolling a stainless steel cart on which rested two bowls filled with salad. Chadwick waited until she left before raising his glass.

"Here's to a successful collaboration."

Ray clinked. She'd heard about these guys. She knew she was a catch, but perhaps Hollywood had learned something from the women's movement. In any case, she was no push over and had no intention going to bed with this flounder. She ate most of the salad. Isadora appeared unsummoned and replaced the bowl with a glazed platter. The pheasant bore chevrons from the grill, side of gleaming baby carrots, garnished with unknown green slivers.

"What makes the salad Magdalena?"

"I don't know. Perhaps she had a garden."

"To Magdalena." Ray was feeling the booze, but she'd felt it before. Training with Nelson Ferreira had given her new confidence. She liked sparring. She got a perverse glee taking down bigger men. The expressions on their faces! She'd even managed to take Josh down once while they were play sparring, and he'd laughed and pulled her down with him.

The sun was setting when they finished dinner.

"Would you like to take a dip in the pool?"

"I didn't bring a suit."

"I believe I have something that would fit you."

"I'll bet you do, Shawn. Dinner was fabulous. Your place is fabulous. You are fabulous. But I'm not going to bed with you. I'm a good Midwestern girl who has a serious boyfriend and my parents were Methodists."

Disappointment flickered, but Chadwick bore up well. "Well of course not. I hope you don't think I'm one of those Hollywood types who tries to bed every pretty girl that comes along."

"Why aren't you married?"

"I was married but it didn't work out."

"Do you have a girlfriend?"

Chadwick blushed, then blanched. "I'm seeing some-one."

He called an Uber.

CHAPTER

49

UNEXPECTED RESISTANCE

Fitch hunkered in his vehicle in the parking lot of a Day's Inn in Minot. He'd pulled in because they advertised free wifi and he needed the bars. He got the bars. He used Google Earth to pore over every inch of the North Dakota/Saskatchewan border looking for a point of entry. A blank spot in the northwest quadrant beckoned. There was nothing there but isolated ranches, farms, and prairie. The four-wheel drive Rav4 would be able to roll across the prairie unimpeded.

There was always a chance its theft had been discovered. He parked the vehicle on a side street in downtown Minot and walked to Waldo's Cafe, a locally owned business, where he ordered a Denver omelet and coffee. The Scandinavian Heritage Association museum was across the street. He wished he had time to sight-see, but he had to catch that bitch before she got to wherever she was going. It made no sense. She was headed toward British Columbia. A search revealed wild animal sanctuaries in the area. Birds, wolves, and bears. That was it. No tigers. Why would they? She wasn't about to drop Genghis off at any of those locations.

He topped off at a Sinclair station that looked like it hadn't changed in fifty years, except for the gas prices. Three eighty-seven for regular. He headed north west on Fifty-Two, then west on Five. He passed a herd of buffalo behind a barbed wire fence. A narrow dirt road ran north between the buffalo herd and rolling prairie of public lands. The dirt road petered out at a ridge. Fitch stopped and got out. Empty beer bottles and cans surrounded a makeshift fire circle. Brass littered the ground. Crouching, he examined the casings. Mostly thirty ought six with a smattering of two two threes. He wasn't much of a gun guy. He knew which way to point the pistol, but Capadona was a boneroo gun nut and they'd spent hours plinking away at his farm. Capadona thought it would be a good idea to keep wild animals as a status symbol, like Mike Tyson and Pablo Escobar. But what good were they when nobody knew, and nobody came to visit?

In a fit of boredom, Capadona had spotted several deer into the forest and they'd spent the afternoon tracking them. They managed to bag one, but since neither knew how to butcher a deer, they left it where it lay.

Fitch gazed north through binoculars. Aside from a small farm, there was nothing as far as the eye could see. The land looked as it had since before Columbus' arrival. It would be dark in eight hours. He decided to remain in place and make the crossing at night. He'd be less visible that way. If the land was consistent from here to Canada, he would have no trouble. He'd brought a pair of bolt cutters to take care of fences.

He'd been doing blow for so long it had become a way of life. His sinuses were constantly inflamed, he had little appetite, and yet he continued to gain weight. He felt exposed on the bluff. He worked the vehicle down a steep grade studded with boulders and pulled it beneath a sandstone overhang that looked as if it might collapse at any moment. He had eighty-five thousand in a bank in the Caymans, twenty-two thou in his checking account. He needed those Pandas. He had no choice. He wanted to teach that bitch a lesson she would never forget. Fitch had never killed anyone. He wasn't a fighter, like Capadona. He was a manipulator and planner. Once he got the money, he would fly out of Canada using a fake passport. Someplace warm. Maybe the Caymans. But first he'd have to convert the gold to cash. That wouldn't be a problem. Capadona knew guys.

Fitch hadn't reached out to his old friend for fear that Capadona was also under investigation. He wondered if he should reach out. He pulled out his phone. No bars. He was in the middle of nowhere. Fatigue washed over him. Lowering the driver's seat, he lay back and slept. When he woke it was dusk. Time to get moving. Fitch got out of the car, relieved himself beneath the overhang, and headed north on the rolling prairie, studded here and there with stands of cottonwood. The lone farm gleamed palely to his right as he bore north, guided by the North Star. He had been traveling for two hours, at speeds under thirty, sometimes slowing to a crawl to negotiate wrinkles in the earth or jumbled rocks, when his headlights fell on two pale ruts worn into the ground. They may have dated from the nineteenth century. Wagon wheels. He followed them, headlights picking out coyote eyes that gleamed for an instant and then turned tail.

He stopped for a bump, shaking out a tiny pile on his hand by the overhead light. Snork. Light went off, car went on. The trail twisted around sandstone buttes and rumbled over a creek. He entered a small woods comprised mostly of cottonwood and willow. Stars appeared intermittently through the branches. As he emerged from the woods, a massive bulk stood astride the path. Fitch stopped, trying to understand what it was. Two dull red eyes glared back. Some kind of animal. He blipped the horn. The thing didn't move. He gave a solid blast. The thing lowered its head and pawed the earth.

Belatedly, he recognized a buffalo. What the fuck! What was a buffalo doing out here in the middle of nowhere? Weren't they all fenced in? He locked the doors and looked for a way around the behemoth. Steep gradients rose on either side. He could either climb the gradient and waste his time bushwhacking over unknown terrain, or get that buffalo to move. He reached for the Colt underneath the passenger seat. It was doubtful anyone would take notice if he fired. He turned off the headlamps and surveyed the horizon. Nothing. No gleam from remote farms. He may as well have been transported back to 1880, except for the Rav4, of course.

He could hold the pistol one handed out the window, but that wasn't what he'd been taught. If he eased out of the driver's seat, stood behind the door and fired through the open window he should be all right. But what if the buffalo charged? One lousy bullet wasn't going to stop that thing. He needed a howitzer. What if it rammed the vehicle rendering it inoperable? It might be wiser to just stay where he was until the buffalo moved on. But who knew how long that would be? Certainly Gena wasn't standing around waiting for him. He shouldn't have done that line. But what's done is done. He was sick and tired of the dumb brute blocking his path. Anxiety gripped him, a need to get going.

He eased the door open and stood behind it, gripping the auto in both hands. He aimed over the animal's head so it would see the flash. He squeezed the trigger. The sound was deafening.

The buffalo charged.

CHAPTER
50

DOWNPOUR

Gena headed north on Forty Four, to hook up with Ninety Seven at Dawson Creek in British Columbia. Genghis lolled fat and lazy in the back. He would not need another meal for three days. If she drove twelve hours a day she could be there in two days. She'd examined the maps and decided to release Genghis in the Togiak Refuge, where they had already been spotted. The farther west she drove, the more likely Genghis was to encounter other tigers, but she'd taken too many chances already. A wilderness like Togiak was big enough to sustain an apex predator like Genghis. There was no shortage of wildlife. She'd thought about freeing him in Canada's Buffalo National Park, but Genghis was American, and deserved to go all the way.

She thanked God every other mile that the big cat had trusted her this far. She would not let him down. This was her life's mission. She just hadn't known it until recently.

Her career, meeting Fitch, moving to the Tiger Sanctuary, everything had prepared her for this moment. She remembered her parents sitting at home on a Friday night watching a movie called *Save the Tiger*. She had no idea what it was about, but the title resonated and here she was.

By some fluke of nature her radio pulled in a contemporary rock station playing only Canadian bands. The only Canadian band she could name was Rush. Wayne had taken her to a concert when she was in high school and she was a huge fan. She had no idea only three guys could make that big a sound. CFBR out of Calgary was blasting Sloan, a band she'd never heard. She dug it. She would pick up some Sloan when she got the chance. No downloads. Gena demanded physical product, an antediluvian attitude she'd inherited from her grandparents, who loved to play Count Basie on their turntable. She would sit in the sofa in their living room—she could almost smell the lavender room freshener—and pore over the liner notes for hours. She had a cell phone and a lap top which she used to watch movies in flight. And that was it. No iTunes, no Blue Tooth, no Alexa. No thank you.

She felt anonymous and safe. If they hadn't caught her by now, they weren't going to. It was clear sailing from there to Alaska. The only problem was how to smuggle a tiger across the border. She'd figure it out. Minutes later, pendulous clouds gathered over the mountains and rumbled. It was going to rain. She turned west at Essex Slave Lake on Two, the lake blue in the midday light. Soon the winds would come and it would turn gray and frothing. If the rains became too severe she'd have to pull over. She was driving up into the mountains. Flash floods could wipe out whole towns. In 1997, a flash flood in Fort Collins, Colorado, dumped fourteen inches in thirty-one hours. Whole trailer parks washed out to the east. A half dozen people drowned. The high-water mark was ten feet above the ground.

She learned this researching an opponent who came from Fort Collins. Deborah Murray. Girl could hit, but Gena won on points. Not that she hadn't tried to knock Debbie out. She landed over a hundred head blows in that fight and Debbie just kept on coming. Great cardio, but she lacked finesse and in the end Gena won all three rounds.

Two hours later she was headed uphill toward Dawson's Creek, which had a dozen campgrounds. She would avoid that at all costs. They were too close to their destination to risk everything for a good night's sleep. Several vehicles were stopped up ahead. As Gena pulled up behind, she saw a half dozen elk crossing the highway. The clouds were closer now, clearing their throats. Water rushed by in the drainage ditch. Fir trees everywhere.

Gena rummaged around in a plastic grocery bag, searching for the Slim Jims. She'd hit the road as soon as she got up and hadn't got around to eating until now. The bag also held Li'l Debbie doughnuts, Planter's Peanuts, and a six pack of Celsius energy drink. Ripping open the Slim Jim, she clenched it between her jars like a cigar and twisted a Celsius loose. Holding the Celsius between her thighs, she wrenched the pull tab open. She set the Slim Jim in the center console while she drank. An acrid odor filled the cab. Genghis was relieving himself in a dainty squat.

The clouds dominated. She saw the wall of water rushing down the mountain, rain so dense it seemed impenetrable. Slowing to twenty, Gena looked for a place to pull over. Everyone turned on their lights. The lights behind her faded. Perhaps they had turned around. She could see no lights in front. The rain hit the vehicle like gravel. She felt Genghis' mood swing from relaxed to agitated. She had to find a place.

Her lights almost missed the dirt road running north off the highway, dipping into the rushing drainage ditch, rising precipitously and disappearing among the Douglas fir and burr oak. Engaging the four wheel drive, she carefully turned onto the dirt road. The van wallowed but pulled its bulk up out of the ditch and churned forward with a determined grip. Gena's visibility was about ten feet. She followed the forest trail as it wound through a wilderness area, ridge after tree-capped ridge. They were alone in the universe, out of touch with the world, their vehicle the only sign of modernity. Grinning, Gena gripped the wheel imagining her great-grandparents homesteading in Nebraska. Heading west with oxen-drawn carts, willing to endure extreme hardship to find a home. Make their mark.

The Transit struggled up a steep rise until the rear wheels found traction and boosted it onto a table, a clearing in the forest. The headlights' cylindrical beams shined on dark green pine ten feet ahead. A dark gap indicated the road continued, but Gena thought they had gone far enough that day. Genghis had been indolent until the rain. He had calmed down some, but he would calm down further if she went back there and held him. She peeled a Slim Jim and poked it through the screen.

"Treat?"

Genghis sniffed, yawned, turned away. Gena stuffed the Slim Jim in her mouth, unlatched the screen and crawled through.

CHAPTER 51

SETBACKS

Josh crossed Saskatchewan in four hours, narrowly avoiding a summons for speeding. The fuzz buster went off a mile out of North Battleford and he gradually applied the brakes, like an elderly valet. He drove sedately past a Loblaw billboard where a Mountie waited, licking his chops and rubbing his hands. Josh grooved to Steve Earle's *Guitar Town*, with Mellencamp's *Scarecrow* in the batter's cage.

Ninja had fixed a mount for his notepad as part of the dash. He could see at a glance where Gena was, until the storm arrived. He watched it roll toward him from twenty miles out, a solid wall of gray from the ground up. He couldn't differentiate between clouds, rain, and land. It was all one. He barely beat the rain to North Battleford, a town of fourteen thousand, stopping at the first motel that was open, The Klondike, a rambling one-story structure with lights on in the middle of the day. Free wifi. HBO. What was it about HBO? Josh rarely watched television. He'd watch select movies that Ray wanted. Mostly he listened to records. Josh parked under the roof in front of the one-story office, ran inside, registered, handed the clerk sixty dollars, and drove to his unit six doors down.

He was soaked through between the car and the door. He stripped and took a hot shower. He went through his leather overnight bag and found clean underwear, jeans, socks, and a Paul Butterfield T-shirt. It would be pointless to order a pizza in the downpour. He leaned back on the queen-sized bed and turned on the big flat screen. The cables were underground. A hundred masked thieves had rampaged through a Bloomingdale's in NYC, taking an estimated seventy-five thousand dollars in merchandise. Eighty masked thieves rampaged through a Jared's in Minneapolis, taking an estimated two hundred and fifty thousand dollars in merchandise. A hundred masked thieves rampaged through a Home Depot in Marin County, taking an estimated eighty thousand dollars in merchandise.

Ten thousand people, most from Central America but many from Asia, were marching through Mexico to enter the United States through the Southern Border. Josh changed the channel.

He watched a sit-com that consisted entirely of insult one upsmanship. He switched to a basketball game, but there were slogans painted on the floor at each end. He switched to a shopping network and watched an attractive woman demonstrate a flame thrower. "It's ideal if you live in a northern clime and have to cope with frozen driveways or walks."

He called Ray. She picked up on the second ring.

"Hey babe, what's going on?"

"I just got back from Los Angeles."

"I didn't even know you were going!"

"Neither did I, until two days ago. Ainsley Cruikshank said Chadwick Productions was flying me out to discuss turning *Kung Fu Musical* into a film."

"Great! How'd it go?"

Ray laughed. "Went great, until the great Chadwick propositioned me at his house. When he realized I wasn't going to go to bed with him, he put me on an Uber and I was outta there in the morning."

"So that's it? The only reason he flew you out there was to get laid?"

"Well, I don't know. There was a woman there, Melanie Hofstetter, who seemed genuinely interested. And Ainsley told me not to worry, other studios are interested. Frankly, I was glad to get out of there. The flight was so bizarre. Some woman was breast-feeding her hairless cat. She caused a scene and we were almost forced to land in Denver. Somebody filmed it and it's up on the internet. Would you like me to send you the link?"

"That's all right."

"When are you coming back?"

"Soon. I'm in Saskatchewan. I should be able to catch up in a day or so."

"Saskatchewan? Are you kidding?"

"No. Somehow, she sneaked that tiger into Canada. She's headed to Alaska to turn it loose."

"Well why don't you just let it go? That seems like a win-win all around. If what you said is true, that tigers live in Alaska, won't it be happier there? There's so much wilderness. It would rather eat a deer than a human, don't you think?"

"I don't know. I have to find out what's happening. They hired me to do a job. Returning without the tiger is only an option once I ascertain that the tiger is alive, and well, and doesn't pose a threat to anybody."

"I miss you so much! I want to make love to you so bad!"

"I feel you."

"Want me to talk you off?"

"No. I want the real thing. Besides. The rain's letting up and I have to hit the road."

"Come back to me!"

"I will."

Just talking to her aroused him. He shook it off and looked out the window. The rain had receded to a steady drumbeat, the worst having passed. Time to hit the road. He filled up at an Esso, three fourteen a gallon for premium, a buck cheaper than in the states, grabbed a road map and headed west on Canadian Highway Sixteen. A mile out of Battleford, the car tilted and weaved. He pulled onto the narrow gravel shelter and got out. His left rear tire was flat, a nail head flush with the rubber. It was a bad place to change a tire but he had no choice. Josh had ditched the ridiculous emergency tire, replacing it with a new Michelin identical to the others. While the car rested on its haunch, he loosed the lug nuts with his wrench. He'd replaced the standard jack with a Pittsburgh Three Ton from Harbor freight. A semi sounded its horn a quarter mile downhill and he got out of the way while it passed, kicking up a spray of water that hit him on the other side of the car.

He cranked the jack until the tire was off the ground, took it off, wrestled the replacement tire and wheel out of the trunk and used a hand pump to fill it to forty pounds, slid it onto the bolts, tightened the nuts by hand, lowered it to the ground, and applied torque, tightening the nuts to specs. The left front tire looked low. He went around the car with a tire gauge and his hand pump bringing all tires up to forty. An hour later, he pulled back onto the highway. Two hours later he crossed into Alberta. Flashing lights and backed up traffic up ahead. He pulled up to the line of a dozen vehicles waiting for the signal, turned off his engine and got out. A handful or drivers stood by the side of the road. He went up to them.

"What's going on?"

"Rock slide. They say it could take hours to clear it out."

Josh returned to his car, lowered his head and said, "Dear Lord, if you could see fit to expedite that rock slide…" He stopped. God didn't need petty shit like this.

CHAPTER
52

ONE THING AFTER ANOTHER

The buffalo hurtled toward Fitch like a meteor. Fitch had no time to do anything but squeeze the trigger. As the planet loomed he squeezed and squeezed. The planet hit the open door, slamming him painfully backward. He fell on his ass. He thought he was dead. A great stillness settled on him. Was this death? An instant of recognition before oblivion? Seconds passed.

Fitch was alive. He'd bruised his elbow and back when he fell on a rock. The buffalo was dead. It lay next to his vehicle, a ton of meat and fur. Holding onto the door he stood. Holy shit. He'd killed a buffalo! Fitch couldn't believe it. Exhilaration puffed him like a party balloon.

I killed a buffalo.

He wished he could take the body with him to show people, but it would have to remain his secret. He wasn't in the country legally, and no doubt the damned thing was protected. He wished he knew how to skin it so he could make a robe. He would have to leave it where it lay for the carrion and the birds. He pulled out his phone and snapped several pictures. The corpse lay halfway in front of the car. He backed up, angled the lights toward the beast and took more pictures. He could always delete them. It was a greater high than blow. He got in the car and drove north, more focused and determined than he had ever been. This was a sign. His new life was about to begin. A man who could kill a buffalo could do anything.

He was on fire. Two hours later he emerged near Carnduff. An hour later, as dawn broke, he hit Highway One and headed west at seventy-five, five over the limit. When his radar detector squawked, he took his foot off the gas and let the car slow by itself, cruising through hamlets at a sedate twenty-five. Luck was with him. He had been blessed by the buffalo gods. He was bullet proof. He was in Alberta by noon, stopped at Medicine Hat to get a reading. No reading. Cloud cover was too intense. It didn't matter. He knew where she was going. All he had to do was get ahead of her and wait for the weather to clear. She couldn't chance exposure. She had to be driving slowly. She'd always been a timid driver, obeying all the rules, never straying above the limit. That should have been a sign. He had no time for such craven souls.

Ahead lay the Rockies under heavy cloud cover. His satellite phone wouldn't work there, but he had a hunch where she was going. She'd told him that bullshit story about tigers in Alaska. What a fool. Releasing a valuable animal like that in the wild where it would likely get shot by some hunter.

***

Fitch determined his best shot of getting ahead of her was through Prince George on Sixteen, and to shoot up Thirty Seven, then take One to the coast. He dare not cross back into the United States. A few tiny settlements clung to the base of the peaks. He pulled into an Esso station in Prince George. It was fourteen hundred miles to Tetlin Junction, Alaska. How far would the Rav4 go on a tank of gas? He popped the glove compartment, burrowed around and found the driver's manual sealed in a zip lock. He flipped through the index. The Rav4 could do four hundred and seventy miles on a full tank. Three and a half tanks to Tetlin. It used a two and a half liter four cylinder making two hundred horses. Compared to his Mercedes, it was a Big Wheels toy. As he shoved the manual back in the glove box, papers shifted revealing a small zip lock baggie filled with white powder.

Glancing furtively around, he unsealed it and dipped a finger, bringing it to his gums, which numbed instantly. Another sign. The gods were truly with him. He estimated the baggie contained an eight ball, more than enough to sustain him on his drive. He shook a little out on the heel of his thumb and snorked. Although he wasn't hungry, he went into the gas station and picked up several Gatorades and a hot dog which he stuffed into his mouth like a log going into a wood chipper. He used a stolen credit card.

As he snaked up into the Rockies, he turned on the radio, but the only stations he could get were all news, with a Canadian accent, and some deranged preacher hectoring his flock. The news was all about the Canadian National Hockey Team, and the departure of their star goalie. They had three months to get their shit together or they were doomed. Fitch switched to the in-dash CD player. *John Denver's Greatest Hits*. Fuck it. He'd travel in silence, save for the constant burr of the tires on the blacktop, as it rose into the mountains. Traffic was moderate, with vacationers towing massive trailers and self-enclosed motor homes. He dogged a motor home for nine miles before the road straightened sufficiently for him to pass. He floored the pedal and the Toyota gathered its skirts and cruised by just as a semi appeared from around a bend heading his way in the left hand lane.

This was going to be close, but he'd be damned if he'd slink back into line. He mashed the gas to the floor, gritted his teeth and hung on. As the semi barreled down on him, it hit the air horns, the bellow of an enraged beast. He squeezed in front of the motor home with twenty feet to spare, and now the motor home was honking in outrage. It reminded him of *Jurassic Park*. He half expected a buffalo to step into the middle of the road. Or polar bears. What did they have up here, anyway? He'd seen a movie once where Alec Baldwin and Anthony Hopkins crash landed in the Alaskan wilderness and almost got eaten by a grizzly bear.

Fuck it. Fitch was no fool. He'd brought two hundred

rounds, minus nine he'd unloaded on the buffalo. As he
turned left, a moose stepped onto the highway a hundred
feet ahead. Holy shit! A wall of meat! Fitch stood on the
brakes and the vehicle shuddered and skipped, threatening
to do a three-sixty until he lifted his foot and it settled down
just in time. He approached the moose slowly. The dumb
thing stared. He laid on the horn. The moose crossed the
road and disappeared into the forest. It was just one thing
after another.

CHAPTER

53

YUKON TERRITORY

Gena pulled into Swift River on August 5 under a clear, cool sky, two days after leaving Alberta. There were a scattering of buildings and a hilarious motel that looked like a blank billboard. Swift River was a service stop on the Alaska Highway, and its only residents worked for highway maintenance, or the handful of necessary services that invariably sprang up around any permanent settlement. The motel. The Yukon Tavern. A service station. She was so close she could feel it. Genghis felt it too and had been unusually restless on the ride up.

She pulled into the service station and topped off. A mechanic wearing a fleece-lined jacket with the seamed face of a coal miner sauntered over.

"Where you headed?"

"Alaska."

"You're almost there. Vacation?"

"I'm moving there."

The mechanic eyed the Sprinter. "Nice van."

"Yeah, I squeezed everything I could into it. Are there any camping grounds around here?"

"Not really. The motel's pretty cheap."

"I'd rather camp."

"Well, it's pretty much all public land around here, so if you find a flat spot, you could probably squat for twenty four hours and nobody'll say boo."

"Thanks."

She pulled out onto the Alaska Highway and headed west. Traffic was moderate, mostly long haul truckers and family campers. A group of bikers swept around her. The Jugan. Gena was attuned to bikers because Wayne was one, although unaffiliated, and wore "LONE WOLF" colors, which she thought was hilarious. She only caught a glimpse of the Jugan, but they appeared to be large, middle-aged men.

An hour outside of town she might as well have been on the moon. The highway was the only sign of civilization. She saw a dirt road running off to the south, toward a derelict barn a hundred yards from the highway, partially concealed by rippling hay. In the distance stood a spidery fire tower. The Transit jounced like a water bed as it went over humps and bumps. The area around the barn was flattened by recent mowing. There was an ancient tiny house trailer just behind it that looked like it hadn't been lived in for decades. She parked outside and entered the old building, beamed roof visible twelve feet overhead. Cardboard boxes peeked out from the loft. There were four stalls, all empty, and the cardboard box to a Toro Power Max. The barn's double rear door was latched. She went up to the door, tried it, pulled on it, leaned on it. It was solid. The front door was flexible steel that rolled up onto racks like an electric garage door. A light switch just inside held eight switches, each labeled in ancient embossing gun. A lights. B lights. C Lights. Workbench. Garage door. She flipped the switch and pushed the button. Screaming like a wendigo, the segmented ceiling rumbled down its grooves. A series of sixty-watt bulbs hanging on wires straight down from the ceiling provided light. Gena hit the garage door like Reggie White. It hardly budged.

Okay.

Genghis would get a break from the truck, at least for the night. She opened the door again and drove the van into the barn. Once in, she lowered the garage door and opened the back of the Sprinter. Genghis regarded her with indifference, still digesting his meal of two days ago. Meals. Never had a tiger eaten so much in so little time.

Gena grabbed a flashlight, filled a galvanized pail with water from a fixture bracketed to one of the six by fours holding up the roof. She set the pail down where Genghis could see it and set out to explore her temporary camp. There was nothing of value. Even here, on the fringes of civilization you couldn't trust people to leave stuff alone. Empty grain sacks and petrified cow pies indicated it had once held livestock. She climbed the ladder to the loft, eight feet above the ground. Genghis could do that in one leap. A filthy mattress lay on the unfinished lumber with a wooden milk crate as a side table. An old wick lamp sat on the box, smelling of kerosene. A dark blanket was bunched up at the bottom, and a paperback book upside down. Gena picked it up.

The North Waters. Looked cheerful. She put it back down. A mosquito buzzed her ear. She flattened it against her neck.

When she looked down Genghis was just below, looking up. She gasped. She'd never even heard him move. She lay on her belly and smiled.

"Hey big guy. Almost there. Few more days."

Genghis yawned and shook his head. He went to the pail and daintily spooned, pink tongue flashing. She thought about showering with the hose, but the water would be freezing. On the other hand she stank. She could use the hose to swamp out the Sprinter.

Gena climbed down. Genghis looked up, stretched lazily and leapt into the cardboard box where he curled up and went to sleep.

Gena found a stack of towels back by the restaurant size sink standing against the wall. Next to it was a sit-down toilet. Gena stripped and went to work, squealing at the shock of cold water, toweling herself, leaping into a fresh set of underwear, cargo pants, and a hoodie. It was in the fifties. Washing her clothes in a bucket, she rinsed them in another bucket, rang them out, slipped out through a human sized door next to the steel garage door, and hung them to dry on an old saw horse. She dragged her sleeping bed up the ladder and went to bed.

She got up once in the middle of the night to take a pee. She thought of squatting over a hole in the floor. "Oh, come on, girl. You're not that far gone."

It was dark out, though she'd left the barn lights on. Halfway down the ladder her heart skipped a beat. Where was Genghis? She looked all around.

"Genghis! Genghis, who's a good boy?"

Nothing.

Gena dropped to the floor and headed for the van. There he was, flaked out in the box, sleeping. Gena turned out the lights and returned to the loft. Dreamed she was running with gazelles in Africa. Dreaming she was boxing Muhammad Ali. The sudden racket of birds woke her. Daylight shined through chinks in the roof and walls. Gena sat up, stretching out her back like a great cat, waking up in stages. It was freezing. She pulled on the pants, boots, and hoodie and stood. She walked to the edge of the loft. Sun shined beneath her from the open back door. Gena fairly leaped down the ladder, rushing from stall to stall, finally to the truck. The back was empty. Somehow, Genghis Khan had figured out how to open the back door.

Maybe this was a sign.

Maybe this was it.

A car pulled up.

CHAPTER
54

ONE LAST KISS

Gena grabbed the only weapon she could find, a pitchfork, and ran out the back door. It faced away from the highway not that anyone could see through all that wheat. Gripping the pitchfork in her right hand, she worked her way slowly around the building, crouching behind a pile of hay as a gray Subaru Forester stopped in front of the barn.

Fitch stepped out. She almost lost it right there. She wondered if she ran him through, would they ever find the body? Would Genghis come back and eat it? She giggled. She was the tiger's procurer. Thumbs hitched in belt, Fitch looked around like he owned the place.

Christ, she wanted to wipe that smug smile off his face. Fuck it. She wasn't afraid of anybody, certainly not that fool. She stepped into the clear holding the pitchfork American Gothic style.

"What are you doing here, Fabian?"

Fabian twitched like a frog. He reddened, then blanched, and then a sly grin crept round.

"I've been looking all over for you."

"How did you find me? What the fuck do you want?"

"I want my tiger back."

"Oh bullshit, Fabian. You don't give a flying fuck about Genghis, or any of the animals. You never have."

"How can you say that? I've saved countless wild animals."

"Bullshit. Why are you even lying to me? Are you trying to impress me? Get back in my good graces?"

Fitch shook his head. "Gena, Gena, Gena. I want my truck back too. You can have this fine Forester. We'll just switch cars and call it a day."

"And what? You let me keep Genghis?"

"Well, he'd clearly rather be with you than me. Where is he?"

"He's in the wind. He got out during the night."

"Got out of what?"

"The barn."

"I don't understand how you got this far without it killing you."

Go ahead. Run him through like a cooked yam. Maybe Genghis was free. Maybe it was for the best. The Yukon was good enough. It had all the wilderness and wild game a tiger could want. It was too bad there were no other tigers within a thousand miles, but she was no matchmaker. Look at who she'd chosen.

"That's all you want? The truck?"

Fitch smiled. "Well, not all. Aren't you curious how I found you?"

"No."

"There's a transmitter in the vehicle. I'm surprised at you, Gena."

"It was a spur of the moment thing, like when you bailed from the Tiger Sanctuary."

"I just want to fuck you one more time."

"Excuse me?"

"Let's go in the barn. Take off your clothes. You must have a sleeping bag or something. We can spread it on the hay."

Gena laughed. "Tell you what, Fabian. Let's you and me throw hands. Best two out of three wins."

"You gonna lose the pitchfork?"

She tossed it on the ground and went into a fighter's stance. "Come on, Faby baby. Let's do it."

Fabian reached behind him for the forty-five.

"Oh, you lying sack of shit."

"You didn't expect me to play fair, did you?"

"So you gonna shoot me, Fabian? Are you a murderer too?"

"You really hurt me, Gena. I thought you were the one."

Gena laughed. "Oh please. So what? I take my clothes off or you shoot me?"

"Yup. But don't worry. I'll only wing you. You'll still be alive to enjoy it."

Gena bolted for the back of the barn. For a minute, Fitch just stood there, bewildered. He squeezed off a round but by then she was around the corner.

Gena was too smart to go back in the barn. She disappeared into the wheat south of the highway. The bullet answered her question whether he'd actually kill her or not. Of course he would. She always knew he would. She'd just lied about it to herself. She'd had dreams of a fairy tale romance, eloping with Prince Charming, and living in his castle for the rest of her days. She ran zig zag through the wheat, and because she was an athlete and kept in training, she far outdistanced the soft and wheezing Fitch.

She broke from the edge of the field. Fifty yards of tundra ended at a dense pine forest. She ran over the ground careful not to step in sinkholes. Ponds glittered through the trees. An eagle soared overhead.

She ran through the trees, needles falling on her, branches clinging. She ran toward a clearing with a pond. The trees came right up to the water. She almost ran into the freezing pond. She worked her way clockwise around the edge, stepping on boulders and deadwood. The pond connected to another. A beaver dam lay between them. Gena edged past the beaver dam wondering what she was going to do. It was in the forties and while it would warm up during the day, she was lost in a wilderness. Her only chance for survival was to return to the highway and flag down a motorist. There was nothing south of her but mountains and wild game.

Through the trees she glimpsed some kind of tower.

She bushwhacked through a dense thicket, emerging in a clearing with a little hill on which rested an industrial water tank tower with a lookout cabin fifty feet above the ground, reachable by a zig zag ladder.

She wanted to climb that tower. But what if Fitch showed up? She'd be trapped. Still, from up there she might be able to spot civilization. Maybe there were flairs or a mirror. She'd be able to see the highway.

She sat, panting, on the concrete base of one of the legs. Mosquitoes swarmed her face and bare arms. She wished she'd brought insect repellent. She waited for her breathing to return to normal. She listened. The wind in the trees, the cry of contentious birds, the ripple of water. She was thirsty. A fast moving creek snaked its way by the tower. She squatted by the creek and lowered her cupped hands. Christ it was cold, but she'd never tasted anything so sweet. She crouched drinking until she had enough.

Maybe Fitch would give up. He really wasn't very brave. He had the truck. He didn't need her. She returned to the tower and with a sigh began to climb.

Fitch stepped from the woods holding the pistol. "Come down here."

Gena half turned. "You again. Why don't you just leave?"

"Oh no. I promised myself one more time. At this range, I can't miss."

"So if I fuck ya you'll leave me alone?"

"You bet."

"Fitch, you're such a liar."

"Listen. I'm not a bad guy. You told me you loved my cock. Nothing's changed."

"One fuck and then you leave? You don't hurt me?"

"Why would I?"

She dropped to the ground. "Where we gonna do it? In the beaver dam?"

"Take your clothes off. We'll do it standing up."

Gena peeled off her wet boots. She reached for her zipper. Genghis Khan flowed from the forest and seized Fitch by his head and shoulder. Fitch screamed and fired once before dropping the pistol. Genghis dragged him into the trees.

Genghis snarled and ripped. Gena saw flashes of golden fur and Fitch's corpse flailing about like laundry in a dryer.

CHAPTER 55

GONE WITH THE WIND

Genghis chewed thoroughly. Gena knew not to approach him while he was eating. She picked up the forty-five and ejected the cartridge from the chamber. She stuck the pistol in the back of her pants and waited a half hour until after the tiger stopped eating. She followed the trail of blood into the woods. Fitch parts all over. A leg here, an arm there. His headless torso half submerged in a sink hole, head gone. Genghis wasn't hungry. He'd dismembered Fitch for fun.

Gena forced herself to retrieve Fitch's wallet and car keys, an aerosol can of Off! No sign of a phone. He must have left it in the car. She sprayed her arms and hands, wiped the insect repellent on the back of her neck.

"Genghis!"

The wind whistled through the branches. The birds called.

"Gennnnghissssss!"

This was it. She'd wanted to hug him one last time before letting him go. At least she'd saved his life. And he'd returned the favor.

"Goodbye, Genghis," she said softly. "I never loved a man the way I love you. I hope you meet a mate."

Shoving Fitch's wallet and keys into her cargo pants, she followed her trail in reverse, where she'd flattened the tundra on her mad long rush. The fire tower disappeared behind the trees as she dead reckoned her way back to the barn. She followed the serpentine path through the hay. It would disappear in a day or two. Gray clouds appeared in the west, but nothing like the downpour she'd encountered earlier.

The ground squished where she stepped and her feet were wet and cold by the time she could see the old red barn through the hay. She walked around to the front where Fitch had left his car. She didn't recognize it. He must have switched vehicles to avoid detection. She slid in behind the driver's seat and looked around. A satellite phone lay on the seat. That's how he'd tracked her. Fitch had been right. She'd been a fool to take off in that truck and assume nobody could find her. She got out and opened the rear passenger doors. The vehicle was stuffed with camping equipment including a rumpled sleeping bag and an air mattress. The key was in her pocket. At least she could drive away.

A vehicle nosed down the dirt road. She got out of the car and waited, pistol in her waist. A silver Chrysler 300 with Wisconsin plates nosed into view. An athletic looking man with a burr skull, arms covered with tats got out.

"Gena Kropenski?"

"Who're you?"

"Josh Pratt. Private investigator. The Wild Animal Initiative hired me to bring back Genghis Khan."

"You're too late. He's gone."

"Gone where?"

Gena gestured all around. "Who knows? I brought him this far."

"Is this your vehicle?"

"No, it belongs to, or rather I should say it was being driven by Fabian Fitch."

The man looked startled. "Fitch? Here?"

"Not any more. Genghis killed him."

"And he left you alone?"

"He likes me."

"Miss Kropenski, I'm no expert. You would know more about this than me. Is this a good place to release a Siberian tiger? I know what you were trying to do. I can't believe you made it this far."

Gena's mouth was a slit. She shook her head. "It's a lousy place. We're nowhere near the Bering Sea. There isn't another tiger within a thousand miles of here. He'll live and die a lonely death but at least he'll be free."

"Do you think he has a taste for human flesh?"

Gena nodded.

"Well, that's not good. We can't in good conscience leave him wandering around."

"Well, I don't know what we can do."

"We could trank him if we could find him, but how do you find a tiger in an immense wilderness like this? Was he wearing a tracking device?"

"No. I really don't think there's any danger of him attacking anyone. There's plenty of game out there."

"Once a tiger tastes human flesh they become dangerous."

"He didn't eat me."

"I have no explanation."

"That tiger loved me and I loved him. He would never harm me. In fact, he appeared just as Fitch was about to rape me. I never thought I'd see him again."

"Are you serious?"

"Yeah."

"Are you driving that Mercedes van?"

"Yes. It's in the barn."

"Show me."

She led the way around back. The lights were still on. Josh shined a flashlight through the van's back door, pulled out a disposal blue face mask and nitrile gloves and put them on.

"I guess I got used to it," Gena said.

Josh got in the van and duck walked forward, poking through the straw. "I thought cats were supposed to be clean."

"Genghis's personal hygiene is very good."

"You got a broom or something? Let's clear this hay out."

Gena returned with a push broom that Josh used to sweep the back clean, exposing the metal floor. He went over every inch with the flashlight, feeling in nooks and crannies with his fingers. He pulled up the floor rug and tossed it out.

"What are you looking for?"

"The transmitter."

"Why?"

"If Fitch planted this transmitter he must have had a reason."

"Maybe he just didn't want anybody to take his truck."

The metal floor looked factory stock. He jumped out and shinnied beneath the chassis. And there it was, a disc the size of a half dollar, glued to the frame. He used a knife to pry it loose, crawled out and handed it to Gena.

"So that's how he found me."

"He would need a satellite phone to track you in this wilderness."

"He had one. It's in his car."

Josh hit the garage door button and went to Fitch's stolen vehicle. The satellite phone was on the passenger seat next to a standard smart phone. Jackpot. Josh dug Roth Eisely's card out of his wallet. Eisely answered on the second ring.

"Roth Eisely."

"Mr. Eisely, it's Josh Pratt."

"Uh oh."

"No sir, I just want to ask you a few questions." Josh gave an abbreviated account of how Genghis arrived in the

Pacific Northwest. "Sir, my question is this. Does that tiger pose a threat to human life?"

"Yes."

"Sir, would it be possible for you to come up here and trank it? I can arrange for the correct dose. Just tell me what kind of rifle you plan to use."

"I'd have to rearrange my schedule. We're about to break ground on a new development."

"Sir, I know it's a lot to ask, but I'm pretty sure the Wild Animal Initiative will pay your expenses and perhaps even a bonus, and if they don't, I will."

"I keep a Challenger 350 at the Dane County Airport. I'd have to recruit a co-pilot. The earliest I can leave would be tomorrow morning. I'm looking at a map of British Columbia. There's an airstrip less than fifty miles away. Pine Lake. You should know that it costs about three thousand dollars an hour to operate, and we're talking a six hour trip. So right away, we're looking at expenses in the thirty-five thousand dollar range."

"Thank you, sir. I will check with WAI and get back to you shortly."

"Josh, I can't ask you to do this. You've already done enough."

"Pretty sure WAI will pick up the tab."

"It's a fool's errand. We'll never see Genghis again. What are you going to do? The two of you hiking through British Columbia?"

"I have an idea."

HA! TORO!

While Gena returned to Fitch's car to take inventory, Josh called Mandy Palmer.

"Josh. I was beginning to think you'd disappeared."

"I'm in Yukon Territory, Mandy. Genghis Khan is up here somewhere. We're going to try and tranquilize him and transport him to Alaska."

"What? Hang on a minute. I'm at a dinner party."

Josh winked at Gena.

"All right. You're in the Yukon?"

"Yes. I followed Gena Kropenski here. She took off with the tiger just two days before the raid. She loves Genghis Khan, and is taking him to Alaska where he can be among his people."

Palmer laughed nervously. "Josh, are you serious?"

"Yes I am. Did you know there were Siberian tigers in Alaska?"

"We've been hearing those stories for years."

"It's true. I looked it up. There's a photograph of a tiger feeding on elk in the Togiak Refuge. I can send it to you if you like."

Silence.

"Mandy, are you there?"

"Yes. I'm just trying to wrap my head around this. It never occurred to me before. But you're nowhere near the Togiak."

"I have a plan to tranquilize Genghis and take him the rest of the way. I've contacted an experienced hunter who is going to arrive here in twenty-four hours to fire the trank."

"How are you going to find him? Tigers can range up to four hundred miles."

"I'd tell you but you'd laugh."

"Try me."

"I'd rather not. Let me just go ahead with my plan and see if it works."

"That's a lot to ask."

"That ain't all. Are you willing to fund this expedition? The hunter with whom I spoke estimates thirty-five thousand dollars in expenses."

"Can't you find a local hunter?"

"This guy specializes in big game. He's tranked big cats before."

"The people with whom I'm dining are on the board. Let me sound them out and get back to you. What happens if you fail?"

"First of all, you don't have to pay me for what I've done. You asked me to deliver the tiger to the Wild Animal Initiative and I'm unable to do that. Secondly, I would be willing to help underwrite these expenses."

"You have that kind of money?"

"I just got a letter from the UN. They're awarding me three and a half million dollars."

"For what?"

"Compensation prize. All I have to is give them my social security and bank numbers."

"Huh?"

"You wouldn't believe the mail I get. Want to see the letter?"

"Never mind."

"I have some savings."

"Let me get back to you."

Gena entered the barn holding a tiny plastic bag filled with white power. "You know, I used to do a snort now and then but being with Fabian cured me of that. I came close to choking him out a couple times, but it would have killed him. He had a couple thou in his billfold. You can have it."

"Won't you need that?"

"I saved most of my winnings. I'm still renting a room from Austin Bear for one fifty a month."

"Can't beat that."

Josh fetched a crowbar and pliers from his trunk and returned to the van, tapping the ribs and bars that added rigidity to the body. He paused over the right wheel well, tapping and listening. He turned and tapped the rib of the left wheel well. They both had a peculiar dead quality as if they weren't hollow. He used the crowbar to rip open the bottom of the lateral girder and the edge of a black box appeared. He had to rip the girder away from the wall to pull out the black box which was two feet long and heavy. There was one on the other side too. Setting it on the floor, he released the two clasps and lifted the lid. Five gold Pandas gleamed in the weak light coming through the van windows. Josh gripped one. They were five deep. Twenty-five gold Pandas. He picked one up, flipped it, caught and covered it with his hand.

"Call it."

"Heads."

Josh uncovered the heavy coin showing a panda. "It's yours."

She laughed. "No, seriously. Who gets this?"

"We do."

"How are we going to get it back into the United States?"

"How'd you get that tiger into Canada?"

"Oh man, that wasn't easy. I just lucked out. There's so much unprotected border between the two countries...I crossed over from North Dakota. I don't think I could ever find that route again."

"Well lucky for you, the whole thing is recorded via that transmitter. As to who's going to drive it back, we'll figure that out later. I entered legally. If I tried to drive it back, you'd have to reenter the US through immigration and they'd find out you didn't enter legally."

"Or we could both go back in your car."

"Let me think about that. Each of those coins is worth two thousand bucks. There are a hundred. They're worth about two hundred thousand dollars. We can split it, after I pay Roth's expenses."

"You keep it. I insist."

"Maybe we should just bury it here."

Gena's face lit up. "Like buried treasure!"

"Yeah. We could plant clues. Make it a treasure hunt."

Gena laughed. "But seriously. I'm in enough hot water without being caught sneaking across the border with gold coins."

"We have to figure how to get you back without additional penalties. I think that when the full extent of Fitch's dealings become known, you'll have a great deal of sympathy on your side. I think I can persuade the Wild Animal Initiative to get behind you. Do you know about the meth lab?"

"What meth lab?"

"It was in one of those pole barns on the property. It hadn't been used in a while but there were enough ingredients still stashed to blow up half the state."

"I didn't realize what a scumbag Fabian was. I was so naive."

"Did you meet Tony Capadona?"

"Oh, the great Capadona! Fabian's godfather. Never did."

"He was there the night you fought Byam. He's the one who spiked her drink."

"Why?"

"He's a gambler. He fixed the fight."

"How do you know that?"

"I had a little talk with Tony. I wouldn't be surprised if he's out of the country now. I've watched you fight. Do you think you'll go back?"

"I don't know. It all seems to distant now. And the police have warrants out on me."

"I think that when the truth is revealed, they'll drop all charges. I know some very good lawyers. You're going to need money to pay them."

"Nobody's going to believe this story anyway."

"They will if we provide pictures."

"What pictures?"

"You coaxing Genghis back in the van. Driving to Alaska. You letting him loose."

"How the fuck do you plan to get Genghis back here?"

Josh grinned, crouching.

"Uh oh."

Josh slid out the end of the van and pointed to the cardboard box.

CHAPTER
57

THE BOX

Fitch's stolen vehicle was a treasure trove. It contained a camping stove, packets of dried fruit, beef jerky, and a case of bottled water. Josh had brought his own sleeping bag and they bedded down for the night, Josh on hay in the barn, Gena in the back of Fitch's stolen car. The satellite phone woke Josh at four am.

"I'm taking off in one hour. I should be landing in seven hours, weather permitting. I'll call you once we get clearance."

"You can do that?"

"I have a satellite phone. It doesn't interfere with navigation systems. The FAA lies."

"Very good, sir. We'll be standing by."

Josh phoned Ninja.

"The number you are calling is not in service at this time."

Ninja phoned back three hours later.

"The fuck you callin' me at six in the morning?"

"I'm sorry. I forgot the time zone difference."

"Fuck you at?"

"British Columbia."

"Fuck you want?"

"How's Fig?"

"She's fine. She's right next to me now. I'm in your office cleaning up your shit."

"What shit?"

"Spyware, malware, your computer looks like a leper colony."

"Don't mess up my settings. Last time I had some guy in to clear it up, I had to reregister with every site and do new passwords. I hate those fuckin' things! I had one password I used for everything and then it was gone."

"What's your password?"

"Hardlyableson, only the 'L' is a one and the 'O' is a zero."

"Clever. I'll try not to fuck it up. I'll write your new passwords down and pin them to your bulletin board. How's it going?"

Josh gave Ninja the rundown. "With any luck, I'll be home in five days."

"Five days?"

"Yeah. If we catch him, we got to see him into Alaska and then I can head home."

"Don't get any tickets."

Josh phoned Ray.

"When you coming back, Red Ryder?"

"Should be home in five days if everything works out."

"Did you find the tiger?"

"We're close. He's running around loose here in British Columbia. Got a big game hunter coming in to tranquilize him so we can drive him to the Togiak Refuge."

"What's that?"

"Wildlife refuge in Alaska. There are other tigers there."

"How do you know?"

"I've seen photographs. It's been verified."

"How do you plan on catching up with him?"

"It's a secret. I'll tell you later."

"Come home in one piece."

"I will. Love you."

"Love you."

Josh wandered the property. It was just an abandoned barn in the middle of nowhere. Oil stains on the floor indicated it had once held machines. He put on his fleece-lined jacket and watched Gena shadow box around the floor.

"That's one way to keep warm."

"Yeah, I don't know what I'm gonna do. This seems to be the high point of my life. I don't know what I'll do afterwards."

"You could write a book."

"I can't write."

"You find a writer. You tell him you have a terrific idea for a book, he should write it, and you'll split the profits."

Gena laughed. "Maybe. Do you know any writers?"

"No."

He slipped off his jacket and shadow boxed himself. They shadow boxed around the floor leaving curving trails in the straw and dust. Eisely phoned at two.

"We'll be landing in fifteen minutes."

"We're on our way."

Josh used Google Earth to locate the airport. It was forty miles away. Traffic on the Alaska Highway was sparse, sparser still when they turned north on a gravel road that wound among pine forests, emerging on a slight rise to reveal a startlingly blue lake next to which was a three runway rural airstrip with a Quonset hut office. A twin engine private jet sat on the tarmac, a couple of old pickups parked next to the office. Josh parked next to a pickup. Two men came out of the glass door to greet them, Eisely carrying a rifle scabbard and a backpack, and another man, slight, in a leather jacket with crew cut red hair, also carrying a backpack. The man in the leather jacket lit a cigarette.

Josh introduced Gena. They shook hands.

"This is my co-pilot Dave. He's coming with us. We'll need all hands on deck to move that tiger."

"What's there to do around here?" Dave asked in a whispery voice.

"I suppose you could hunt moose," Gena said.

"It's only legal if you go with an outfitter," Eisely said. "Let's go. The sooner we wrap this tiger up, the sooner we can go home."

Eisely and Dave shifted their gear into the Chrysler's trunk.

Forty-five minutes later they pulled up to the barn. Josh sprung the trunk so Eisely could retrieve his equipment. Dave reached for a cig. Eisely put a hand on his arm.

"Dave, you're gonna have to hold off on that."

Dave put the pack away.

"What are you using?" Josh said.

"G2 X-Caliber. It's an air gun designed specifically to tranquilize animals. Good up to forty yards. I brought five rounds of tranks."

A crease appeared between Gena's eyes. "You won't hurt him, will you?"

"It'll leave a bruise, but when he wakes up he won't even remember it. Animals are funny that way."

Josh grabbed Eisely's backpack from the trunk. "You re-member when you told me tigers were among the few wild animals who bore a grudge against humans that hurt them?"

"That is true."

"Genghis Khan ate Fabian Fitch."

Eisely's eyebrows rose. "Whoa."

"He also killed two men who tried to rape me."

"I didn't know that," Josh said.

"I'm telling you. If the one guy hadn't had a gun, I would have taken them both out."

"That makes him a man killer," Eisely said. "It raises ethical questions."

"This place we're taking him," Gena said. "It's a remote

wilderness area that already contains tigers. We're here to save the tiger, not worry about whether he's going to chow down on tourists. I doubt there are any tourists where he's going."

"I'm only here to trank him. Then I gotta go back."

"We understand, Mr. Eisely. We're grateful for your service, and we'll pay for your expenses."

"How you going to do that?"

Josh and Gena looked at each other.

Josh turned toward the barn. "Follow me."

Eisely got a whiff of the van and turned away. Josh set a black display box on a makeshift table, two sawhorses and a slab of plywood. Eisely felt the coins, held them up to the light, jiggled them in his hand.

"Where'd you get these?"

"They belonged to Fabian Fitch, the dude behind the Tiger Sanctuary. He followed Gena here to recover them. Gena did not know they were in the van she took to transport Genghis. That's why he was chasing her. Each of those is worth about two thousand dollars. Twenty should pay for your expenses, and for Dave. I assume he's not along for fun."

"How did Fitch find you?"

Josh pulled the transmitter from his pocket. It was the same size as the Panda. "Take the Pandas. You can fly it back into the US a lot easier than we can."

"Fine. Let me think about that. It's not a bad idea. I can land at a regional airport and nobody will say boo. Now how do you propose we get that tiger in my sights?"

Josh pointed to the box.

Eisely grinned. "No, seriously."

Josh pointed to the box.

"That's the damndest thing I ever heard."

"All cats love boxes."

"It's true," Gena said. "He slept in that box."

"Where will we put it?"

"There's a place out back where he ate Fitch. Don't they return to their kills?"

"Some do, some don't. What the hell. Let's give it a shot."

TIGER IN A BOX

They put the box at the base of the fire tower. Eisely and Dave had brought their own sleeping bags. Eisely brought night vision goggles, and concealed himself in gorse on a slight rise one hundred feet from the box.

"Why don't you use the tower?" Josh said.

"I pee off that thing in the middle of the night, the tiger will smell it."

"Yeah," Josh said, "but won't he hang around until you come down for breakfast?"

"Ha ha. No. It's better if he thinks he's safe."

"You told me that tigers bear a grudge. Gena, did Fitch ever abuse Genghis?"

Gena looked away. "He used an electric cattle prod."

Eisely sipped coffee from a thermos. "Conceivably, you're the only person in the world he won't eat. In fact, your interaction with this tiger has no precedent. I've never heard of a wild animal behaving like this."

"I can't explain it. I love him and he loves me."

"You oughta write a book about it."

They used Fitch's camp stove to heat up canned beef stew. Dave pulled out a bottle of Johnny Walker and they toasted Genghis. All except Eisely, who left for his blind while it was still light. David threw his sleeping bag down in a stall. Gena took Fitch's inflatable mattress ad laid it the back of the van. Josh took another stall. He had a hard time falling asleep, thinking about Ray. Her scent. It was maddening. When he was with her, she'd drive him crazy, trying to get him to watch Anderson Cooper or some such shit.

Josh finally drifted off only to be wakened by what sounded like a free-for-all among wolverines. Howls, shrieks, bellows. Maybe it was a bear. Or bears. He hoped they didn't come in the barn. He had to take a leak. He wondered if he laid a perimeter of piss around the doors if it would dissuade predators. It worked for animals. He got up, went out back and looked up. The Milky Way gleamed from a million points of light. There was no artificial light up here, nothing to dim the heavens. Made him want to go camping. Ray wouldn't go for that. Her idea of roughing it was a Motel 6.

The night had quieted, but still whispered and muttered. It was a balmy August night in British Columbia, in the fifties. Leaves rustled. Creatures chittered. Crickets played a slow waltz, not the furious bluegrass of the lower forty-eight. It smelled of pine. He looked up. A shooting star blazed across the sky.

"Dear Lord," he said, "help me smuggle this tiger into Alaska. It's not for myself that I ask. It's for the tiger."

He returned to the barn and fell asleep. The next thing he knew Gena was shaking his shoulder.

"Get up. We got him."

Josh sat up. "Huh?"

"Genghis showed up in the middle of the night, curled up in the box, and Eisely nailed him in the shoulder. Says Genghis will be dopey and manageable for at least three hours. We've got to get him in the van now."

Fifteen minutes later, Gena, Dave, and Josh pulled up to the cardboard box in the shadow of the fire tower. Eisely sat on a rock nearby drinking from a thermos. Gena backed the van up to within a few feet from where Genghis slept, curled up like a domestic cat, softly snoring. Josh and Gena took pictures.

"Roth, would you crouch next to the box?"

Roth, grinning. Josh and Gena took pictures.

"Do we lift the box, or try to take him out?" Gena said.

Eisely walked around the box. "It's a pretty sturdy box. If we each take a corner we should be able to get him in. Gena, you up for this?"

"I can bench press two hundred pounds."

They pulled the rear doors all the way open. Each took a corner, Josh opposite Eisely.

"All right, keep your spines straight," the hunter said, "and bend at the knee. On my word, one, two three, heave!"

The box rose from the ground. The center sagged, but did not break. Genghis' tail flicked. They slid the box onto the steel floor and closed the doors. Josh held his hand up for a high five. High fives all around.

Dave pulled out a pack of American Spirits. "Now can I smoke?"

"Knock yourself out," Eisely said. "I have just one question. How do you plan to smuggle this tiger into Alaska?"

Josh grinned. "Two words. Indian reservation."

"What reservation?" Gena said.

"Tsimshian Chilkat, which straddles British Columbia and southern Alaska. We can use a logging trail to get in. Then we go to the tribal elders, show 'em what we've got, and ask for their cooperation."

Eisely shook his head. "That is fuckin' genius."

Josh counted out twenty of the Pandas. Eisely put them in his backpack. "It's pretty informal up here. I don't think we'll have any trouble. And we'll land in Rhinelander and rent a car."

Josh turned to Gena. "I'll drive these guys back to the airport and then I'll follow you west. Let's take a look at the map."

They examined Gena's old *State Farm Road Atlas*, and the Canadian map Josh picked up at the Esso. Gena would take the Alaska Highway to Whitehorse, with Josh following. Gena had the only working phone, because it was a satellite phone and didn't rely on towers. She would wait for Josh to appear and then they would caravan west to the

Tsimshian Res, which straddled the BC/Alaska border.

It was seven-thirty when Josh pulled over in Whitehorse. His phone was working. Gena was waiting for him on the shoulder north of town. Josh pulled up behind her and joined her in the van.

"How's the big guy?"

"Slept the whole way. He's just now coming out of it, but he's groggy."

Josh peered through the steel fence. Genghis' tail flopped over the side of the box and swished back and forth.

"Does he need to eat or pee or anything?"

"He won't need to eat for three days. I should reach the reserve by then."

"How you gonna get in? Won't there be a booth or something?"

"There will probably be some rangers or something, but the whole area's a wilderness. There are no roads in. I don't need to enter the reserve to turn him loose. We'll just choose a remote spot and say goodbye."

She sniffled. Josh opened his arms and she clung to him sobbing.

"It's gonna be great," Josh said. "It's a win-win situation. Genghis goes free, and hopefully one of these days he'll meet a nice attractive female, and they'll settle down and he'll get a job."

Gena laughed. "Josh, I don't know how I can ever thank you."

"Don't worry about it. You ready to go? Or do you want

to crash?"

"The faster I deliver Genghis, the better. Let's go."

"Okay, I won't call you while we're driving, but if I flash my brights at you I want you to pull over."

"Why?"

"You never know. Sometimes I get hunches."

CHAPTER
59

I HOPE YOU LIKE SALMON

The Tsimshian Reserve straddled the border near Stewart, a rugged coastal area marked by granite cliffs and endless rows of pine marching toward the horizon. Josh led the way, praying that his old Chrysler with two hundred and twenty thousand miles would survive the rough forest trails. Gena used Google Earth via the satellite phone. It was Thursday, at least they thought it was Thursday, a week after Gena had fled the compound. They followed the rugged road west until it opened into a field, village in the distance.

As they got closer, they saw that the Tsimshian village consisted mostly of prefab single family dwellings and trailers, many with flower gardens out front in the brief summer. A pale yellow pole barn with old pickups and a Studebaker out front was the biggest building in town, and served as town hall and recreation center.

Gena pulled into a gravel parking lot boarded by rough

logs. Josh parked next to her and got out. As they approached the town hall, the door opened and two men came out, both with long gray hair tied in ponytails, one in coveralls and a red cotton shirt, the other heavy cargo pants and a leather jacket. They stood in front of the building, waiting.

Josh and Gena approached. "I'm Josh Pratt, a private detective from Wisconsin, and this is Gena Kropenski, an MMA fighter. You may know her as Queen Tiger. We're taking our tiger to a game preserve where he can live with others of his kind. We'd like permission to travel through your village."

The shorter of the two, in coveralls, looked the other man. "Is there something we can do for you?"

"Yes. Let us pass through with our tiger."

"Your tiger."

"Yes. He's a Siberian tiger named Genghis Khan. He weighs seven hundred pounds."

"Maybe seven hundred and fifty," Gena said.

The short man had Asian features, a potato nose, and unibrow. "Show me."

They walked toward the van.

"Genghis has been tranquilized, but he is always dangerous," Gena said softly. "So if you don't mind, I'll open the front passenger door and you can take a look through the mesh screen. Don't make any sudden movements."

Gena opened the passenger door. It didn't squeak. She nodded.

The shorter, who seemed to be the leader, climbed into

the truck on his knees and looked in back. He looked to his companion and mouthed the words, "holy shit." He lingered a minute, then got down.

"Doug, take a look."

Doug, who was built like a wide receiver, followed. He stared a long time. He got out and they shut the door as quietly as possible.

The leader gestured toward the building. "Come inside. Let's talk."

Inside was linoleum floor and two pool tables at one end of the long building, office, counter and private rooms lining the back wall.

"My name is Joseph and this is Doug." He led the way to a folding banquet table. "Pull up a chair. You want coffee?"

"Wouldn't mind," Josh said.

Joseph gestured toward a sideboard holding a commercial coffee dispenser. Josh looked at Gena. She nodded.

Joseph and Doug waited until Josh and Gena sipped some coffee. Joseph turned his hand palm up on the table.

"Where'd you get that tiger?"

"Are you familiar with the Tiger Sanctuary in Wisconsin?"

"No."

Josh gave them the run down, leaving out Capadona and his dead ends.

Joseph turned to Doug. "You ever hear of tigers in Alaska?"

Doug nodded his head. "Yup."

"Why didn't you tell me?"

Doug shrugged.

Joseph folded his hands. "Why don't you folks spend the night here. We got a couple rooms with bunks."

Josh turned to Gena. "We got time for that?"

"I'm beat. I hardly slept a wink last night. Genghis will be fine."

"I wonder if you have some larger enclosure we could put him in. A garage or something, something bigger than that truck."

"Well, we do got the garage. We'd have to move a few things, but how do you plan to get him back in the truck?"

"He'll do as I ask," Gena said.

"You some kind of shaman?"

Gena laughed. "No. But that tiger and me share a special bond. I don't know if you've ever experienced something like this, to bond with a wild animal. I'd trust him with my life. In fact, he's saved my life twice."

"How's that?"

Josh nudged Gena under the table. "She can't explain it. It's a spiritual thing."

"Well, what the hell. What else we have to do?"

They moved a commercial fishing boat on a trailer out, a frame holding four aluminum skiffs, and an old International Harvester station wagon. The garage had four bins. They used a front loader to bring in several loads of hay from the stable and left one door open while Gena backed up the van. They cleared well back as Gena got out of the cab and opened the rear door.

Nada.

Josh counted to two hundred when Genghis poured out of the back of the van, yawned, and padded off to a pile of straw. As soon as Gena pulled the van ahead, Joseph shut the garage door.

"Doug, tell people not to go in the garage."

A dozen children and some women stood around watching. Doug cupped his hands.

"Don't go in the garage!"

"There's a tiger in there," Joseph added.

A young woman with long black hair, wearing blue jeans and quilted vest, said, "What's going on?"

Joseph nodded toward Josh. "You heard the man. Go on up to those windows and take a look. Lift the young ones up so they can see him. His name is Genghis Khan."

The women laughed. The children giggled. A little boy went up to the nearest window and started jumping up and down. A young mother chased after.

"All right! All right! But you have to use your imagination."

She held him up so he could look in the window. He squealed in delight. The woman set him down and turned. "They aren't lying."

Soon, word spread throughout the village. Everyone filed by the garage staring through the windows. Some took pictures. Gena warned them not to use flashes, but nobody had a flash camera. Everyone had smart phones. An impromptu party broke out in the lodge. Joseph and Doug hauled out beer and Canadian liquor. The women went to work cooking and baking.

"You don't have to do all this for us," Gena said.

"Well, it's not every day a tiger passes through here."

"Really," Josh said. "We're happy with pizza."

Joseph winked. "I hope you like salmon."

CHAPTER 60

DRUNK OCTOPUS WANTS TO FIGHT

Josh woke as dawn slanted in through the triple paned window in a room containing a cot, a thin mattress, a wood-burning stove, a cheap desk and a computer. Josh visited the communal shower and washed for the first time in four days. Tables in the big room were covered with paper plates and Red Solo cups. Josh had never tasted salmon that good. He cleaned off the tables, putting the trash in barrels.

He went into Joseph's office, with the big window looking out on the yard, and wrote him a note.

Dear Joseph: "Thank you for your kind hospitality. If ever you should need my services, please don't hesitate to call. God bless you and your people."

He left his card on top of the note. He carried his backpack out to his Chrysler and prepared to drive off the way he'd come in. The night before, he and Gena had divvied up the rest of the Pandas. There were thirty left. Gena took twenty and Josh took ten. He jammed them into the back seat cushions.

He drove. He drove toward the rising sun with a Packer cap pulled low. The Chrysler would do about four hundred on a tank of gas. He had enough to reach Hazleton. He could top off there. He listened to Tower of Power. Why not. There wasn't a Mountie within a hundred miles. Tower of Power made him drive one hundred and forty miles an hour. He slowed down when he saw a herd of elk crossing the road a quarter mile ahead. He gassed up in Hazleton. He made it all the way to Calgary before pulling into a Best Western. It was midnight by the time he got out of the shower. He thought about calling Ray, but settled for sending her a text message.

Mission accomplished! On my way home. Love you!

Her phone call woke him the next morning. He looked at the bedside clock. It was eight.

"Hey babe."

"How'd it go?"

"I left Gena and Genghis in Alaska. It's up to her now, but I have a feeling she'll pull it off. All the hard work is done."

"Call me when you stop for the night."

It took three more days to get home. He listened to the same Tower of Power record three times. Crossing the border at Northgate, North Dakota, the American customs agent waved him through with a yawn. When he pulled into his driveway at nine pm, Ninja's SUV was gone. Fig bellowed from inside the house as if she could sense her master's return. Perhaps she could. Josh entered through the kitchen and Fig was all over him, wagging, slobbering, whining in happiness. Josh sat on the floor while she covered him with fur and slobber.

Josh stood. There was a note on the fridge.

"Dear unreconstructed redneck: I have taken up residence in an undisclosed location! You know how to get hold of me. This is an invoice for nine thousand eight hundred and seventy-five dollars and sixty-six cents, mostly for dog services. You may remit at your leisure. I am gainfully employed by an underworld boss seeking information on other underworld bosses. It's been fantastico! Until we meet again, tata! Your pal Ninja."

Josh phoned Ray. "I'm home!"

"I'll be right over."

Josh went into the basement. Everything was as it was before Ninja arrived. The house was immaculate. He went into the kitchen and opened the fridge. Ninja had bought bacon, cheese, and a bottle of Möet and Chandon with a red bow on it and a note: *I know what happens next.* He'd even vacuumed the floor.

Josh showered and put on clean clothes as Fig announced Ray with a twenty-one bark salute. She appeared at the door wearing a long raincoat and flew into his arms. They went inside and she dropped the raincoat revealing black lace panties and bra. Fig tried to follow them into the bedroom but Josh gently shooed her out.

"You will be rewarded with treats."

He brought the champagne and two flutes into the bedroom. They barely sipped before they were at each other. They lay in bed panting listening to Fig whine and scratch the door. Josh got up, pulled on a pair of pants and let her in. Fig leaped on the bed and licked Ray like she was a buffet table until laughing and shielding herself, she got up.

"Now I need another shower."

"Fig's saliva cures cancer."

Neither had eaten dinner so Josh thawed a thin crust pizza. They sat in the living room with Sinatra on the stereo.

"Tell me."

Josh told her the whole story from when he crossed into Canada, leaving out Gena's encounter with the would-be rapists. That was her business. It was midnight when he finished.

"That should be a movie," Ray said.

"I told Gena she should write a book about it. Oh, I almost forgot. Let me show you something."

He went into the garage and dug around in the back seat cushions, retrieving the pandas. He laid them out on the low table in the living room. Ray picked one up.

"Where did you get these?"

"They were concealed in Fitch's van. No wonder he was so eager to track it down."

"Why didn't he take the van in the first place?"

"Too conspicuous. He fled because he panicked."

Fig insinuated herself between them.

"So is *Kung Fu Musical* dead?"

"No! I forgot to tell you! Ainsley phoned me today and said that Webflix is interested! They showed it to Blaine Hunter and he's interested! They want to fly me out again next week. This time, I'll insist on going to Disneyland."

"Who's Blaine Hunter?"

"He directed *Drunk Octopus Wants to Fight* and *The Jumping Jehosaphats*!"

"I have not heard of either of those."

"That's one of the things I like about you. You're completely oblivious to popular culture."

"I watched *Sons of Anarchy*. I got it out of the library."

"I'm beat. Let's go to bed."

"All right."

CHAPTER
61

JOURNEY'S END

The Togiak Refuge was more beautiful than Gena could have imagined. Had she proceeded on her chosen career path as an MMA fighter, she never would have seen it. All she would have seen was the insides of airports and arenas. Maybe Abu Dhabi, which hosted its first women's fight in 2019. With over four million acres, the Togiak Refuge was the fourth largest wildlife refuge in the United States. Its southwest border was the Bering Sea. There were no roads to the refuge. She pushed the Sprinter to its limit over dirt roads and manadnocks, avoiding the coastal village of Togiak where US Game and Wildlife had a field office. She saw wolf, moose, bears and elk. The chassis scraped on rocks as she wound among towering granite peaks carved by glacial ebb and flow.

Before she left the Tsimshian village, they had loaded her up with enough smoked salmon to open a deli, as well as pemmican and moose jerky. In the two days since, Genghis had become his old self, restless, playful, and affectionate. It had been five days since he last ate but at no time did he exhibit aggressive behavior toward her. It was almost as if he knew.

The satellite phone indicated that she was one hundred and twenty miles inland at Togiak. The middle of nowhere. Even now, in early August, the wind caused her cheeks to go numb when she exited the vehicle. She had passed numerous lakes and creeks tumbling down from the Ahklun Mountains. Some of the lakes were quite large. She pulled up on the banks of a long finger lake running north and south. This was Togiak Lake, the heart of the refuge. It was near here that a game camera had snapped the iconic picture of a tiger feasting on a reindeer. She hoped that tiger was female and that she was still around.

Gena sat behind the wheel for a minute, her heart filled with joy and sadness. They had come so far together and now it was time to say goodbye. She turned in her seat. Sensing her mood, Genghis cozied up to the grill and let her ruffle his ears.

"This is it, big guy. It's been quite an adventure but now you're home. I hope you'll like it here. There's plenty of game for you to hunt, and there should be other tigers around. At least I hope so. You ready?"

Genghis looked at her with soulful eyes and growled deep in his throat.

"All right, big guy. Let's get 'er done."

Zipping her down-filled parka, she stepped out of the van into frigid cold, went around to the back and opened the doors. Genghis crept forward. She sat on the floor of the bay and Genghis laid his head in her lap for the last time, rolling to the side for a belly rub. Tears filled her eyes. She hoped someday to meet a man she loved as much as this tiger.

She stood and motioned toward the wilderness. "Go."

Genghis leaped out of the back of the van and ran north.

A LOOK AT: FLORIDA MAN BY MIKE BARON

MIKE BARON DELIVERS A RIOTOUS, HEART-FELT AND ULTIMATELY UPLIFITING STORY IN FLORIDA MAN.

Gary Duba's having a bad day. There's a snake in his toilet, a rabid raccoon in the yard, and his girl Krystal's in jail for getting naked at a Waffle House and licking the manager.

Gary's a redneck living in a trailer by the swamp. But he's got dreams, big dreams. Every time he tries to get ahead, fate deals him a low blow. But then he gets lucky...

With his best friend, Floyd, Gary sets out to sell his prized Barry Bonds rookie card to raise the five hundred needed for bail. But things always find a way of getting out of hand.

"Florida Man will make you laugh out loud. It's sui generis."

AVAILABLE NOW

ABOUT THE AUTHOR

Mike Baron is the creator of Nexus (with artist Steve Rude) and Badger two of the longest lasting independent superhero comics. Nexus is about a cosmic avenger 500 years in the future. Badger, about a multiple personality one of whom is a costumed crime fighter. First/Devils Due is publishing all new Badger stories. Baron has won two Eisners and an Inkpot award and written The Punisher, Flash, Deadman and Star Wars among many other titles.

Baron has published ten novels that span a variety of topics. They have satanic rock bands, biker zombies, spontaneous human combustion, ghosts, and overall hardboiled crimes.

Mike Baron has written for The Boston Phoenix, Boston Globe, Oui, Fusion, Creem, Isthmus, Front Page Mag, and Ellery Queen's Mystery Magazine.